Return to Chateau Fleury

Return to Chateau Fleury

Elizabeth Pye

Return to Chateau Fleury
Copyright 2017 by Elizabeth Pye
A Writers Lair publication
Printed in the United States

This book is a work of fiction. This story, including names of characters and incidents, are products of the author's imagination or are used fictitiously.

ISBN-13: 978-0-9982130-1-9
ISBN-10: 0998213012

Original watercolor cover design by Barbara Parish
Author's photograph by Sandy Seeley

Also by Elizabeth Pye

Silk or Sugar

To My Mother

A belated thanks for surrounding me with books.
Your love of reading inspired me to seek
the adventure of a good tome.

Acknowledgments

A special thanks to Amy Jenkins, my abiding friend and critique partner, who endured an untold number of Chapter One rewrites.

I'm most fortunate to be associated with the High Desert Branch of the California Writers Club and the Romancing the Page critique group. A heartfelt thank you to Roberta Smith, Marilyn Ramirez, Holly La Pat, Anne Fowler, Lorelei Kay, and Ann Miner for their savvy suggestions for the improvement of the manuscript.

I'm beholden to Jenny Margotta for the final editing and for shepherding *Return to Chateau Fleury* to publication. Additionally, I appreciate the willingness of Kathy Puffer and Angie Horn to review the proof copy of the book.

I'm most grateful to Barbara Parish for the beautiful, original watercolor cover design.

French Revolution Horror

Prisoners condemned to die
at drop of guillotine blade.
Their goodbyes said,
innocent blood is shed.
Too many orphans cry—
Seine River runs red.

By Elizabeth Pye

Author's Notes

I don't know how to explain my time travel experiences, but they've had a profound effect on me. I feel a wisdom that I'd lacked before the new millennium; hence, my desire to write this novel. In 2007 I completed the first draft of *Return to Chateau Fleury,* a work of fiction inspired by my vivid past life regressions to the French Revolutionary period. All of my life I've been partial to things French, especially, those from the time of the eighteenth century Bourbon kings. For example, my favorite furniture is the Louis XV rococo style.

I've been fortunate to travel to France several times in recent years and have focused on chateaux and cathedrals in and around Paris and the Loire Valley in search of a connection. I'm charmed by the Cathedrale de St-Gatien, also known as the Cathedral of Tours, and have had several unexplained experiences there. Perhaps they're from the collective consciousness first suggested by French sociologist Emile Durkheim in 1893 and later expanded upon by Carl Jung, Swiss psychologist and psychiatrist. Or are they explained by the many-worlds interpretation of quantum mechanics which suggests all possible alternate histories and futures are real, each representing an actual universe—everything that could possibly have happened in our past—but did not—has occurred in the past of some other universe?

I've taken care to represent the historical figures written into my story as accurately as possible. My research includes both primary and secondary sources. I have read memoir accounts, historical reports, and other writings to gain useful insights. All other characters are entirely products of my imagination.

CLAIRE BENNETT'S FEMALE FAMILY LINE TO MARQUISE MARIE DE FLEURY

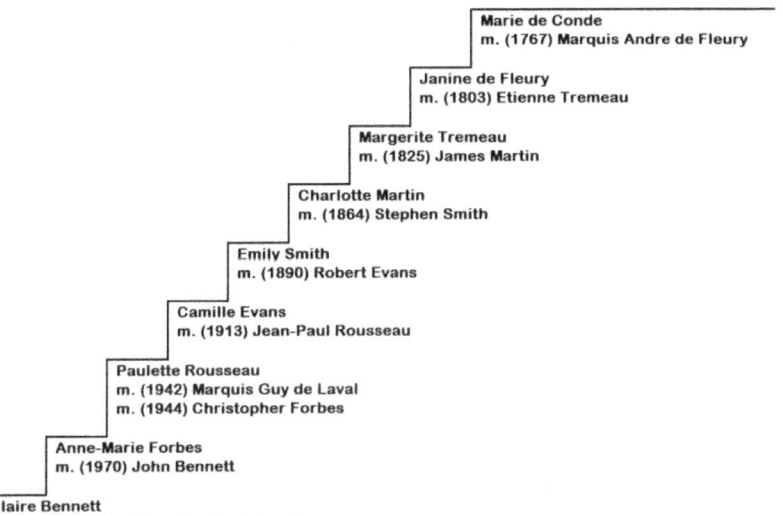

Marie de Conde
m. (1767) Marquis Andre de Fleury

Janine de Fleury
m. (1803) Etienne Tremeau

Margerite Tremeau
m. (1825) James Martin

Charlotte Martin
m. (1864) Stephen Smith

Emily Smith
m. (1890) Robert Evans

Camille Evans
m. (1913) Jean-Paul Rousseau

Paulette Rousseau
m. (1942) Marquis Guy de Laval
m. (1944) Christopher Forbes

Anne-Marie Forbes
m. (1970) John Bennett

Claire Bennett
m. (1998) Marquis Marc-Claude de Laval

Chateau Fleury –April 15, 1793

Philippe, L'Égalité! Le Duc d'Orléans betrayed us, as before he betrayed our dead King Louis. He has given our scent to the wild dogs of the Jacobins and Montagnards, who lust for blood and power. The 'Men of the Mountain' . . . these revolutionary extremists will be satisfied with no less than the annihilation of all those who oppose them. Chateau Fleury, and for that matter all of France, is no longer safe for us. We must repudiate the hostile womb of our motherland or perish . . . as was the fate of our King. In a few hours my husband will go to arrange our exodus. This afternoon Andre and I made a blood oath to seal our eternal love.

    (Taken from Marie de Fleury's diary)

Chapter 1

As dusk fell outside the bedroom windows, Marie reluctantly moved from the comfort of her husband's arms. Their entwined bodies resisted the separation necessitated by the unrelenting gravity of unfolding events. Oddly, she took solace in the pain in her fingertip, a reminder of the binding oath made earlier in the day. She fought the throbbing thoughts bombarding her head. What might happen if Andre were recognized on the street? His arrest would almost certainly lead to a sham case before the tribunal and then . . . the scaffold. She rebuked herself, for if ever, this was the time to draw upon her faith in miracles.

Andre must return to us!

Marie swiped a telltale tear from her cheek as she watched Andre pull on his jacket. He came to her, drew her to him, and gently kissed away a second tear.

"I promise I'll be strong," she whispered. "It's just . . . just that I'm worried about Janine. If only she could be spared all of this."

"Our best hope is to stay with our plan of action."

Marie saw the strain on his creased brow. "You're right. You know you can rely on me."

"I've said my *au revoirs* to Janine. She's remarkably brave." Andre gave Marie a prolonged kiss before he disappeared into the night.

Marie stood by the window, looking in the direction she thought he would take. A dog began to bark nearby and Marie held her breath. "What's next?" she breathed out loud. Finally, convinced no one was coming to harm them—at least for now—she allowed herself to relax a bit. All was quiet again.

Thank God, the animal has stopped its incessant yapping!

She watched and listened for any sights or sounds that would bode poorly for Andre's successful departure from the chateau. Seeing or hearing none, she turned slowly and climbed the stairs toward her boudoir. The stillness threatened to swallow her into the hollow emptiness of the chateau.

Marie's lady of the bedchamber followed her up the stairs. "Madame, I'll bring you a tray of warm milk and toast."

"*Merci*, Cecile." Marie knew it didn't matter to her dear, loyal Cecile whether she was hungry or not. Her faithful servant knew her well and sought to comfort her. After all, she'd been with the family since Marie was a baby—thirty-five years ago. Without conscious thought, Marie slipped into her dressing gown and sat at her elaborately carved desk. She dipped her quill into the ink and began recording the fast-moving events of the day in her diary.

Before long, Cecile stood at the door with a tray. "You need to eat something," she said as she studied Marie's face and set the meager meal on the desk. "Don't you worry, *Monsieur le Marquis* will take care of things. As soon as he gets back, you and *Mademoiselle* will leave these dangerous parts."

"What would I do without you?" Marie said. "You always console me no matter how grave the situation."

Her kind maid gave her an indulgent smile and hurried from the room. Alone once more with only her thoughts to keep her company, Marie broke off a piece of the fried bread and chewed it slowly—eating just enough to satisfy Cecile . . . she hoped. The warm milk soothed her nerves. She swallowed the last drop before taking off her robe and slipping her diary into its large inside pocket.

As soon as her head sank into the pillow, the lingering scent of Andre carried her back to their afternoon of passion, fueled by exhilaration and desperation. She reached for the gold, heart-shaped locket Andre had given her on their wedding day and cradled it. She'd been thrilled with Andre's gift, but now the treasured item felt cold and heavy, like her heart. She lay awake for a long while, unable to quiet her jumbled thoughts and slipping in and out of awareness until she finally slept.

Shortly after midnight Cecile awakened her. "Those murderers are outside and coming in . . . to search everywhere . . . and go through everything. Ooh, what will become of us!"

"Janine! They must not find her!" Marie's first thought was for the safety of her daughter. A fifteen-year-old girl should not have to endure such frightful events. Resentment and indignation gnawed at her gut. She heard raucous voices and rough laughter, which grew in intensity as she listened. "They're almost here."

Oh, God, Andre!

She leapt out of bed, her heart racing as she pulled on her robe. Ignoring Cecile, she hurried down the stairs, stopping short to hide in the shadows when a loud thud on the door startled her. Would they attempt to break down the door?

The men pounded and shouted, "In the name of the Republic, open this door. *Now!*"

Fortunately for Marie, the butler, one of the few remaining loyal household servants, opened the door. A belligerent intruder snarled, "I have a report that this house harbors royalists. I am an officer of the *Département* and have come to see for myself!" He pushed his way past the servant. Eight of his citizen-guard cronies filed in behind him.

The sabers of the self-appointed servants of the Republic clanged as they walked. "We're here to round up the enemies of the people and make them pay for their treason," one of them shouted as the group detoured by way of the kitchen.

Marie kept still, immobilized in the grip of terror. She could see the frightened butler, his feet fastened in place where he stood by the open door.

The unwelcome men returned from the kitchen, some of them carrying wine bottles and others gnawing on poultry drumsticks as they continued on their self-appointed mission.

Marie crept toward the salon and found Janine there, just moments before the ruffians barged into the room. A man with a scraggly gray beard swore at the women. "*Sacré Dieu!* Where is the rat?"

Another called, "Citizen Andre Fleury! Show yourself."

The chorus of voices chided, "He's here somewhere. Surely, he is not so cowardly as to hide and leave his women defenseless."

The marauders rummaged through drawers, turning the contents out on the floor and rifling through them, all the while muttering about damning documents hidden in secret compartments. "That traitor wrote treasonous pamphlets and letters in support of the royalists. We'll search until we find them," their leader proclaimed.

A grisly-looking, scar-faced guard grabbed Janine's arm. "Oh, *la vache*! I'll take you as my trophy."

Numb with terror, Marie shuddered at the thought of the barbarous things these vipers might do, right then and there.

"We have work to do." A muscular, young guard stepped forward and removed the man's hand from Janine's arm. "Now get on with it. She'll get the punishment she deserves," he said with authority in the absence of the group's leader.

The guard in charge returned to the room and looked at Marie. "Citizenness Fleury, you and your daughter are under house arrest. You will be confined to designated areas in the house. Guards will be on duty around the clock to enforce your compliance with my orders." He stepped within inches of Marie. "Understand?"

Marie instinctively drew away from the putrid odor of rotting teeth that swirled out on the man's breath. Oblivious to her disdain, the man strode from the room as he barked orders and assignments to his subordinates.

Marie took advantage of the men's absence. "Hurry to our rooms now," she said to Janine and Cecile, who had emerged from the shadows. They climbed the stairs together without being challenged. Marie stood by her boudoir door and watched Janine and Cecile move along the corridor to their own rooms.

Once safely in her own room, Marie bolted her door and paced in circles to release her pent-up anxiety. Finally, overcome with fatigue, physically and mentally, she fell into bed in the wee hours of the morning. She was aware of a few stray sunbeams creeping along the floor. Sleep seemed hopeless, but gradually, her rambling thoughts faded to nothingness and she slipped into a fitful slumber interrupted by nightmarish fragments.

She awoke with a start to the deafening silence throughout the house.

Where are the men?

Another day. What would it bring? She knew she had to confront whatever awaited her. She dressed quickly and went downstairs. As she approached the blue salon door, she saw a youthful guard stationed just outside of it. He nodded to her as she came closer.

She entered the room to find Janine and Cecile were already there. "And the knight killed the dragon that threatened the land," Cecile concluded the story.

Marie smiled at Cecile's attempt to comfort Janine by telling her a child's tale of hope.

An apologetic knock on the partially closed door preceded the appearance of the guard. He stepped into the room, took off his hat, and approached Marie. "Do you recognize me, Madame de Fleury?"

Marie turned and forced herself to look straight at him. "No. I don't believe I do."

"Until last month my father was your head gardener. Monsieur de Fleury insisted he leave your service for his own good."

Marie's brow crinkled. "I . . . I do remember you. You're Etienne Tremeau."

He squared his shoulders and looked first at Janine and then Marie. "Madame, I must be brief. I'm here to help you. Tonight, meet me by the stables. I'll escort you to my father's house, where he'll hide you until you can leave town." The young man didn't wait for an answer, but turned abruptly and went back to his post outside the door.

"Non, Maman, we can't go," Janine said. "We will endanger the Tremeau family if we do."

Marie shook her head at Janine. "You must go alone. I'm the one the guards have their eyes on. Only one of us needs to wait here for your father and Uncle Alexandre."

"I want to be here with you," her daughter protested, her eyes moist with unshed tears.

"Janine, my prayer has been answered. Now is your chance to escape this nightmare until it's safe to come home."

"But, Maman," Janine said as she collapsed into her mother's arms.

"It's best this way." Marie held her daughter and stroked her hair.

A few minutes before ten o'clock Marie watched Janine leave the salon and step through the opened, secret panel in the revolving bookcase. Holding a lighted candlestick, Janine made her way toward the narrow flight of stone stairs that led to the ground level of the chateau, as had her father twenty-four hours earlier.

The pockmarked captor spent the night guarding the three women he'd seen go into the salon shortly after he came on duty at nine o'clock. He'd watched with diligence and was certain no one had passed through the door all night. At the break of dawn, he unbolted the door and tiptoed into the room. What a beautiful sight. Visions of the innocent beauty of the young virgin stimulated his imagination.

There they were, all three women, sleeping on the sofas—one, two, three. He couldn't see the object of his excitement but shouted out as he walked past Marie and Cecile, "How about a kiss for this brave soldier of the Republic? How about it, mademoiselle high and mighty?" He reached down and groped at the third form. "What the hell is this?" he yelled as he looked at the limp blanket in his hands. "Where's the girl?" he bellowed. Shaking with anger and frustration, he grabbed Marie around the neck. "*Putain*, tell me now, or I'll kill you with my bare hands! Tramp!"

Upon hearing the commotion, two other guards dashed in with weapons drawn.

"The girl is gone!" roared the first guard, letting go of Marie. "Search outside. I'll make these two talk." He grabbed Marie by the hair, shoved her against the wall, and tried to kiss her.

Marie acted instinctively to protect herself, turning her head and raking her fingernails down his cheek.

His violence had failed to gain any information from Marie or Cecile, and his anger was evident on his reddish-purple face. He lunged at Marie and grabbed her again around the neck. He pushed her to the floor and straddled her, raised his fist, and hit her in the stomach.

Cecile ran from the room, screaming, "Help. Help."

"What is going on here?" the leader of the group called out as he came upon the brutal scene. He rushed over and pulled the man off of Marie. "Get out of here, you crazy idiot. You'll kill her before she is arrested." He extended a hand and helped Marie to a chair.

"The girl is gone," the pockmarked attacker whined. "That bitch," he pointed at Marie, "won't tell me where she is."

The leader turned to Marie. "Either you tell *me* now where she is, or I'll arrest you and send you to prison in Paris—maybe La Force or La Conciergerie—where Citizenness Capet, your queen, awaits justice."

Chapter 2

Boise, Idaho, September 1998

"This time tomorrow I'll be in Paris," Claire Bennett muttered. "Will this be the time for the sins of the fathers to be visited on the succeeding generations?" Her hands trembled as she placed her black leather jacket in her college-days Samsonite suitcase and closed it with determination. Anticipation of the trip was tempered by underlying anxiety. She picked up her purse from the nightstand and sat in her brown swivel rocker. A quick check of her handbag's side pocket assured her that she had ready access to her passport and airplane ticket.

Satisfied, she picked up the diary written by her ancestor, Marquise Marie de Fleury, and began to read the ornate, delicate script.

July 24, 1767 – Paris

I love my new life as Madame la Marquise de Fleury. My husband is wonderful—marriage is heavenly—all twenty days of it. Now I truly know why God created woman. My Andre is full of fire, tempered with tenderness that reveals a deep capacity to love. I find it hard to keep my feet planted firmly on the ground.

But alas, I must make a note of an odd incident at the cathedral, one that I can't get out of my mind. Toward the end of our wedding ceremony, I sensed a negative presence. I looked to my right and saw Louis-Phillipe d'Orléans staring at me. It was as though his eyes revealed the very core of his soul—a soul that harbored the potential for evil. I am troubled by such thoughts.

Claire shook her head and blinked away tears. How sad to

imagine that Marie had sensed the danger posed by d'Orléans—and others of his ilk—many years before his betrayal of the king and those in service to their sovereign. She gazed unseeing at the spruce tree outside her window. "I promise I'll check on Chateau Fleury," she whispered to the memory of the marquise as well as to herself. After closing the tapestry-covered book, she placed it in her carry-on. Marie's gold locket, a treasured family heirloom, was warm against her chest. She'd wear it for safekeeping during the flight.

Claire slipped her purse strap over her shoulder, picked up her luggage, and went downstairs. The aroma of freshly brewed coffee beckoned from the kitchen and brought a comfortable appreciation of her family. Sharing a cup with her mother would be especially welcome today.

"Good morning, dear," Mrs. Bennett said, without turning from the stove.

"Morning," Claire said in a lackluster tone.

Mrs. Bennett turned to face her daughter, concern written on her face. "You've been thinking of the marquise again." Her mother wrapped her arm around Claire's waist, led her to a chair at the table, and sat down beside her. "Don't let such thoughts spoil your time in Paris. You and Michelle will have a wonderful time."

Nodding, Claire squeezed her mother's hand. "I won't let it. But thank you for reminding me, just the same." She feared returning to Paris, where she had been physically ill when she visited the prison cells at the Conciergerie. She had felt the hopelessness of those unfortunate people—as if she were one of them.

Now she had an obligation for she'd promised to accompany the exchange students to Paris and work with them on the final phase of her research project. Always in the back of her mind was the mantra, publish or perish! "As usual, you're right, Mom. I must go."

"You don't *have* to."

"I really do. Dr. de Motte, my former professor at the Paris-Sorbonne University, has invited me to sit in on a committee meeting of the United Nations Educational, Scientific and Cultural Organization. That meeting just might lead to research opportunities that could further my professional goals. I must think about tenure at Boise State."

Paris, September 1998

Slightly disoriented after her long flight followed by an uneasy first night at Michelle's apartment, Claire wondered whether she looked as haggard as she felt. She hoped the brisk walk and fresh air on their way to breakfast at Michelle's favorite sidewalk café would revive her. At least no dreams had kept her awake during the night. Maybe she was too tired to dream, or maybe—and wouldn't that be great—she'd left those annoying interruptions on the other side of the Atlantic. *Don't count on it*, an inner voice warned. She sighed.

Ostensibly, she was here in Paris on a leave of absence to conduct research for publication and to rub shoulders with members of an esteemed international organization. However, she knew deep in her heart that she'd returned to pursue Chateau Fleury and the marquise.

By the time they reached the café along the bustling Champs-Élysées, Claire felt refreshed and ready to start the day. She noticed the sunlight dance across strands of Michelle's sleek raven hair in rhythm with the saucy toss of her head. Even in the unforgiving glare, her friend had not visibly aged a day in the decade since they had been students at the University of Paris.

"*Bonjour*," a serious young waiter greeted them. "What will you have?" He looked at Claire.

"A cheese omelet and *café*."

"Okay." He turned to Michelle, "*Et vous?*"

"Can't you guess what every French girl eats for breakfast?" she said with a good-natured smile.

"Non, mademoiselle," he said.

It was now they noticed he spoke French with a definite German accent.

Michelle seemed to take pity on him. "A croissant and café, *s'il vous plaît*."

Her friend's lighthearted banter carried Claire back to her carefree days as an exchange student. She and Michelle Laval had developed a lasting friendship, although at the time an alliance seemed unlikely—their backgrounds were so different—Claire an ambitious middle-class American and Michelle a fun-loving French aristocrat.

"Forgive me. I've been doing all of the talking." Michelle's head bobbed in time with her expressive hand gestures. "What plans do you have for your time here, other than visiting with me?"

"Now that my students are settled on campus, I'll work on my research and take care of a few other things." Claire adjusted her chair to escape the glare of the morning sun.

"What other things? I have plans for your time."

"I'm not sure when Professor de Motte will want me to visit with her committee. It's for the UNESCO Report on Higher Education for the Twenty-First Century. You do remember that Professor de Motte mentored me while I studied here?"

"*Oui*. How could I forget?" Michelle pushed aside her half-eaten croissant. "Claire, you work too much. You need to get away."

Michelle's words struck a responsive chord. She did need to unwind. Could time in the French countryside rejuvenate her? "Oui . . . right after the first committee meeting."

"The UNESCO committee or another one?" Michelle sipped her coffee.

"UNESCO. The one I want to discuss with Marc-Claude. Thank you for arranging an appointment with him."

Michelle nodded and smiled. "You and he are alike—always working, too busy to have fun. You'll be old before you know it and still not have lived life as it should be."

Claire glanced at her watch—no time to pursue that comment. It was time to leave for her meeting with Marc-Claude. Michelle's brother was an attorney whom she hoped would help her with her Chateau Fleury project. To that end she needed a quiet walk along the Seine while she gathered her thoughts before they spoke.

Most likely the aristocratic attorney would be put off by any suggestion of impropriety of members of his social circle. She'd have to select her words with care. The nobility of France had protected one another since suffering persecution during the French Revolution. An attack on one was considered an attack on all.

Claire touched Michelle's sleeve before she stood and picked up her handbag. "I really appreciate staying with you while I'm here. I'll call before I start back to the apartment."

Michelle rose and brushed an imaginary strand of hair from her cheek before she and Claire exchanged the obligatory *la bise* to each cheek. "*À la prochaine*. See you soon. No need to plan where to go for dinner. We'll stay in while I persuade you to come to Lamont with me."

Marc-Claude Laval closed the folder and shoved it so hard it flew off his desk. "Blast Michelle and her meddling," he mumbled as he got up and walked around his desk to pick up the scattered sheets of paper. His kid sister couldn't resist worrying about his social life. He knew he shouldn't let her get to him. But she did. She had asked if he would advise her *college friend* about Gypsies or some such thing, to which request, he'd pointed out that his specialty was international business law.

His sister seemed to have no appreciation for the demands of his practice and his responsibilities to the European Union—probably because she only worked part-time . . . and only when she felt like it. He wished she would stop urging him to date more often. She did it for their parents rather than for him.

Marc-Claude was of the opinion that his father criticized him because of his own unhappy marriage. His parents used to argue a lot until General de Laval learned that silence kept the peace. After that they managed to maintain a sham marriage and lead separate lives in opposite wings of the sprawling chateau. *If I can't expect a better marriage than theirs, I'll remain single.* Regardless of Madame de Laval's wish for him to marry Felicity de Fleury, he wasn't motivated to do so. Felicity was too much like his mother—she always had to have the last word.

Claire walked along the Champs-Élysées toward the Place de la Concorde. Michelle was a gem to broker a meeting with her brother, a successful international-law attorney who served on a committee of the European Union. She'd tried to rationalize that she needed his opinion about the legal hurdles faced by third-world-nation women who sought a higher education. But her underlying motive was to gather information about Chateau Fleury—the ancestral home of Marquis Andre de Fleury's family since the sixteenth century.

She'd first read the Marquise de Fleury's diary as a child and since then had fallen under its spell. The words on the pages tugged at her heart. She couldn't seem to distance herself from them. As irrational as it might appear, she felt compelled to find out more about Chateau Fleury and the secrets buried there. She wondered if somehow the essence of the marquise remained in the stones of the chateau. Would it bring her closer to Marie de Fleury to be in the physical location where she had spent so many hours? Sometimes, she felt as though Marie was trying to break through the time barrier that separated them.

Claire intended to seek Marc-Claude Laval's advice about the chateau, but he had no knowledge of her intentions. She had no right to take up his time with what would seem to him a frivolous pursuit. She tried to assuage her conscience in that she hadn't revealed her primary desire to Michelle. Her ancestors' estate had been seized during the Revolution in 1793 and later reclaimed on behalf of the family by an imposter using the de Fleury name—an injustice Claire seemed unable to ignore, try as she may.

Claire's pace slowed when she reached the Place de la Concorde—the site of the 1793 Place de la Revolution, home to Madame Guillotine. She felt dizzy and sank onto a nearby bench as a gray cloud engulfed her. *What is happening to me?*

Dazed, she looked around. She saw nothing through the ominous fog but she heard phantom-like sounds of jeering crowds, creaking cart wheels and horses' hooves striking stone.

She struggled against the pull into darkness. She looked behind her and to the sides but saw nothing out of the ordinary. Raising her hand to her throat, she clutched her heavy gold locket. The buzzing in her head grew louder. She staggered to her feet and began to walk, arms outstretched, feeling her way through the mist. A raw, searing pain sliced through her neck and shot through her head. Disoriented, she heard tires screech and felt a rush of air before her hands connected with something solid—a man's rough hands.

"Why don't you watch where you're going?" After screeching to a stop, the black-haired man had climbed out of his cab, slamming the door shut. "Are you okay?" he asked as he peered at her.

"Oui, monsieur." Seeing no one inside, Claire pulled open the back door of his taxi and flopped onto the seat.

The cabbie got into the driver's seat and looked at her in the rearview mirror. "Where to?" he said, fiddling with the radio dial.

"*Vingt-cinq* Rue de Victoires." Claire sank into the shabby back seat. "Drive around for twenty minutes or so before getting me there. And please stop at the first place you see where I can get some coffee. I desperately need a cup." She closed her eyes and stilled her mind, although true meditation was out of the question just yet.

The lurching ride suddenly changed as the cabbie turned into a McDonald's and screeched to a stop. "Coffee time," he said, exiting the car without waiting for her.

Claire shrugged her shoulders to relax her tense muscles.

I shouldn't have come here.

She went inside, ordered a coffee to go, and went out to wait for the driver. Some minutes later he returned and soon they were traveling along the Rue de Rivoli. She kept track of their location by noting the familiar landmarks they passed. They'd gone by the Tuileries Gardens and the palatial Louvre Museum before they picked up their coffee. Now out of the window she saw the Hotel de Ville for the second time.

Before they reached the Banque de France a second time, the cab turned onto the Place des Victoires, rounded a corner, and stopped by one of the historic Mansart-designed buildings that housed Laval and Associates. The driver turned to face her. "Ninety francs, mademoiselle."

Claire gulped and handed over one precious Paul Cézanne portrait—a 100-francs note. Somewhat intimidated by her surroundings, she knew she faced another challenging encounter inside. She couldn't let that aristocratic Frenchman Marc-Claude Laval deter her from her personal mission. She'd keep their conversation formal and try to maintain her dignity at all cost.

She reexamined the pros and cons of broaching the subject of Chateau Fleury at all. The stakes were high. After all, she hoped to become associated with people at UNESCO, people with whom he interacted. However, at the moment her desire to find out about the fate of the chateau and the descendants of those who had stolen it overrode her pride and professional aspirations.

"Bonjour, mademoiselle." The Laval and Associates' receptionist studied her with a quizzical expression.

"Bonjour. I have a ten o'clock appointment with Monsieur Laval."

"May I get you something to drink?"

"*L'eau,* s'il vous plait."

The trim woman ushered Claire to a tapestry-covered Louis XV-style chair and soon returned with a glass of water. "I'll let Monsieur Laval know you're here," the receptionist said before returning to her desk.

"Thank you." Claire sipped the water and studied the elegantly appointed reception area. Three matching, tapestry-covered walnut chairs and a sofa upholstered in a nubby brown fabric completed the seating arrangement. Laval's office was in the high rent district—outside her budget. She wouldn't be there if this were not a complimentary consultation.

Like a mother hen, the receptionist kept an eye on her. "More water?"

"No more, merci." After waiting for what seemed an eternity, she glanced at her watch. Forty-five minutes had passed.

I'll never get used to the French attitude toward time.

As if reading Claire's mind, the receptionist stood. "Mademoiselle Bennett, come with me." Claire followed the slender suit-clad blonde to a spacious office at the end of the corridor. "Mademoiselle Bennett is here for her appointment, Monsieur Laval," the receptionist said before she turned to leave.

The tall, dark-haired Frenchman approached and took Claire's hand. "*Enchanté.* I'm Marc-Claude Laval. Please be seated." With a light touch to her arm, he guided her toward an overstuffed, maroon leather chair and sat on a nearby matching loveseat. *He's smooth as satin.*

Claire was not prepared for his suave good looks. She had pictured him as a stuffy, nearsighted older man. Michelle's reference to him as her learned older brother, a Rhodes Scholar at Oxford, had misled her. Contrary to her preconceived notion, the man was vibrant—simply put, handsome.

Like a jaguar—sleek and muscular. Those alert golden eyes won't miss a thing—always one step ahead of his prey.

"Thank you. It's nice to meet you."

"Dr. Bennett, Michelle often speaks of you. She tells me you teach French at Boise State University."

Leave it to Michelle to make the introductions. "Yes, that's correct. And, please, call me Claire."

The warmth of his smile carried over to his voice. "Likewise, call me Marc-Claude." His eyes held hers for a brief moment before he spoke again. "Do you come to Paris often?"

Claire relaxed in his presence in spite of herself. "Not often enough," she replied, resisting the distraction of his easy manner.

"Do you enjoy your work at the university?"

"Very much. I enjoy teaching. And of course my research keeps me busy."

"Research, oui. My sister said you're completing some research while you're here and have appointments at UNESCO. What is the topic of your research?"

"It involves a group of university exchange students. They've taken my training workshop and now they're here to practice what they've learned."

An easy smile played at the corners of his mouth. "Training, eh? What kind?"

Had she imagined a teasing tone in his voice? She dismissed the thought. "Cross-cultural training. The idea came from some of my faux pas while I was an exchange student."

"Cultural misunderstandings are quite embarrassing," he said. His English accent was such that even the Queen would approve.

"You admit to such experiences?" Claire responded in her best French.

He smiled and looked her in the eye. "*Une fois n'est pas coutume*. Just this once."

Seeing the amusement in his eyes, she laughed. "My workshops address cultural shock and misunderstandings."

His expression grew thoughtful. "Ummm, that idea has merit . . . for businessmen *and* women." When she nodded, he continued, "I believe you have questions for me about human

15

trafficking of women."

"That's correct."

"I don't know how helpful I'll be. What information would you like?"

She sensed his steady gaze, feeling a warm flush rise up her neck to her face, but she kept her eyes lowered and fumbled with her notes, hoping he wouldn't notice—not likely, given his keen perception.

What's the matter with me?

She inhaled the subtle bouquet of his woodland aftershave, determined not to respond to it. "The EU has sponsored research on trafficking under its Sexual Trafficking of Persons program. Various agencies keep statistics and records on the cases." Claire paused. "However, problems remain. How familiar are you with the issues?"

Marc-Claude leaned back in his seat. "I have no firsthand experience with such cases."

"There is an acknowledged problem for these women," Claire said. "They become just a number on a piece of paper with few options open to them." She jotted a note on her pad before she looked up, her eyes meeting his. What are France and the EU doing about it?"

"Europol reports are compiled from information supplied by member-state national law-enforcement agencies. The statistics are only as good as those provided by the local or regional law-enforcement offices."

"To your knowledge, are there any services to assist women who come to the attention of the authorities here in Paris?"

Marc-Claude picked up a legal pad and pen from the coffee table and made a few notes. "Not that I'm aware of. But I'll see if I can gather more information for you and let you know what I find."

"Thank you." Claire took a deep breath and slowly exhaled. "I do have another matter I'd like to discuss . . . if time permits."

He raised an eyebrow. "*Certainement.* What is it?"

"It's more of a historical question than a legal one." Claire cleared her throat.

"Eh . . . of course." Marc-Claude glanced at his watch.

"I'm sorry. I should have mentioned it to Michelle, but I wasn't sure whether to bring it up with you."

"What's the question?" He regarded her with somber curiosity.

"My family members are the legitimate direct descendants of the Marquis and Marquise de Fleury, owners of Chateau Fleury in the Loire Valley before the Revolution."

A fleeting look of astonishment crossed his face. "You must be mistaken."

She pulled a small book from her purse and handed it to him. "This diary belonged to Marquise de Fleury. Janine, the Marquise's only surviving child, added some brief notes at the end of her mother's diary."

Marc-Claude's eyes focused on a mille-fleur paperweight on his desk. "Janine . . . *beau prénon.* Beautiful name."

"Janine wrote of the horrors of the French Revolution. Her parents were guillotined in 1793." Her voice breaking, Claire paused and pressed her hand to her throat.

Marc-Claude placed his hand over hers for a brief moment before getting up. "*Excusez-moi.*" Taking two bottles of Perrier from the small refrigerator by his desk, he returned, handed one to Claire, and sat, placing the other on the side table.

"Merci." Claire nodded toward the Perrier. "After their death, Comte Louis de Fleury, planned their escape from France. But before they could get away, Janine saw him killed."

"By the revolutionaries?"

"Non, stabbed on the chateau grounds by a stable hand who then stole his identity."

Marc-Claude tapped his fingers on the side of the loveseat. "During that time our society collapsed around us."

"Janine recorded that some years later an imposter, calling himself the Comte de Fleury, returned to France and laid claim to the family assets, including the chateau."

Marc-Claude's brows drew together in a frown.

Undeterred, Claire removed the gold locket from around her neck. "This is a family heirloom." She opened the large, ornately engraved, heart-shaped locket and handed it to him. As their fingertips met, a bittersweet yearning touched her.

"The Marquis and Marquise?" He cupped the locket in his hand while lightly running his index finger along the elaborate raised design. His expression defied interpretation while he studied the miniature painting of the young bride and groom.

"Yes." For an uncomfortable moment, Claire lowered her head and fought the urge to cry. She wanted to grab the locket from his hand and change the subject before she fell apart in front of him.

Marc-Claude looked from the miniature painting to Claire and back again. "Remarkable resemblance. Your features are similar to those of the Marquise."

"You think so?" She reached for the locket.

He ignored her outstretched hand and remained silent for a moment before he returned it. "Tell me more about Janine's escape."

"After her uncle's death, Janine feared she'd be next. She went to Bordeaux with the help of the gardener's son."

Marc-Claude's expression stilled and grew serious. "To help her would have meant risking his own life."

"Yes, he was a brave man, a very special man."

Marc-Claude's voice softened. "Where did she go after she reached Bordeaux?"

"To her betrothed's family. She accompanied them to New Orleans."

"Thank God. Eh . . . did she return to France and lay claim to her family property?"

"She did return to France some years later but ran into difficulties when she tried to challenge the fraudulent claim."

He nodded. "Returning émigrés often faced drawn-out legal proceedings when challenging ownership of property."

"It was more complicated than that. Janine finally gave up on the property but wanted the family history recorded. That's why she added notes to her mother's diary."

Marc-Claude remained silent, his expression unreadable.

Why doesn't he say something? Claire closed her eyes and stroked the book cover. "While I'm in France, I want to pick up where Janine left off and add to the notes in Marquise de Fleury's diary."

"How can I help you?" Marc-Claude held her gaze.

"What were the legal requirements for returning émigrés to reclaim their property?"

"The established social structures, including the legal system, were in disarray during the revolution. Afterward, many fundamental assumptions underlying the entire legal system changed."

She grimaced. "Was there any clarification of the conflicting laws over the years?"

"The Napoleonic Code of Eighteen-Ten, the French Civil Code, sought to mix aspects of revolutionary law with pre-revolutionary law and is the foundation of our laws today."

Without thought Claire blurted out, "What about the provisions in the new Nineteen Ninety-Four Code?" She froze.

Where did that come from? If I believed in ghosts, I'd think I'm possessed.

"I thought you needed to ask me questions," Marc-Claude said, his mouth tight and grim. "It seems this is an unnecessary consultation, since you have already researched it yourself, you should know it doesn't apply." He glanced at his watch and stood.

Apparently, she had been dismissed. Had she ruined everything? How stupid—she needed to keep his goodwill.

Chapter 3

Marc-Claude thought better of sending Claire on her way. Her claim might bring a horde of reporters to Chateau Fleury—to say nothing about his own doorstep. He didn't have time for such distractions. "I apologize for my reaction a moment ago," he said. "I confess, I am puzzled as to why you led me to believe you sought counsel."

For a moment Claire stared back in waiting silence, as if trying to process his change of attitude. "I'm sorry I was less than straightforward in my request."

"I suggest we start over. As it happens I also have a personal interest in the de Fleury family."

Claire looked at him as if she couldn't believe she'd heard correctly. "It's my turn to be surprised," she said with a nervous laugh.

"I have a standing reservation at the Café de Flore. You're welcome to join me if you'd like to compare notes."

She nodded. "Oui, that sounds nice."

Marc-Claude's silver Peugeot was parked in a shady spot, yet the warmth of the sun reached through the leafy-green canopy along the tree-lined sidewalk. He opened the passenger door for Claire to step inside. With thoughts bouncing around in his head, he sought a strategy for damage control concerning her allegations. Aristocratic French families abhorred unfavorable negative publicity and protected one another as much as possible.

Claire appeared to have calmed down. "Umm . . . coffee smells good," she said, looking at a nearby sidewalk café before slipping onto the seat.

Would you like a cup of *chocolat* or café?" he asked.

"Not now, merci."

He closed her door, went around to the driver's side, and climbed in. There would be plenty of time for coffee at the restaurant. As he drove toward their destination, he considered how a routine morning had been disrupted when the attractive, middle-class American came to his office and made claim to his cousin's property. No matter how convincing the story she told, it couldn't be true.

The Count de Fleury isn't the Count de Fleury? Preposterous!

He was conflicted about going to lunch when he felt he could better use the time for his upcoming trip to Ankara on behalf of Turkey's bid for European Union membership. Why had he allowed her to annoy him so? He could have suggested a meeting at a later date, allowing time to plan his response.

Too late for change.

He'd just have to strategize while they were together. As they merged with traffic, he asked, "How long have you lived in Boise?"

"My great-grandfather moved there during the nineteen twenties." Claire glanced at Marc-Claude. "He opened a department store, and our family has been there ever since."

Marc-Claude nodded as he drove across the Pont des Arts and continued on Boulevard Saint Germain, his thoughts occupied with the slender young woman beside him with the auburn hair. What was it about her that reminded him of the Marquise de Fleury? Her smile? Her oval face? Her Mona Lisa eyes? Yes, all of the above. Could she be descended from the de Fleury family? How else could he explain the diary and locket? Perhaps she had picked them up at an auction or an antique shop.

No doubt she'd be a challenging opponent. Her educational and professional accomplishments were impressive. He'd have to pay attention to stay a step ahead of her. "Is your family still in the retail business?" he asked. His question had a purpose. Genealogical research on her family most certainly was in order—on both sides of the Atlantic.

"Not anymore."

Marc-Claude slowed as the lunch-hour crowds spilled onto the wide street like swarming bees. No doubt the crisp, sunny day was responsible for bringing them out in droves. "Retirement or wanted a change?" He slowed to allow space for a shapely, blonde biker to move ahead of him, but he paid her no mind—Claire filled his thoughts.

Claire tugged on her handbag strap. "Unfriendly takeover by a large, out-of-state corporation."

He shook his head. "There's too much of that happening today." He pulled into a tight space that exceeded the length of the car by mere inches. "The restaurant's just across the street."

Plush red carpet led them into the mirrored and mahogany interior of the Café de Flore. Marc-Claude's eyes lingered on Claire's graceful, willowy figure. To his critical eye her long legs deserved better than her practical, one-inch heel, black pumps.

His thoughts turned to their morning session. She'd been emotional while telling her story and would have garnered some sympathy—not his usual response—if she hadn't made such a ridiculous claim. He prided himself on reserving judgment, allowing for rational analysis of the facts.

"Bonjour, Monsieur Laval." With hand extended, the maître d' clasped Marc-Claude's hand while casting an approving glance at Claire. The men bantered about the large number of people in the restaurant as they walked to Marc-Claude's usual, secluded corner table.

Along the way Marc-Claude spotted a newspaper reporter from *La Figaro* and quickly turned away from him.

No time for a quasi-interview about Turkey's latest bid for EU membership.

He succeeded at remaining unnoticed—one small victory at least.

After the maître d' seated them and departed, Claire studied the menu. "What do you recommend?" she asked.

"The coq au vin is excellent . . . or if you like shellfish, the coquilles Saint-Jacques."

She tilted her head as if making a weighty decision. "I'll have the coq au vin."

Marc-Claude nodded toward the waiter who stood a discreet distance from them. The server approached the table. "Monsieur, may I take your order?"

"Oui. We'll both have the coq au vin."

After the waiter left, Marc-Claude focused on Claire. He wanted to understand her . . . get to know the workings of her mind. "What influenced you to study French?"

"Marquise de Fleury's diary and the pictures in the locket."

Makes a good story.

"Interesting how the past shapes the present."

"So why did *you* choose a career in law?" Claire shot back at him.

"As the world shrinks, international law offers a significant avenue for service." While they waited for their meals, Claire appeared to relax and listened quietly as Marc-Claude continued to expostulate on how the world was being reshaped by electronic information technology.

"*Bon appétit,*" the waiter said after bringing their order to them and quickly departing.

Both Marc-Claude and Claire fell silent for a time then Claire cut a small piece of chicken and ate it slowly, as if savoring its subtle flavor. Her expression contented, she said, "This is delicious."

"I'm glad it pleases you." Marc-Claude reminded himself not to be disarmed by his companion.

Claire placed her fork on the plate and took a deep breath. "And did your family history influence your career choice?"

"Not that I know of. I suppose it's possible that Claude de Laval—my namesake—may have. He was Constable of France and as such served as arbiter for the king back in the day."

She smiled with satisfaction. "And now there's no longer a king for you to serve."

Marc-Claude acknowledged her wry humor with a nod. "My service is to the European Union. Its success is important to the future of France."

"In its early years a united Europe seemed to be the impossible dream." Claire said, admiration reflecting in her voice, "Just look at it now."

Her interest in the EU pleased him. "Great strides have been made, yet it remains a work in progress."

Claire nodded. "I'd like to ask about your personal interest in the de Fleury family."

"I have known them all of my life. The de Fleurys are our neighbors in the Loire Valley. Felicity de Fleury, Michelle, and I grew up together."

Claire straightened in her seat and pursed her lips. "I see. Does that relationship create a conflict of interest for you?"

"I hope not. You've raised questions I believe we both want

answered." When Claire remained silent, he sought to assure her. "We can work together or separately . . . whichever you prefer."

Claire looked down at the table and hesitated, sighing. "What fee will you charge me if we work together?"

"No charge."

The lines of concentration deepened along her brows. "We'll work together then."

"Good. As a matter of fact . . ." Marc-Claude paused while the waiter cleared the table.

"What were you saying?" Claire asked after the waiter set two cups of coffee and a plate of cheese and fruit on the table and again departed.

"Would you be interested in adapting your cross-cultural training for groups other than students?"

"Why do you ask?"

"I have a client . . . a successful businessman, who wants to expand outside the EU. Our negotiations with an American firm have stalled."

A thoughtful smile curved her mouth. "Let me guess. Cultural misunderstandings."

"Afraid so. Jacques Tessier is pretty set in his ways and so are the Americans."

Claire set her cup down and gave him her full attention. "I'm sure I can adjust my presentation to meet your needs."

"Many of the same problems surface again and again."

"Such as?" Claire helped herself to a piece of cheese and a cluster of purple grapes.

"For example, Jacques is frugal and closes down when the Americans insist the solution to any problem is to invest more money."

Claire nodded, "I see."

Marc-Claude held her gaze. "Are you interested in putting together a proposal for Laval and Associates?"

She eased into a smile, holding a small piece of cheese poised in one hand. "That sounds intriguing." She nibbled at the cheese. "Ummm . . . let me give it some thought. I'll let you know."

Pleased with the progress so far on that score, Marc-Claude placed his napkin on the table. "Shall we sightsee this afternoon?"

"Oui . . . if you can spare the time."

"Of course. Where to?"

"Montmartre. I've always planned to go there, but somehow it's never happened."

Montmartre. Her answer stirred a memory he'd almost forgotten. "Good choice. It's a laid-back place." He hadn't been there for years. His childhood memories of visiting with his *Grand-mère* Maille evoked a carefree feeling.

The wide Boulevard Saint Germain ended at the Pont de la Concorde. After crossing the bridge over the River Seine, Claire leaned forward, covering her ears.

"What's . . ." Marc-Claude glanced at her.

She pressed her hand to her head. "I . . . I don't feel well."

He slowed the car and pulled onto the sidewalk. "*Mon Dieu!* What's wrong?"

"I . . . I don't know. I'm dizzy."

He got out and raced around the front of the car to open the door. But before he could help her, she pushed her way out and bumped into him. After recovering his footing, he reached out to steady her.

She clung to his hand and leaned against him. "Just give me a minute."

"Take your time." Marc-Claude put his free arm around her shoulder. Annoyed by the impulse to slip his arm down around her waist, he dropped it to his side.

She looked up at him, still clutching his hand, a frightened look in her eyes. "Thank you," she whispered. After another uncertain moment, she let go of him and slid back onto the car seat. "I'm much better now."

What just happened?

Marc-Claude watched her, noting that a little color had returned to her cheeks, before he went to the driver's side of the car and got in. "I'll call Michelle to be sure she's at the apartment to keep an eye on you." He paused for a moment. "If she's not, you can wait at the office for her return."

25

Claire raised an eyebrow. "What about Montmartre?"

"We'll go another time," he said rather too quickly, fighting the conflicting emotions he felt toward her. How could she both attract and repel him at the same time?

"I *want* to go today."

He relented when he saw the stubborn set of her jaw.

Just be done with it!

"Okay. If you're sure?"

By the time they reached Rue Pigalle and began the ascent to the summit, the highest point in Paris, Claire still hadn't caught sight of the gleaming white Basilica of the Sacred Heart, famous in pictures of Montmartre. Boutiques, cabarets, clubs, and cafes lined both sides of the street. The wide boulevards overflowed with a mix of people from many ethnic groups, many in colorful attire. A street-bazaar atmosphere prevailed as they approached Montmartre, *la butt* to the locals.

Claire wondered what Marc-Claude thought of her episode and hoped it hadn't left a negative impression. She had drawn enough strength from the physical nearness of him to ward off the encroaching sounds and visions. His first reaction had been one of concern—all in his favor. He'd been warm and comforting. But she cringed at her own behavior. She'd been so vulnerable.

This is pitiful.

Wanting to prolong their time together, she had all but insisted he take her to Montmartre against his wishes. She sat forward in her seat and looked out of the window. "I haven't even caught a glimpse of Sacré Coeur. Where is it?"

"Hidden behind the buildings. Keep watching. You'll see it soon."

True to his word, she saw the top of the church come into view. "There it is—so imposing, so beautiful."

Marc-Claude darted into a parking space that opened up on Rue de Antoine. "We'll take the cable car up this time."

Claire looked at the ribbon of steep stairs. "I don't mind taking the stairs."

"Better ride today. There's plenty of walking up and down hills after we reach the top."

Although crowds pressed onto the cable car platform, Marc-Claude and Claire found two vacant seats on the second car to arrive.

After getting off the sleek *funiculaire* at the Place du Tertre, they mingled with the crowds of people milling around and going in and out of shops or sitting at the small café tables along the street.

"Let's get to the main attraction." Claire waved toward the huge church.

"Agreed." Marc-Claude reached for her hand as they navigated their way through the wave of tourists pushing toward the basilica.

She couldn't deny the well-being she felt with him by her side. She hesitated as they reached a candy vendor's stall at the edge of the street. "I haven't had cotton candy since I was a kid." She looked with longing toward the pink, cloud-like puffs of sugar.

"Would you like some?"

She thought better of the idea. "No, thank you."

Marc-Claude let go of her hand when they reached the open space near Sacré Coeur. Dozens of street artists filled the square, waiting to sketch a portrait onsite, to sell a completed painting, or both.

"Let's take a look." Claire moved a few steps ahead and waited for him while watching one of the artists at work. The tensions of the day evaporated in the carefree environment as she let go and enjoyed viewing the well-worn easels and artists' trays covered with bright globs of oil paints. Display stands and tree trunks supported paintings in various stages of completion. Autumn-colored leaves swirled around the cobblestone square. Whiffs of turpentine permeated the air around unfinished oil paintings.

"Ready to take a look inside the church?" Marc-Claude asked.

"Yes."

After climbing the steep stairs and getting closer to the basilica, Claire spotted a small sign by the closed doors. It read: Mass in progress. Disappointed, she looked at Marc-Claude. "Oh, no, we won't be able to go inside today."

"Not today. Turn around. You'll have to be content with our

great view of the city."

"What do you say to a cup of *chocolat chaud* while we enjoy the scenery?" She didn't wait for his answer before ordering two cups of hot, creamy sweetness at a nearby beverage stand.

"Merci," Marc-Claude said as she handed him one.

"My pleasure." Claire sipped her own as Marc-Claude and she moved to the fence near the edge of the square. Enthralled by the panoramic vista, Claire pointed and said, "There's the Eiffel Tower." Moving her finger to the left, she said, "And somewhere about over there is Michelle's apartment . . . and your office." She turned to Marc-Claude, noting his amusement.

He smiled and inclined his head. "We can stop by an art gallery on the way out."

"I'd like that."

The Roberto Santoni gallery stood wedged between a *pâtissterie* and wine store. The tempting scent of baked pastries filled the air. Three of the artist's oil paintings dressed the first-floor studio window of the slender, four-story building. Marc-Claude and Claire stopped for a moment to look at them before entering the gallery. Inside the room, warm-apple-pie-scented reed diffusers failed to disguise the trace of turpentine fumes. Marc-Claude and Claire strolled around the long, narrow gallery, pausing at artwork of interest. An easy touch on his sleeve drew Marc-Claude's attention to the framed oil painting of the Montmartre vineyard just ahead of them.

Claire stopped in front of it. "I like this one."

Marc-Claude moved to her side, his heart skipping a beat. He recalled seeing it with his Grand-mère. He had especially liked the expansive rows of grapevines clothed in autumn-colored leaves; but as a ten-year old boy, he had missed the artist's depiction of affection between young lovers—the focal point of the picture. Now, twenty-three years later, it triggered a soft yearning to settle down with the right woman—if he ever found her. "So do I. Too bad it's not . . ."

"*Désolée* . . . eh, it's not for sale." Motioning to the sign neatly printed beside it, the young sales clerk approached, turning her lithe body toward Marc-Claude. Her gaze steadfast, she added, "The owner displays a few pieces from his private collection, and this is one of them. But most of what you see *is* for sale. *Je m'appelle* Nadia. I'm at your service, Monsieur Laval."

"Merci, Mademoiselle." Marc-Claude pressed Claire's arm and began moving along the exhibit toward the door.

Nadia followed along with them. "Madame de Maille painted it. I'm sure you must know . . . although I haven't seen you here before. I recognized you from your pictures in *La Figero*."

Marc-Claude walked faster, hoping to make it to the door before the girl volunteered any more information.

Determined not to be thwarted, Nadia kept pace and stepped in front of him. In a low voice, she said, "Your cousin, Felicity de Fleury, stopped in recently."

Marc-Claude ignored the remark and cursed his decision to bring Claire here. The twit had divulged information he hadn't wanted Claire to hear just yet. Now he *was* on the defensive.

Claire's expression said it all. Her face clouded. She strode to the door and turned to face him. Her solemn expression revealed her displeasure.

He stopped beside her and said, "Time to start back."

When they stepped outside, they were promptly rebuffed by a cold wind.

Claire broke the silence. "You neglected to say you have *de Fleury cousins*. What else have you neglected to tell me?" The chill in her voice matched the cold wind in their faces.

"Claire, I'd rather you hadn't learned it this way. Keep in mind we've just met today. There are many things you don't know about me nor I about you."

She looked crestfallen. "It's about trust. You could have told me. I need to have confidence in you if we are to work together."

"You're being unfair by implying I have been less than forthright. I recall you were less than straightforward about the purpose of your office consultation. To put this in some perspective, I understand you're passionate about the de Fleury family history. I am too."

"Yes, of course. I'm sorry you seem loath to give credence to my concerns."

Marc-Claude needed to distance himself from her. "We've both had a long day and mine isn't over yet. I'll get you back to Michelle's apartment." He rued taking the afternoon off for the disastrous trip to Montmartre. He had work waiting at the office that couldn't be delayed until morning. The finishing touches must be made to the EU committee report and faxed to Brussels before the end of the day. He had also promised to have a position paper in the mayor's hands by nine o'clock in the morning. And he'd had more than enough of Mademoiselle Bennett's mercurial moods. He'd leave it to Michelle to contend with her.

Chapter 4

One week later Michelle's 1965 Austin-Healey convertible roared along the A10, whisking Claire to the Loire Valley. Leaving Paris did little to ease Claire's reservations about Marc-Claude's trustworthiness. Perhaps he would make that a non-issue—she hadn't heard from him in over a week.

"Claire . . . Claire! You haven't heard a word I said." A note of irritation registered in Michelle's voice.

"Oh, sorry." Claire kept her eyes on the fields of aging yellow sunflowers, standing so close together their heads bumped into each other. An uneasy feeling gnawed at the pit of her stomach. She couldn't deny she felt attracted to Marc-Claude, as he'd scarcely been out of her thoughts. But the flutterings in her lower regions in anticipation of their next meeting were born of anxiety rather than desire. Or so she tried to convince herself. She hoped her anxiety had little to do with him but stemmed, instead, from their conflicting interest in de Fleury research. Although still smarting from the way they parted after their visit to the art gallery, she had prepared a draft proposal for the cross-cultural workshop—in case he asked for it.

In spite of her disappointment in Marc-Claude, her week had gone well. After Dr. de Motte's first committee meeting, Claire got caught up in the plight of Gypsy youth in France. She planned to prepare a preliminary report for Dr. de Motte. Who knew, it could lead to a committee assignment. By keeping busy she had felt like herself again.

Michelle tapped her red fingernails on the steering wheel. "Shall we a take a short detour around the Gypsy camps while in Tours?"

"Oui, I'd like that," Claire said, grateful for the opportunity.

"It won't take long. And on the way you'll want to see the beautiful gardens at the museum," Michelle said. As usual, her voice was cheerful.

Claire appreciated her friend's effort on her behalf. "You've missed your calling. You'd be a great tour guide."

"You're not the first to tell me."

"Have you been to Roberto Santoni's gallery in Montmartre?" Claire probed for tidbits of useful information.

Michelle shook her head. "I don't recall it. Another tour destination for us?"

"If you like abstract art, Santoni's works are pretty good." Claire judged from her answer that Marc-Claude hadn't told his sister about the less-than-ideal way they had parted, so she felt free to probe further. "How long has Chateau Lamont been in your family?"

"Forever almost. Construction began in the fourteenth century with the first Count de Laval."

"Ooh. Now I understand why Marc-Claude feels such a strong tie to his heritage." She'd done it again—steered the conversation to Marc-Claude. It seemed that thoughts of Michelle's brother had a way of intruding, no matter the topic of conversation.

"Oh yeah, he's really into it—being the heir apparent and all," Michelle said with a Gallic shrug.

The city of Tours lay before them as they drew near the bridge across the tranquil Loire River. Michelle exited the A10 and drove the short distance into town. With a flourish she pulled the car to the side of the narrow, cobbled street across from the Cathedral of Tours.

Claire's entire focus was on the Cathédrale St-Gatien. "Let's take a peek inside." She had an overwhelming urge to go inside the magnificent church.

Michelle gave her a curious glance, but all she said was, *"Bien sûr*. Of course."

They crossed the street and entered the majestic house of worship, passing the remnants of a tour group. A couple of sightseers approached a few minutes later. "Could you give us directions to St. Martin's?" one asked in a heavy German accent.

"Oui." Michelle turned to Claire. "I'll get a map from the car." She and the tourists left the building.

In a quandary as to why she was drawn into the cathedral, Claire sat down on one of the plain wooden chairs facing the elegant altar. Swaddled within this historic work of art, she lost all sense of time. The towering stone walls, more than a hundred feet high, drew her eyes to the thirteenth century stained-glass windows of the upper portion of the gothic-style apse.

Buzzing in her ears preceded a floating sensation. She felt constricted as though bound by a tight corset, and she fought to regain control. Redirecting her attention to her surroundings, she lifted her eyes to the rib-vault ceiling of the choir and looked over her shoulder at the great organ, silent now but bathed in light from a large stained-glass window.

Nearby, the tomb of the two children of King Charles VIII and Anne of Brittany reposed. Carved stone angels and child-like effigies topped their elaborate resting place. Although a warm day, a chill hung in the air. Footsteps echoed softly at the rear of the church. A slightly musty odor hung in the air. Was she the only soul still in this cavernous building?

To Claire's amazement a vision, an image like that in her locket of Marquise Marie de Fleury wearing her wedding gown, glided toward her. Immobilized, Claire's awareness seemed to alternate between the bride of long ago and this image now before her.

She closed her eyes and focused on sitting on the chair. She realized she felt a pounding in her head and the headache grew until it was all she could focus on.

Now that you are here, we shall return to Chateau Fleury. The Marquise's words ran through Claire's mind.

"Come on. Time to go." Michelle said, firmly placing a hand on Claire's shoulder.

Claire shook her head to clear it and peered at her friend. "Ooh . . . okay." Still somewhat disoriented, she stood on shaky legs and followed Michelle outside.

Twittering sounds, like hundreds of birds, came from a densely leafed tree by the car. Where were they? Could Michelle hear them? Claire paused and looked up at the canopy of green but saw no birds.

It's all a hallucination.

Chagrined, she climbed into the car. By the time she managed to fasten her seatbelt, Michelle had merged with the boulevard traffic.

"Sorry I took so long. After I sent the tourists on their way, I saw this marvelous display of jewelry and I just had to look. And then

I couldn't make up my mind which one I wanted." Michelle jiggled her arm to reflect sunlight off the chunky bracelet around her wrist.

"No problem. Time stood still while you were gone."

Michelle gave Claire a perplexed look and extended her gold-laden arm. "Like it?"

Claire examined the gold jewelry of alternating links of smooth and matte-brushed finish. "It's beautiful."

No doubt the bauble cost a king's ransom.

Michelle's preoccupation with her new purchase allowed time for Claire to reflect on the meaning of the odd happenings at the cathedral. The experience would have been pleasant had it not been so bizarre.

I have to get a grip.

As the car moved past the familiar sites, the old part of the city soon gave way to modern buildings and homes. After driving about twenty minutes, they entered an industrial area and Michelle gestured to the right. "There's one of the Gypsy encampments."

Claire's attention turned to her surroundings. An expansive, empty plot of land, enclosed by a chain link fence, was packed with trailers, trucks, and other modes of transportation. Contrary to what she'd expected, many of them were not rattletraps; rather, they appeared to be in fine condition. Some new.

"We've been overrun with these people since the dissolution of the Soviet Union. They bring crime wherever they go. They're here today and gone tomorrow, making it hard to control any illegal behavior."

"They need opportunities," Claire said. "Education and jobs."

"They don't want to change their lifestyle. They're nomads and don't want to stay anywhere long enough to be educated or hold a job."

"That could be . . . or is it the only means of survival they know?" Claire countered. "At any rate, I hope to learn a lot more about them in the coming weeks."

"Good luck."

They left town and traveled in silence along the open highway.

Claire braced for disaster as Michelle suddenly accelerated and turn to the left from the main highway. "Are we about there?" she asked when she recovered her voice.

"Almost." The car climbed along the steep, wooded driveway toward the chateau.

It was a picturesque drive. Autumn leaves danced on the road ahead. The midnight blue of the brooding sky created a striking backdrop for the splashes of red, gold, and green of the forest. Fallen leaves turned the moist road into a colorful mosaic. A pungent odor of damp, decaying foliage filtered into the car.

"Welcome to Chateau Lamont-sur-Loire . . . the modest abode of the de Laval family." The levity in Michelle's voice did little to disguise her affection for her home.

As they drew closer to the chateau, Claire confronted her concerns.

Will I be welcome in the de Laval's home after they learn of my reason for coming to the Loire Valley? Even worse, what if Felicity is here?

The multicolored forest gave way to an expanse of manicured lawns surrounding the visible sides of the authentic fortress-castle. Although perched on the edge of a cliff, the chateau stood securely anchored to the ground. Its five, round stone towers, each capped with a blue-gray slate roof, soared above the horizon. An aura of make-believe seemed to surround the house.

"Wow. It looks like a hotel or museum," Claire said.

Maybe this isn't the best place for me. Perhaps, I should forget *the past.*

What she needed was a confidant, but something told her Michelle would not be a good choice.

Michelle nodded. "In a way, I suppose it is a museum. However, it's home to me."

"I guess that's why you haven't completed your degree. You're stuck in the art department, if I recall correctly."

"You may be right. I'm a hands-on person. I love my time at the museum and my restoration work."

"Restoration work? How do you mean?"

"I restore damaged paintings."

"I didn't know. I think I can understand how you got

sidetracked." Claire stared ahead at what looked to be a drawbridge no less.

For once Michelle didn't have a ready quip. "Old Tour de Laval, the *grande* tower with the crenellation and parapet around the roof, dates from the fourteenth century." Michelle pointed to the largest tower. "That's Guy de Laval's defensive tower, the old keep."

Claire nodded. She hadn't expected Michelle's family home to be quite so awe inspiring. There seemed to be spires, chimneys, and bell towers everywhere, rising at varying heights from the roofline of the monastic-looking old chateau. Its early history was evident from the crenellated wall around the top and the narrow slits just big enough for an arrow directed at the enemy. She surmised that the door set into the roof provided access to a place of rest and protection for the defenders of the castle. "How long did it take to complete all of this?"

"More than a hundred years."

Looking at the rough-hewn donjon and its tiny window openings, Claire wondered what modern conveniences existed inside. The exterior defensive design conjured visions of men dashing in and out, supplying munitions to guards and bells tolling all the while they were under siege.

"Do you find it comfortable?"

"I do." Michelle laughed. "But I don't know about your room in the unfinished, haunted tower." She waited for a reaction.

"You're not serious," Claire said.

"Don't worry. It's not cold and damp."

"You little minx!"

"Improvements and changes have been made over the years, mostly to the private living areas. We've retained the historic features of public rooms. They're much as they were in their fortress days—but your room isn't there."

The car tires rumbled across the drawbridge as they passed between the gate towers into a central courtyard. Michelle pulled into one of the parking spaces along a colonnaded walkway.

"It feels good to get out the car," Claire commented as she stretched and breathed in the fresh, moist air. The view across the rugged landscape to the river seemed to go on forever. "What a view. It's beautiful here."

Inside the defensive walls, the architecture assumed a more

domestic appearance. Each of the three wings, anchored between towers, had no feel of a fortress. Claire admired the beauty of the arcades along the front of the two renaissance-style wings.

Michelle opened the car trunk and unloaded the bags, handing Claire's to her. She motioned toward a slanted doorway in one of the towers across the courtyard. "This way to Tour du Grand Escalier." The old guardroom led to a huge stone staircase and the upper floors.

Inside the spacious room, Claire was amazed to find it filled with suits of armor and ancient weaponry. "This room is obviously a weapons museum," she commented. Gesturing toward a glass display cabinet, she shuddered and hurried past it. "A pretty grisly cache."

"Oui. We've had centuries to add to our collection."

Claire noted a lock on one of the cabinets, but she continued without stopping to look at the treasure trove of daggers, knives, and guns.

"Don't ask me about th e history of the pieces. Marc-Claude can tell you, though. He knows what they were used for, dates, and family connections." Michelle's words carried around the room.

As they left the chamber and approached the massive spiral staircase, Michelle gave Claire's arm a playful pat. "Upstairs we'll leave the oldest wing of the house and go to your room."

Along the broad, curving stairwell, carved motifs on the limestone wall changed from late Gothic to Italian Renaissance, in effect transforming the fortress into a palace. Along the walls the pilasters and ogee arches morphed into exquisite scrolls of classical acanthus leaves, carrying the eye to de Laval family armorial shield.

The stairs took them to a large anteroom. Michelle opened the middle door of three, heavy, wooden ones. "This way."

A thick French-blue carpet hushed their footsteps along the hall. About midway down the corridor, Michelle said, "That's my bedroom." She gestured to a dark wooden door with a carved orchard scene.

"Nice. Is my room nearby or in another wing?" Claire asked. So often great houses had a guest wing, and she didn't like the thought of the isolation.

"It's at the end of the hall," Michelle said as they continued on their way. She stopped at a door decorated with a carved hunting scene and turned the well-worn brass knob. "Here we are. This is your room.

Remnants of daylight filtered through the tall diamond-pane windows of the tower bedroom. The view looked over the treetops and down the steep slope to the Loire River. Logs crackled in the fireplace, sending deep gray shadows dancing around the room. "You can use the armoire or the closet to hang up your things." Michelle gestured and pushed a door open. "And there's the bathroom."

Claire moved closer and peeked inside. "Looks like I have everything I need."

"Just let me know if you think of something later. *Le diner* is at eight." Michelle glanced at her watch. "It's only four now. I'll stop by for you about six. It'll give us time to go by some of our public rooms on our way to the salon for cocktails."

"Sounds good," Claire said, relieved to have some quiet time before meeting General and Madame de Laval.

Alone, Claire took stock of the guestroom amenities. Would she find a good night's sleep here? She flipped the light switch. Identical bronze bedside lamps promptly erased the gyrating shadows. Her breath caught in her throat as her eyes settled on the bed.

What a magnificent piece of furniture.

Two carved wooden angels, cheek to cheek, sat above the detailed tapestry portion of the headboard. Had she seen a picture of it or a similar one somewhere? It felt so familiar. She ran her fingers along the patina of an angel's head and breathed deeply, wondering whether she could recall where she'd seen one like it. No answers came. She chastised herself. It didn't matter. Not only was it beautiful, it looked comfortable.

That's what's important.

Claire couldn't resist folding back the floral-print bedspread and lying on the soft mattress.

This is good.

She wanted to forget about cocktails and dinner and stay right where she was for the rest of the night. That not being a viable option, she got up and unpacked. After she freshened up and changed clothes, she still had plenty of time before dinner, so she sat by the window and looked at the view of the Loire.

As the sky darkened, hazy images of the bed in a different but equally grand room came and went. A sense of foreboding marred her enjoyment of its beauty. Claire's heart raced. Her teeth chattered as if lost in a snowstorm in her summer nightgown.

So cold.

She couldn't think straight. She sat immobilized and struggled to breathe until the clock chimed six times and jarred her from her irrational torment.

Chapter 5

While Claire waited for Michelle, she scrutinized her image in the full-length mirror, satisfied she looked no worse for wear. She wanted to make a favorable impression on Michelle's parents. Yet she felt at a disadvantage as she didn't travel in aristocratic circles. She had little knowledge of the nuances of dressing for drinks at country estates. The simple linen dress of royal blue and matching heels shouldn't raise any eyebrows—she hoped. Claire glanced at her watch, noting Michelle should arrive any moment. *It'll be okay,* she reassured herself as she heard a tap and opened the door.

Michelle wore a skimpy aqua silk dress with most of its fabric in its long sleeves. She pursed her lips, "You're dressed like you're going to a campus event."

Claire gave a silent groan. "And you look like you're going to a nightclub."

"Not to worry. We're expressing ourselves." Michelle hugged Claire. "I like you just the way you are."

"Thank you. Enough said."

"Actually, it's not." Michelle sobered. "I must forewarn you that my parents will subject you to an inquisition. Don't let it bother you. They do that to all of my friends."

They descended the stairs and passed the *grande salle à manger*, the large medieval dining room in the public area of Chateau Lamont-sur-Loire. "We'll stop in there on the way back," Michelle said.

When they entered the *petite salon* in the family's private quarters, Claire found the transition to the room elegant yet intimate. The walls by the fireplace absorbed the golden glow of lighted candles from the silver candelabra on the mantle. The orange-red flames of burning wood in the fireplace reflected on the Versailles-patterned parquet floor. A table held an arrangement of variegated ivy and tiny yellow, white, and pink rosebuds surrounded by crystal decanters and glasses, bottles of champagne, and a selection of wines. Platters of cheeses and grapes sat nearby. No detail had been overlooked.

Monsieur and Madame de Laval rose from a settee and came to

meet them. Madame's pink, light green, and yellow tweed Chanel suit matched the colors of the flowers on the coffee table. Clearly, the woman was obsessed with detail.

Claire noted the strong physical resemblance between Michelle and her mother: both were slender, of average height, and had dark hair. However, that's where the comparison ended. Madame's stiff formality promised none of Michelle's easy-going attitude toward life.

Claire turned her attention to General de Laval. He stood with a commanding air of self-confidence, his military posture evident. She half expected to hear him bark out some kind of orders. His navy-blue jacket fit perfectly across his broad shoulders; definitely, not an off-the-rack uniform.

"Maman, Père, may I present Claire Bennett."

The general's steady gaze—not unlike Marc-Claude's—held Claire captive. "*Bienvenu chez nous.* Welcome to our home," he said. He carefully studied her before he averted his eyes. Although Michelle had alerted her to her parents' ways, Claire wondered whether she received increased scrutiny because she was American.

Madame de Laval turned to Claire. "Please be seated." When Claire took the indicated chair next to Michelle, Madame de Laval turned her attention to her daughter. "Have you spoken with Marc-Claude about when he'll get here? You know how he is. Work, work, and more work, without a thought of his familial responsibilities at home." Madame passed a glass of champagne to Claire and continued, "Why do I have such thoughtless children?"

"Maman, he'll be here in plenty of time for the fundraiser."

"What do you mean in plenty of time? Felicity needs him now. You know how busy she is with her volunteer work and fundraising activities."

"There's no need to worry about Marc-Claude."

Madame scowled at her daughter. "You should take a page from Felicity's book and spend more time on Loire Valley projects. That lovely young woman works tirelessly for others. She takes care of her ailing father, volunteers at the museum and other charities, and still manages to fulfill her business obligations in Paris."

The General set down his brandy snifter and focused on Claire. "You may not know this region is known as the *Jardin de la France.*"

Frowning, Michelle said, "The next thing Père will tell you

is . . ."

"Michelle, enough." Her father gave her a withering look.

Taken aback by his stern rebuke of his daughter, Claire said, uncertain of his response. "Oui, I'm aware that Tours is often referred to as the Garden of France."

Madame raised her ridged shoulders an inch higher. "Lamont fruit will be served at dinner tonight," she said with an imperious lift of her chin.

"Our commercial crops are sunflowers, roses, and chrysanthemums," Monsieur said.

Michelle gestured toward the window outside. "We also send surplus fruit and vegetables from our orchards and gardens to the local market in Tours."

Eager to dispense with the pretense of pleasantries, Claire nodded and responded, "The outdoor markets are wonderful."

Madame de Laval filled her own etched-crystal flute after no one else asked for refills. "Claire, tell us about yourself . . . and your family."

Here it comes.

"My mother, brother, and I live in Boise, Idaho."

"Michelle says you're a university professor," General de Laval said.

"Yes, I am."

The General nodded. "A worthy profession." A faint trace of approval sounded in his voice.

Chalk up one for me—one point at least.

Claire glanced at Madame but before Madame could pose another question, Michelle said, "Claire's always known she'd be a professor." Michelle smiled at Claire and continued, "She's missed out on lots of fun because of it."

Madame de Laval's apparent preoccupation vanished and she snapped at her daughter, "You should be more goal-oriented yourself."

Wow! What authoritarian parents—of adult offspring, no less.

Claire clasped her hands. What had she gotten into with her visit?

The General cleared his throat. "The Idaho . . . for what agriculture and industry is it known?"

"Boise is surrounded by fertile valleys. You may have heard of

Idaho potatoes, but it also has a thriving grape and wine industry."

With an indulgent look, he said, "California wines . . . oui. Idaho wines . . . non."

Madame changed the subject. "Michelle, what have you planned for Claire's entertainment while we're all attending the reception for the Friends of French Architecture and Arts?"

"That's easy. She'll come with us," Michelle turned to Claire. "It's Saturday evening."

Claire felt caught between rejection and welcome. Madame had made it clear she did not expect her to attend, and Michelle made it equally clear she planned for her to be there.

"No more tickets are available," Madame said, regarding her daughter. "It's quite an undertaking for Felicity . . . especially now that her father is ailing." Madame turned to Claire and explained, "The event is of interest to those who are dedicated to the preservation and maintenance of our national treasures. Our nation has a rich heritage that the French people must work to preserve."

"I'm sure I can get Claire a ticket." Michelle locked eyes with her mother. "She appreciates our efforts to protect our history."

"You know Felicity is counting on Marc-Claude." Madame de Laval rang for the butler then lifted her chin and addressed Claire. "They are practically engaged."

Claire's back stiffened. What was the woman's point? Had Marc-Claude mentioned her to his mother?

General de Laval gave his wife a disapproving look and glanced at Claire before returning his focus to his wife. "You know, dear, Marc-Claude doesn't always do things your way."

The conversation continued along the same lines, with withering looks and innuendos from Michelle's parents. In Claire's opinion, her evening with the senior Lavals couldn't end soon enough.

Mercifully, Michelle finally rose and saved Claire from further tedium. "Please excuse us. We have things to do before dinner." After they were out of earshot, she said, "I hope Maman didn't offend you. Sometimes she is so insensitive."

"I got her point."

"She wants to be a grand-mère and expects Marc-Claude to fulfill her wish."

"You promised to show me the grande salle à manger. Let's

stop by there now."

"My thoughts exactly."

When Claire stepped into the room, she felt centuries removed from the Laval's salon. The old room whispered of its medieval past. The sparse furnishings consisted of a rectangular rectory table with chairs along the walls, which were adorned with huge tapestries depicting hunting and harvest scenes in muted colors of red, gold, and blue. "What gorgeous tapestries. I feel like I've stepped back in time."

"I thought you'd like them," Michelle said. "Tomorrow we can go into town and visit the museum, or we can take a bike ride along the nature trail."

"A bike ride sounds good . . . and so does the museum." Yes, both things appealed to her. The bike ride would work out tensions, and the museum might reveal something about Marie and Andre de Fleury. She needed to evaluate it and gather as much information as she could in the time she had. "Let's do both."

"We could. The trail leads into town." Michelle led Claire from the old room. "We just wouldn't have as much time for the museum."

"Okay. That's the plan."

"Are you awake?" Michelle called from outside Claire's bedroom door.

Claire rolled over and looked at the clock. *Gosh, almost 7:30.* "Come in."

Michelle bounded into the room, dressed in tight jeans and a form-fitting sweater that showed off her trim body. Her black hair, cut in a chic, straight style, emphasized her valentine-red sculpted mouth and hazel eyes. "How'd you sleep?" she asked as she flopped onto a pink brocade chair.

"Not as well as hoped . . . overtired I think."

"I'll go easy on you today," Michelle promised.

Claire grabbed her robe from the foot of the bed and slipped into it. "A quick shower and I'll be good to go."

"I'll wait." Michelle began to tap her fingers on the arm of the chair in time to a melody only she could hear as Claire hurried into the bathroom.

After her shower Claire pulled on a pair of jeans and a long-sleeved T-shirt and returned to the bedroom. "I'm glad we're cycling. Goodness knows, I need the exercise."

"We'll take the trail along the river and get to town in time for a little sightseeing before lunch."

After a light breakfast of croissants and coffee, they headed for the garage complex. The morning sun shone through the branches of a tree, casting an abstract pattern on the walls of the converted stables. The building housed cars and trucks of various kinds. At one end various bicycles and numerous motorcycles occupied designated parking spaces. Grasping the handlebars of a red bike, Michelle said, "Choose one."

Claire stopped in front of an aqua-colored Peugeot racing bike. She lingered a moment before moving on and getting astride a blue one.

"Marc-Claude's matches your outfit. Too bad it's a guy's bike."

"A Peugeot bike and car, too? He must have stock in the company?"

Michelle shrugged. "May have."

The sound of an approaching car intruded on the quiet of the morning and Claire looked around in time to see Marc-Claude's Peugeot draw near and come to an abrupt stop in one of the garage parking spaces. From the driver's side he swung his long legs out of the open car door and climbed out. A shorter, heavyset man emerged from the other side and met him in front of the car.

"Marc-Claude! Maman's waiting for you." After exchanging the requisite kisses and hugs, Michelle linked arms with the other man. "Hey, Jacques, *Ça va?*"

Unprepared for Marc-Claude's arrival, Claire hesitated before getting off her bike. How would he react to seeing her, and what could she say to him?

With no hesitation he came to her. "Claire, good to see you," he said, greeting her with a quick kiss to each cheek. "I'm sorry we parted the way we did the last time. Truce?"

"Yes." Relieved, she clasped his outstretched hand. She doubted Madame de Laval would be pleased.

"Good." He started to turn but stopped and looked back at her.

"We're good," Claire said.

"We'll talk more later. And I'll share some human trafficking information that you may find useful." Marc-Claude gestured at her bike. "Cycling?"

"Yes."

"Where to?"

"Sightseeing and lunch in Tours."

"There are plenty of places to see. If we agree to work together, we can take breaks from research to visit places of interest."

Any remaining resolve to resist him dissolved under the magnetic depth of his golden eyes. "You're quite the negotiator."

Michelle slipped her arm around her brother's waist and interrupted to introduce Claire to Jacques. "Join us for a ride," she said to the men and got back on her bike.

Marc-Claude shook his head. "Can't right now. How about meeting you for lunch? Chez Monteau at twelve-thirty?"

"You're on," Michelle said.

Claire got back on her bike and followed Michelle from the garage area. They picked up a paved road and followed it around the side of the chateau until it narrowed into a winding dirt path down a steep hill toward the Loire. At the river's edge they connected with the cycling trail and headed for Tours.

Riding alongside Michelle, Claire said, "Your mother speaks as if Marc-Claude and Felicity are an item? Are they?"

"Why? Do you have a thing for him?"

"A thing? Don't be silly. We've just met." Heat crept up Claire's neck to her cheeks. Had Michelle noticed?

"He's not engaged. I don't think he knows what he wants." Michelle sighed. "It's my parents and Felicity who want the marriage."

Claire noticed a dragonfly flitting around a bush. "I don't want to upset anyone."

"Now, what might you do to cause that?"

"Marc-Claude and I have plans to work together on a couple of projects."

"So?"

"I don't know."

"Don't worry so much."

46

"I'll try to follow your advice."

Michelle faced her with a determined look. "*I* am going to marry for love."

A bee buzzed around Claire's head. She waved it away. "There must be mutual love, trust, and *respect* before I marry *anyone*."

"My parents think Jacques and I should marry, but . . . I'm not sure whether I love him enough."

The path narrowed, forcing them to ride single file for a short distance before it widened again. When they could once again ride side by side, Claire continued, "Your parents take an active interest in your lives." She hoped she hadn't stepped over the line, prodding too much.

Michelle showed no concern. "It's our way. Marc-Claude expects it. I just *can't* accept it."

"He wants to please them?"

"I suppose. I think the day Marc-Claude was born, Père set out to train him for the military."

"Seriously? How?"

"In every way. He called him his little warrior. He pushed him to win every race he entered to the point that Marc-Claude stopped cycling for a while."

"That's sad."

"If he didn't win, Père was beastly. I'd slip away and cry for Marc-Claude, who mustn't show any emotion."

Claire imagined little Michelle wanting to protect her brother and regretted bringing up bad memories.

"One time I asked Père not to be so cruel. He said that it was not my concern."

"Maybe your father didn't know how to respond."

Michelle shook her head. "Before then I'd adored him. Things changed between us after that."

To change the subject Claire said, "What did Marc-Claude say about that?"

"Nothing. I don't know whether he even noticed. My father often told the story of our grandfather's death during the war. He'd say, 'He died honorably in defense of France, as many Lavals have.'"

"Perhaps he'd heard that when he was young and wanted to protect the family honor," Claire offered.

"Yes, and Père won. Now they think alike, although Marc-

Claude refused to follow him into a military career." Michelle lowered her head and gripped her handlebars until her knuckles whitened.

They rode in silence to the end of the trail and slowed before entering the busy city boulevard. Riding for several blocks and passing shops on a side street, they came to the cathedral. They left their bikes at Cathedral Square and took their backpacks from the wire bike baskets. After they'd passed the church, the Musée des Beaux-Arts came into view.

"The museum is housed in the pre-revolutionary home of the archbishop," Michelle said. "Felicity volunteers here. Maybe you'll meet her today."

Was Felicity cold and efficient like Madame de Laval or a French sex kitten like Michelle or . . .

"I could spend hours in here." Michelle brushed a leaf from her shirt as she and Claire entered the museum's ornate archway.

The buildings and grounds showcased architectural periods beginning with the Gothic cathedral period through the eighteenth-century neo-classical design of the Archbishop's Palace. Claire hoped to find paintings or sculptures that might depict the de Fleury family. Perhaps something even remained that had belonged to the Archbishop de Fleury, who lived there for a time before the French Revolution.

The two young women walked toward the museum past the aged Cedar of Lebanon tree, reputed to have been planted by Napoleon Bonaparte. Witness to sweeping changes over its lifetime, the tree's branches reminded Claire of huge arms draped in green velvet. On the other side of the walkway, she noticed a lily pond, its dark waters brightened by floating pink, red, and yellow blossoms. Formal French gardens graced the approach to the imposing stone building.

Michelle led the way inside. "Bonjour, Madame. Is Felicity here?"

The woman behind the counter greeted them and said, "Not today."

Thank goodness, she's not here.

Claire relaxed and looked forward to an enjoyable day. She

was not disappointed as room after room of the old palace displayed its extensive collection of period furniture and paintings. She moved through the galleries on the first floor at her own pace, leaving Michelle in the midst of a deep conversation with the receptionist. When Michelle caught up with her in the Louis XV-period exhibit room, Claire said, "This collection is wonderful. I'm surprised there aren't many people here."

"The tourist season is past . . . not like in Paris, where it's endless."

"It's nice not to be rushed through the exhibition." Claire indulged herself by imagining everything as it might have been before the French Revolution. She felt at home in the antique-furnished rooms of wood-paneled walls, fine silks, and tapestries. Michelle moved on ahead of her. But she expected Michelle to very soon be back downstairs, talking with her friend behind the counter.

By the time Claire reached the third floor, she was alone. She wandered along and came to a painting of an old chateau. The gold-tone nameplate read: Chateau de Maille. *Hum . . . Maille.* Marc-Claude had mentioned his Grand-mère Maille. There could be a connection. Claire glanced up when she heard footsteps.

Michelle slowed her pace as she approached Claire and pressed her hand to her stomach. "*J'ai faim!* I'm hungry. It's about time to meet Marc-Claude and Jacques for lunch."

"Time already?" Claire felt a rush of anticipation at being with Marc-Claude again. She'd ask him about the Maille chateau.

They picked up their bikes, rode a short distance, and stopped in front of a white, stone-faced building. The mingled aromas of sizzling steaks and freshly baked bread beckoned them into Chez Monteau.

Claire ran her hand across the surface of the building. "What kind of stone is this?"

"*Tuffeau.* The limestone from the Loire region."

After Claire and Michelle were seated, and while waiting for the two men, Michelle continued chattering. Claire nodded in polite response until the waitress interrupted the monologue.

"What can I get you to drink while you wait for the others?"

"A bottle of Vouvray wine and some water." Michelle turned to Claire. "At the reception tomorrow you'll meet some of our neighbors and friends. You'll fit right in if you talk about historic preservation and the arts."

The longer they waited for the men, the more irritated Claire became. She'd thought Marc-Claude wanted to make a good impression, and she'd expected him to already be at the restaurant when they arrived. Instead, he had disappointed her again. But she couldn't help watching for him while trying to keep her mind on what Michelle was saying.

"Claire, you haven't heard a word I said." Michelle stared at her. "Sometimes you really act weird."

Claire's hand trembled as she lifted her glass and sipped the mellow wine in an effort to stall for time. She cast a covert glance at Michelle and hoped she didn't notice. "I . . . I don't know what's happening to me. Maybe I'm losing it." She reached for a tissue and daubed her moist eyes.

Michelle waited in silence.

"Strange things have been happening since I arrived in Paris."

"Things? What kind of things?"

Words began to flow like a ruptured dam as she released the pressure of her pent-up tension. "At times it's as though I'm living in scenes from the past—sort of a time warp. It's like viewing a double-screen television. All my senses are in two places, back in the time of the French Revolution and the here-and-now."

"Ooh! Such as . . ."

"Well . . . to begin . . . I, ah . . . I had a vague feeling of anxiety when I came to the Place de Concorde on the way to Marc-Claude's office. The feeling grew stronger until it almost overwhelmed me. I seemed to be at the square during the revolution."

Michelle consoled, "Perhaps you were overtired and keyed up about your meeting? Your mind blended your knowledge of the history of the square into your perceptions. I'm sure under the right circumstances that could happen."

"I wish it could be explained away that easily. I had another time-warp experience after we got here yesterday."

"Umm . . . really?" Michelle looked at her watch and motioned for the waitress to take their order. "Men!"

Because neither was interested in eating, they ordered a single sandwich to share. As they waited for the food, a sinking feeling clutched at Claire's heart. Marc-Claude had not even called to say they weren't coming. "To answer the last question you asked before we ordered, yes, in the cathedral."

"You seemed disoriented when I came back to pick you up. What happened?"

"I went back in time and saw a vision. Somehow, I knew it was seventeen sixty-seven."

"That's exciting."

Claire nodded. "The odd thing about it is that I recognized the Marquise de Fleury."

"Seriously, Claire, this is fascinating. I believe many things are possible . . . even those considered to be in the realm of the impossible." She paused as the waitress placed the sandwich and a second plate on the table. "I have a friend, Susan Fisher, who's a hypnotherapist. She's told me about some of her clients who have had similar experiences."

Claire was relieved that Michelle didn't seem shocked. "Fascinating is *not* the word that I'd use for it," Claire admitted.

"Susan tells me that oftentimes there is a triggering event that causes such experiences, whether a debilitating phobia, an illness, or flashbacks such as you've described."

"A triggering event?"

"Yes, something that disturbs a subconscious memory. She suggests that many of these problems have their roots in our unresolved past lives."

"Oh, come on now. Past lives?"

"It's an intriguing concept. The idea of unresolved problems originating in childhood is widely accepted in the professional psychological community. Some professionals suggest that it goes back beyond childhood to past-life experiences."

"You're suggesting reincarnation?" Claire asked.

"Yes, it makes sense to me. Whether or not a person believes in past lives, hypnotherapy sessions bring about miraculous healings."

"I'd like to think there's some reasonable explanation for what's happening to me."

"Tell you what. When we get home I'll give you a book Susan recommended about work done in the field, including case histories."

Claire smiled for the first time since sitting down for lunch.

"Thanks for giving me hope."

"That's what friends are for. Besides, I've read a lot on the subject and am considering a past-life regression myself."

"Why? Do you have past-life memories?"

"None that I remember . . . that's why I'm going to have a regression."

Claire shook her head. "I don't know what to think."

"Wait until you read some of the case studies. Shall we get started back?"

"I'm ready."

"We'll take the highway rather than the bike trail . . . it's faster."

Claire looked forward to returning and reading Michelle's book but was delayed when, on their way up the driveway, a car approached behind them. Marc-Claude and his mother waved as they went by.

Between breaths Michelle muttered, "That's strange. I wonder where they've been. Where's Jacques?"

Claire sped up the hill, making use of her sudden adrenaline surge.

Out of sight, out of mind, I guess.

By the time they reached the garage, Marc-Claude waited alone by the bikes as Claire and Michelle pulled into the shade and got off. Hands on her hips, Michelle stared at her brother. "And where were you and Jacques at twelve-thirty?"

"You know where we were."

"How should we know? For sure you weren't where you said you'd be."

"Didn't Maman call to let you know I was taking her to the dentist?" As Marc-Claude watched Michelle's expression, a dawning look of awareness crossed his face. "Tell me she did."

"No, she did not. Since when do you take her to the dentist anyway?"

He kicked the ground. "I don't believe this. She said she'd called and explained the situation to you."

"Sorry, she didn't," his sister said.

"Her car wouldn't start and she had an unbearable toothache. The dentist said he'd see her right away . . . so I took her." Marc-Claude shook his head and turned to Claire. "I'm so sorry about this misunderstanding. I had no idea you didn't get the message."

Claire nodded, not looking at him, and followed Michelle to the house. *Misunderstanding—right!*

Chapter 6

Claire gazed at the oversized mantle clock as she waited in the library for Michelle. She tried not to think about Marc-Claude but couldn't help but wonder if his story about his mother was true. Would Madame stoop to such a ploy to keep him from a lunch appointment with her?

Footsteps echoed behind her. Claire looked around and saw Michelle, book in hand. *Hypnotherapy: Case Studies . . . must be the one she promised me.* She took the thick, brown-covered book from her friend's outstretched hand. "Thank you."

"I hope it's useful," Michelle said. "Before you get started, I want you to know that Marc-Claude was deceived by Maman this morning."

"Did he ask you to tell me?" Peeved, Claire added, "Quite frankly, the whole thing sounds unlikely to me."

"You're mistaken. I know Maman. And he did *not* ask me to speak to you about it. He was angry and embarrassed. He couldn't believe she'd gone to such lengths to keep him from lunch."

Claire sighed and shook her head. "Every time I think I know what's going on, things aren't what they seem."

"I just thought you should know." Michelle looked out the window. "There's Jacques now . . . be back soon."

After watching Michelle disappear through the French doors, Claire opened the book and scanned the table of contents. At least she could get started reading. She snuggled into the buttery-soft leather sofa by the huge fireplace. She had just finished the first chapter when a rush of air from the opened terrace door distracted her. Expecting to see Michelle, she was surprised to see Marc-Claude, who paused as he stepped inside. "Come on in," she called.

"It's chilly out there." Marc-Claude edged closer to the fire, rubbing his hands together. "It's chocolat chaud weather."

Her will to remain aloof dissolved. "Hot chocolate does sound good."

He went back toward the door and pressed the intercom button on the wall. "Hey, Jan, a pot of hot chocolate would be great in the library now." He slipped off his suede jacket and eased into the chair nearest Claire. "I hope the lunch appointment fiasco hasn't spoiled our chance to work together."

Claire regarded him with somber curiosity.

Madam wins if you walk away.

"Never mind. It was just lunch." She smiled and changed the subject. "What information do you have for me about human trafficking?" She didn't dare mention the subject of contention between them and create more friction. Chateau Fleury should be left to unfold during their research.

Marc-Claude's expression revealed no reaction to her flippant comment. "I asked a friend, a *commissaire* in the National Police, what's being done about human trafficking. Our laws on prostitution are ineffective and of little help to law enforcement."

"Is there nothing else that can be done?" Claire asked, holding his gaze. "Do you think the laws will be changed?"

"They may be. There certainly is concern about the problem. My friend referred me to a contact in Europol."

"Is it likely that the EU will take some action?"

"I don't know. Work is being done by various agencies. For example, I know of a young Romanian woman who is a member of a sponsored outreach team that seeks to identify and aid victims. If you would like to interview her, it can be arranged."

"I certainly would like to meet her."

Marc-Claude cleared his throat. "Actually, you've already met her. It's Nadia from Roberto Santoni's gallery."

"Oh. I see." It couldn't have been easy for Marc-Claude to mention Nadia, yet, to his credit he had done so. Claire bit her lip and tried to swallow her misgivings. "Thank you. I'd like to speak with her."

"I don't know when Michelle plans to return to Paris, but I have to get back by Tuesday. You're welcome to ride with me."

"I'll speak to Michelle and accept your offer if it's okay with her." Claire hesitated. "There is one more thing I need to ask."

"Oui?"

"Had you met Nadia before we went to the gallery?"

"Non. I had not."

Claire sought assurance from Marc-Claude. "So you know of

no problems with me interviewing her?"

"None that I know of," he replied.

"Good. Now that we've agreed to work together, what can I do for you?"

"I'll need to read your family diary before we start our research,"

She couldn't very well refuse his reasonable request. "I'll get it now."

Dogged by a nagging hesitation, Claire's shoulders slumped on her way up the stairs and down the hall to her bedroom. She didn't like to let the fragile heirloom out of her possession. It documented that her ancestors were the legitimate owners of Chateau Fleury.

Pushing her concerns away, she pulled her luggage from the closet and took the well-worn memoir from one of the side pockets. She sat on the bed and toyed with the thought of telling Marc-Claude she had mislaid the diary. *Not a good idea.* She couldn't in good conscience lie. After all, she had insisted there be honesty between them. Eager to get the deed done, Claire left her bag by the bed and returned to the library, clutching the memoir.

"Back just in time." Marc-Claude poured two cups of mocha-colored liquid and handed one to Claire.

Rather than give him the diary, she laid it on her lap. "Umm, this is good." She sipped the beverage and inhaled the chocolate aroma. The hot steam warmed her face and soothed her jittery nerves.

Marc-Claude leaned forward, nearer to her, and gestured to the book. "What's that scene on the cover?"

Claire's heart did a flip-flop each time their eyes met. She set her ceramic mug down, picked up the diary, and stared at the cover. "I'm not sure . . . I think it's Janine's needlepoint depiction of the harbor at New Orleans." She got up and stood beside his chair, holding the diary closer to him without letting go.

"May I?" He reached to take it from her.

Releasing her grip, she said, "It's very fragile. Please be careful."

He acknowledged her concern with a warm smile. "I will."

Unable to ignore her protective feelings, she watched his every move. He rotated the book around and ran his fingers over the cover before opening it. As if evaluating the paper, he moved his thumb and first two fingers across the yellowed pages. Seemingly satisfied, he leaned back and began reading, stopping only to jot notes on a blue legal pad retrieved from the shelf below the side table.

Claire savored the last of her decadent beverage and felt calmer, confident that Marc-Claude was showing proper reverence for Marie's diary. Forcing herself not to scrutinize his every move, she picked up the hypnotherapy book and began reading. One case study in particular caught her attention. She noticed parallels to her own experiences and made mental notes as she went along.

The monograph recounted the experience of a man who had a recurring nightmare. During a business trip he was overcome with a panic attack and became paralyzed in his right arm. The triggering event happened in an unfamiliar European city while he visited an Opera House. Under hypnosis, a past life regression to the 1800s revealed that at that time the man had been tortured and murdered behind the stage. Was the story true? Who knew? Regardless, his paralysis was cured.

Claire became so absorbed that she ceased to keep an eye on the memoir. But when the diary again crossed her mind, she cast a furtive glance in Marc-Claude's direction and breathed a sigh of relief to see him still there with the journal.

She set aside her book and pondered the seemingly miraculous cure outlined in the description. How had the hypnotherapist gained access to forgotten thoughts and memories? Still, if a regression could cure a paralysis, surely she would benefit from one, too. She tried to think back to the time she'd first had that dreadful nightmare. It must have been about two years ago. Lost in thought, she closed her eyes and took several deep breaths.

Snippets of movie-like scenes from the diary played out before her mind's eye. A younger version of the Marquise Marie de Fleury stood with her mother and father in front of a fairytale chateau. Inside the house Marie danced with her future husband. As the music faded, André kissed her trembling hand. "My pleasure, Mademoiselle de Condé," he murmured.

The scene shifted to a distinguished-looking man who rose from his chair and motioned another man toward the salon. "Best begin with the Articles of the Marriage Contract, and in the meantime, our young people shall converse and become acquainted."

Acquainted, acquainted . . .

The word repeated over and over as the images faded. Yet the emotional power of the scene remained with Claire.

She stretched and wiggled her fingers before realizing that Marc-Claude had spoken to her. "I'm sorry. Did you say something?" Feeling heat rush to her cheeks, she got up and stood by the fire, her back to him.

"I asked whether Janine was acquainted with the stable hand."

She nodded. "But I don't know to what extent."

"More hot chocolate?" Marc-Claude offered.

"Please," Claire said, wondering how long he had been watching her. Had he noticed anything unusual? If so, he gave no indication.

"The memoir is well written. I've already found leads for our research."

Claire sidled up beside him and held his gaze. "I'm glad you're reviewing it."

He smiled in return. "I'm not done yet. Do you mind if I keep it until I finish?"

"Can I trust you?" Claire asked in earnest. Then, forcing a lighthearted laugh, she reached over and patted the book with affection.

"Yes, Claire, and now is the time to begin."

"I agree. Will you return it to me in the morning?"

"First thing in the morning. Okay?"

"Of course." Claire continued, "I hope you can appreciate my concern. After all, it is over two hundred years old."

Marc-Claude nodded. "Completely understandable." He placed the book on the coffee table. "What did you decide about the workshop?"

Claire moved past him and returned to the sofa. "I prepared a brief proposal for you, outlining several options for your consideration. I'll get it to you before the day's over."

"That's good. I'll see how Jacques responds."

As if on cue, Michelle and Jacques burst into the room, laughing at some private joke. "Shssh." Michelle placed a manicured finger on Jacques' lips. "We're not alone." She giggled.

Marc-Claude stood. "Don't pay attention to us."

Like moths drawn to light, Jacques and Michelle gravitated to the fire, she in her signature red casual wear and he in a suit.

Pointing to the silver pot, Jacques asked, "Is it hot? If so I want some."

Marc-Claude poured a cup and handed it to Michelle, who took a sip before handing the cup to Jacques.

"*Chocolat* . . . good idea. I want one, too," Michelle said, her hand outstretched.

Marc-Claude set the pot down after he gave her another cup. "Claire has written up a plan for our consideration about the cross-cultural training I recommended," he said as he came to stand beside Jacques at the fireplace.

"You know I don't believe there *is* a solution." Jacques scowled. "The Americans are impossible to do business with, *mon ami*."

"The stakes are high enough to justify a one-time workshop."

"Laval, you're relentless."

"Think about it. We'll talk later." Marc-Claude clapped Jacques on the shoulder.

A jaunty tune from Michelle's cell phone sounded. "Felicity, how are you?" She strolled to the back of the room before circling back around to the front.

Jacques watched her for a moment then turned back to Marc-Claude. "All right, I'm with you."

"Okay, I'll tell him." Michelle flipped the cover down on her phone, and said to Marc-Claude, "Call Felicity right away."

Marc-Claude nodded to Michelle and excused himself to Claire, "Everything is urgent with Felicity and Maman."

The screeching brakes on Marc-Claude's Peugeot broke the rhythm of the caravan of vehicles along the driveway to the fundraiser. His car missed a red fox by inches, and the startled animal paused to stare before disappearing into the forest. The rippling pattern of luxury cars resumed along the *allée* of white bark sycamores that led into the estate.

Marc-Claude caught Claire's eye in the rearview mirror. "Are you okay?"

"Yes."

Jacques whistled softly. "Mon Dieu."

Marc-Claude shrugged. "Must be chasing a rabbit or something."

The chateau came into view as they rounded a bend in the road. The low-lying vermilion sun cast long slanted shadows of slate gray on the golden façade of the house. Its slender towers, soaring pinnacles and high, gabled windows revealed its Italian Renaissance design. Claire caught her breath—she'd recognize the fairytale castle of her vision anywhere. It was the site of the signing of Marie and Andre's marriage contract. Why hadn't the Lavals mentioned Chateau Fleury?

"*C'est magnifique.*" Marc-Claude glanced back at Claire in the mirror. "Claire, what do you say?"

"It's . . . it's breathtaking." She fought to control her voice. Marc-Claude behaved as if she had known where they were going. Was it possible that Michelle had told her that the event was at Chateau Fleury—and in her preoccupied state of mind, it hadn't registered?

Not likely.

Eagar to see the grounds, Claire looked in dismay as they drew nearer the chateau. The meticulously groomed French gardens of old had given way to simple anemic green grass and smoke-colored gravel. And where were the geometric-patterned flowerbeds abounding with a rainbow of colors? Glimpses of the neglected rose garden and the high plume of water spraying from a horse's mouth at the top of the classic, three-tiered fountain saddened her. She lowered her eyes, closing out the distressing view of the residence. She'd read detailed descriptions by Marie and Janine of the beauty of the gardens and the angel-topped fountain, and now a graveled parking area covered the entire east side of the yard up to the old stables.

The uniformed attendant's impatient hand gesture directed them to park in the next spot in a newly formed row of cars.

Jacques shook his head. "It's a shame the old count doesn't have the inclination or resources to maintain this place," he said with an expansive wave of his hand.

Marc-Claude nodded in agreement. "You know they received a

grant from the Society of Friends of French Arts, don't you? It's earmarked for the restoration of the paneling and gilt in the twin grand salons."

Jacques ran his hand over his thinning hair. "How's the work coming?"

"One salon is completed. Work should begin on the other one any day now," Marc-Claude said, a note of pride evident in his voice.

At the mention of the salon, an image of Marie and Andre's dance together there flashed through Claire's mind. Would she see the actual room tonight?

Jacques looked toward the rows of grapevines on the hills past the elaborate but neglected stables and mused, "Hmm . . . do you suppose those vineyards bring in much income?"

"They'd bring in more if they received proper care," Marc-Claude said.

"I understand that the count's health is failing." With a probing look, Jacques said, "What Felicity needs is an astute husband to help her manage this place."

Marc-Claude ignored the comment and parked beside a large black limousine. When he got out of the car and opened the door for Claire, she accepted his outstretched hand and stepped out, taking a moment to adjust the long skirt of her champagne-colored silk gown. She patted her elegantly-coiffed hair and moved to his side.

Crickets chimed in with their own love songs as classical music from the chateau wafted through the air. Jacques began humming along with the music. "What is that tune?"

Claire ignored the discordant sounds from the woods and hummed along with him. "Mozart?" The closer she came to the chateau, the more anxious she became. Her heart thumped and her hands grew cold. As if reading her mind, Marc-Claude reached for her hand and guided her up the steps, his touch most reassuring.

Within minutes I'll be inside Chateau Fleury!

Chapter 7

Claire sighed as she and Marc-Claude entered Chateau Fleury's spacious limestone gallery. More beautiful than she'd imagined, it brought feelings of awe tinged with uncertainty.

"It's a grand entry, but wait until you see the other rooms," Marc-Claude said as he guided her into the large ballroom.

Claire accepted a glass of champagne from a dapper waiter making the rounds with a tray. The pale green, paneled walls were accented with gold gilt.

One of the newly restored rooms?

Light from two huge crystal chandeliers glittered on silver trays of caviar, smoked salmon, pâté de fois gras, and *pâté en croute*. Claire sensed eyes on her and glanced to her right side. A voluptuous young woman with tawny brown hair approached.

"There's Felicity now," Marc-Claude said.

Claire made a quick evaluation of Felicity. Some men might find her sexy—if they looked no further than her hourglass figure. The rest of the package was nondescript. Striking it was not.

Felicity entwined her arms around Marc-Claude's neck and kissed him on both cheeks, sliding her lips to his. Rubbing against him, she purred, "I've missed you. I haven't seen you for ages."

The brash hussy!

Marc-Claude moved his hands along the back of Felicity's smooth satin dress and stepped aside. "With a schedule like yours, how do you find time to miss anyone?"

Claire distanced herself a few paces toward Jacques, who was talking with a gray-haired woman. However, she could still see and hear Marc-Claude and Felicity's conversation.

"I'll always find time for you," Felicity said in a silky voice. "As if you don't know that."

"How's your father?" Marc-Claude replied in a flat tone,

Felicity's demeanor changed. She pursed her lips and shook her head. "Not good. The doctors aren't encouraging." She slipped her arm around Marc-Claude and drew him nearer Jacques. "I don't think I've had the pleasure of meeting you," she said to Claire.

Quite the actress! She's gone from scheming seductress to distressed damsel, and now she's pretending to fawn over me, all in a matter of minutes.

Marc-Claude edged away from Felicity. "This is Claire Bennett, Michelle's friend from *l'Amérique,*" he said.

"Welcome to our event," Felicity's eyes were appraising as she repositioned herself by Marc-Claude's side.

"Merci." Claire's terse reply was barely polite as resentment and a touch of jealousy threatened her composure. Felicity left little doubt as to her possessiveness toward Marc-Claude. Worse yet, he allowed it!

"What brings you to France?" Felicity asked, firmly in control.

"I accompanied a group of exchange students."

"Oh. That's wonderful." Felicity's predatory green eyes darted around the room. "There's our guest speaker over there . . . with Michelle."

Marc-Claude turned and looked in the direction she pointed. "Where's he from?"

"Paris. You know he's the leading landscape architect in all of France."

"Oh, yes." Marc-Claude nodded.

"Jacques, be a dear and take care of Claire," Felicity said. "Marc-Claude and I must make our rounds." She reached for Marc-Claude's hand. "Come on."

"Tell Michelle I'm looking for her," Jacques called to them. "Claire, let's see where . . . oh, there she is."

Michelle wove through the elbow-to-elbow crowd to reach them, and Jacques slipped his arm around her waist. "May I get you a drink?"

"Not now." She lowered her voice. "First, I have someone for Claire to meet. Wait here."

"Don't be long," Jacques said.

Michelle smiled and led Claire across the room to a thirty-something, conservatively dressed woman. "Claire, I'd like you to meet Susan Fisher, my hypnotherapist friend from Paris. Susan, this is Claire Bennett from the U.S. It's okay to speak French. She's a French language professor. Isn't it wonderful? She's having flashbacks of what seem to be past life memories."

"So nice to meet you," Susan said.

"Claire, you and Susan need to find a place where you can talk."

"Is this a good time?" Claire asked Susan.

"Oui, I'd like to hear about your experiences."

"Wait here." Michelle turned to leave. "I'll ask Felicity where we can find a quiet place."

"That won't be necessary," Claire said, to her surprise. "Follow me." She turned and walked toward the terrace. "This way . . . past those archways over there."

What am I doing?

Michelle frowned. "Where *are* you going?"

"To the rose garden."

I hope.

Susan gave Michelle a quizzical look, but Michelle just shrugged and said, "Lead the way."

Without hesitation Claire led them across the salon and through the archways into the walled area of the garden. Michelle and Susan followed, speaking softly on the way. Claire pressed on. She knew where to go. But how did she know?

The sense of déjà vu drew her onward. In the Marie-and-Andre vision, she hadn't seen the garden. Thoughts pounded against her skull. Somehow she knew of a secluded garden room in a far corner— one with roses and a small shell fountain. She led them past the large central fountain to the far end of the garden and poked her head around a fragrant jasmine-encircled opening in the wall. Her pulse responded to her euphoria. "There it is . . . just ahead."

"So it is." Michelle's voice conveyed surprise at Claire's familiarity with the garden. "You know this place better than I do."

What's happened here?

Claire ran her fingers along the wall and sighed. "Some of these stones are loose . . . and the roses haven't been trimmed in ages, by the look of them."

"These old places need constant attention." Michelle pulled up cushioned chairs to the small fountain. "At least this neglected spot seems to have been spruced up for this event, although no visitors are likely to use it. Please, be seated."

Claire took care to fold her skirt across her lap, keeping it off the ground. "Trimming the roses won't involve much work or expense, but that wall looks like another matter," she said before she sat.

Susan sat in the chair nearest her and started to roll her foot over a loose pebble, first pushing it away and then bringing it back.

Michelle watched Susan's game with the small stone for a moment then said, "I told Claire about your work."

Susan nodded in response.

"She tells me you're a clinical psychologist," Claire said.

"Yes. And I'm also a certified hypnotherapist. Some of my cases lend themselves to the use of hypnosis."

Claire positioned her hands on her lap for renewed assurance that her folded, delicate skirt remained in place. "How do those cases differ from others?"

"Hypnotherapy shortens the process for uncovering troublesome repressed memories."

"She received her hypnotherapy training while working in London. Fortunately for us, she returned to Paris." Michelle glanced at her watch, stood, and pushed her chair back. "Please excuse me. Jacques is waiting for me, and I must get more information from the speaker before I introduce him."

Once Michelle had walked away, Claire adjusted her chair and turned to Susan. "Where were we? Oh, yes, you said hypnotherapy can reduce the time it takes to produce results."

"The subconscious mind can be accessed and work begun in one session. Traditional therapy may take months or years to uncover negative beliefs and perceptions at the root of a problem."

Startled, Claire felt as if a hand had touched her shoulder, and she turned to see who was there. She could swear she'd heard a man's voice whisper in her ear, "I knew I'd find you here." And he was gone—or was it a hallucination, right there in front of Susan?

God help me. I need to understand what is real and what is not.

"I'm sorry. What did you say?" Claire shifted her position on the chair.

"Traditional therapy requires a prolonged search for the root of troublesome issues."

"Do you also help people understand the meaning of their dreams?" Claire asked, not broaching the subject of visions yet.

"Yes. Dreams are another way the subconscious

communicates. During hypnosis the subconscious can be questioned further . . ."

The crackle of footsteps on the gravel path drew Claire's attention. She turned and saw Marc-Claude. He approached and took a deep breath of the jasmine-scented night air. "Peace and quiet for a change," he said, looking up at the night sky.

"How'd you find us?" Claire asked.

"Michelle told me where you were."

Claire glanced up at the sapphire-colored sky dotted with countless golden stars and the silver sliver of a moon. "It's timeless out here."

"I wish I could stay longer." Marc-Claude glanced at his watch. "The speaker will begin his talk in ten minutes. It's about gardens. You won't want to miss it."

"Merci." Claire glanced at Susan and back to Marc-Claude. "We'll be there."

Susan watched Marc-Claude retreat. "Now there's a man who lives by his *noblesse oblige*. He's the one who makes the SFFA the success it is."

"How so?"

"The Lavals hosted the fundraiser last year at Lamont. And Marc-Claude sponsored the food and champagne for tonight. Many of the major contributors are here because of him."

"I'm impressed."

"He's the kind of guy many women fantasize about . . . handsome, charming, power broker from an ancient noble family, and so on."

"Do you fantasize about him?" Claire asked.

"I pride myself on being a realist. I'm not part of his world. *C'est la vie*."

"Susan, I'm so glad we've had a chance to meet. I need your help to get answers about my strange experiences."

Susan took a business card from her clutch and handed it to Claire. "Give me a call when you're ready to get started."

"I will," Claire said. "Shall we go inside now?"

They left the secret garden and followed the last of the main garden visitors through the salon into the library. After finding seats toward the back of the auditorium-style setup, there were only minutes to spare before Michelle introduced Monsieur Landry.

After the lights dimmed, he launched into his presentation, discussing the visuals on a large screen. Haunting violin and harpsichord music seemed to overlay his voice—for Claire's ears only. *So compelling.* She focused on Monsieur Landry's words while trying to ignore the music. She'd be able to comment on the lecture in case Marc-Claude or Michelle asked how she liked it. Besides, the topic of La Notre's famous gardens fascinated her, especially the ones he designed for the king at Versailles.

After the talk, as people congregated in clusters, the buzz of voices increased in volume. When Michelle, Jacques, and Marc-Claude joined Susan and Claire, Marc-Claude drew Claire aside. "Claire, I have something to show you. Come this way." He led her from the room through the salon and into the large entry gallery.

Felicity must have let him off the leash!

"If Monsieur Landry hadn't mentioned the Le Notre garden at Lamont, I wouldn't have known it was there," Claire said as they walked along. "Tell me about it."

"He designed it in seventeen-twenty-one. It's outside the library. The terrace remains as originally designed."

"I must see it before I leave."

"Yes. Words don't do it justice."

The entire gallery floor, the walls, and ceiling of Chateau Fleury were constructed of beautiful limestone. While they moved along the wide hall, Claire observed rosettes of the de Fleury coat of arms anchored at the cross points of the ribbed stone on the vaulted ceiling.

Marc-Claude stopped at a partially closed door and pushed it open. When he motioned her inside, she took a step back. "Should we be in there?"

"It's all good." He turned the knob and led the way into a second salon, a near duplicate of the one they had passed through—except for its neglected condition. A press of the light switch near the door revealed faded blue wall paneling.

Not bad, considering it's two hundred and fifty years old.

Somehow she knew, without looking or asking, that this room opened into the dining room—the room where Marie first met her future husband.

Heavy footsteps announced a uniformed guard before he appeared at the door. "Monsieur, Madame. This room is closed to guests," he said in a brusque tone, betraying his sense of self-importance.

A shadow of annoyance clouded Marc-Claude's handsome features. He spun around to face the guard. "Yasin."

"I'm sorry, Monsieur de Laval, I didn't recognize you. Take your time," he said and retreated.

"At times Yasin shows his rough edges, but he does take his job seriously."

Claire felt less forgiving. "He should be more civil. The people here are invited guests."

Marc-Claude nodded and spoke with passion. "This *boiserie* has remained in pretty good condition compared to the other salon. Most of it requires only a good cleaning."

Marc-Claude's love of Chateau Fleury was obvious. No wonder Claire's claim riled him. What drove his desire for the preservation of the chateau? Did he foresee that one day, via Felicity, it would be his? Claire gestured toward a damaged area on the wall. "What about this?"

"The blemished gilding requires gold leaf restoration."

Claire, too, felt a proprietary attachment to the chateau and wanted its preservation to move forward. Running her finger over the loose and cracking pattern, she asked, "How will they go about the repair?"

"A special glue mixture is brushed over all cracks and flaking gesso. If there are loose gold-leaf chips, another type of glue is injected underneath."

"You speak as if from experience." She acknowledged that he seemed well equipped to bring the chateau back to its former glory.

"I'm quite interested in . . ."

"What *are* you doing in here?" Felicity stood in the doorway, staring at Claire and Marc-Claude. "I've looked everywhere for you." Her petulant remark was clearly addressed to Marc-Claude.

"I'm showing Claire our next restoration project."

Felicity slipped her arm through his, her voice soft. "You're full of surprises. You can't help showing off this project." She kissed him on the cheek. "Come, we have to thank Monsieur Landry before he gets away."

"Go ahead, we'll be there in a few minutes. Claire, you'll want to meet him, too."

"Marc-Claude, come on before he leaves." Felicity ran her fingers over her hair and stared at him. "I'm not leaving without you."

"All right." Marc-Claude stepped away from Felicity and said to Claire, "We'll finish up another time. Let's go."

After the three of them arrived in the main salon, Claire stopped to chat with Michelle and Susan while Marc-Claude and Felicity went ahead.

"We may as well sit down. I have to wait for Michelle, too," Susan said. "She invited me to stay the night at Lamont."

"Good. I hope to see you before you leave."

"Michelle will drop me off at the TVG station early in the morning. I'll take the train and be back in Paris for my first appointment."

"Do you know Felicity very well?" Claire asked.

"Not really. I come to these events and help a bit. She's hard to get to know." Susan nodded. "Secretive. Shyness? I don't think so."

Claire chuckled. "I don't either."

"She's all over Marc-Claude. It probably works against her."

Claire perked up. *I hope so!* "You don't think it appeals to his ego?"

"Oh, it does in a way, but she's suffocating him. Anyway, I doubt he needs her to have his ego stroked."

Claire sighed. "I've been thinking I should be in Paris by the end of the week. Should I schedule a session with you now?"

"Non. Call when you're back," Susan said. As the last of the invited guests departed, Susan said, "I'll see if I can be of help to them."

"Let me know if there's anything I can do for Michelle," Claire said.

Susan rose. "I doubt that there is, but if so, I'll let you know."

A long table and chairs were set up for the small group of sponsors to make a preliminary evaluation of the event. Monsieur and Madame de Laval sat with four other couples, comparing notes. Susan sat across from Michelle and Jacques while Felicity and Marc-Claude occupied the two chairs at the head of the table.

To pass the time while she waited, Claire went into the garden and sat down by the large fountain. The thing that struck her as peculiar was the discordant water flow from the out-of-place horse's mouth atop the *formal* fountain. Soon her thoughts turned to Susan, and what she'd said about Marc-Claude. She relaxed in the stillness until Felicity approached.

"Here you are. I couldn't imagine where you had gone." She sat across from Claire. "I'm sorry you had to fend for yourself tonight," she said with a smile.

Seriously? Who does she think she's kidding?

"Not at all. You had many demands on your time."

"We must get better acquainted. How long will you be at Lamont?"

"A couple more days."

"I'll have you for tea . . . and give you the grand tour."

"How thoughtful. I'd like that," Claire said." She'd take what she could get. Not perfect, but she'd see more of the chateau and have an opportunity to ask questions about what had happened to it over the years—regardless of Felicity's reasons. What was Felicity's ulterior motive for engaging her in conversation? Most likely she wanted to protect what she considered hers—Marc-Claude and Chateau Fleury. That is if she had learned about Claire's claim. Claire's thoughts were interrupted by the sight of Marc-Claude at the open door.

He looked into the garden before coming out and sitting down beside Felicity. "You did a great job tonight. I'm sure we'll be pleasantly surprised at the final tally."

"Merci. Everyone has been great—especially you." She leaned her head against his shoulder.

"And you. I know you've spent countless hours on this event." Marc-Claude gave Felicity a quick hug and stood. "It's getting late. I'd better get Claire home."

Felicity rose and reached for his hand. "No need. Claire can ride home with Michelle and Susan."

"I'm going now. It's anybody's guess how long Michelle will be here." Marc-Claude turned to Claire. "Coming?"

Chapter 8

Marc-Claude and Claire sped into the night along the deserted highway, leaving Chateau Fleury in the distance. Marc-Claude rested his arm on the back of Claire's seat. "Is Fleury as you imagined it from the memoir?"

If only he knew what I know.

"Pretty much." Fighting her impulse to elaborate, Claire kept her answer vague, troubled that he hadn't mentioned they would be going to Chateau Fleury that night. How had he expected she'd react when she realized their destination? It was downright foolish of him not to tell her. But what if he thought she knew. She couldn't be sure, especially with the turmoil created by Madame's interference with their lunch appointment. She controlled her impulse to whine.

Marc-Claude appeared content to dispense with small talk, leaving her to her thoughts. After continuing on the main highway, he let up on the accelerator as he made the sharp turn into the entrance to Chateau Lamont.

"We're here already?" Claire said. "It seemed much farther on the drive there."

"It's about twenty-five kilometers." With an amused smile, he added, "Almost sixteen miles each way."

They shared a chuckle. "I suppose it is," Claire said, appreciating his way of lessening her tension. He made her laugh, and goodness knows, that was something she needed to do more often.

Lamont's massive towers loomed on the horizon, creating a picture-postcard image of a storybook castle. "How long do you think it will be before Michelle and Jacques get back?" Claire had decided to ask Michelle why she hadn't told her the fundraiser was at Chateau Fleury. Of course, Michelle had no way of knowing of her particular interest in it—unless Marc-Claude had told her. Was it logical to blame him?

"Probably not for another two hours or so." Marc-Claude glanced at Claire as they approached the drawbridge gate into the courtyard. "Knowing Michelle, it may not be before dawn." He eased the car into its usual place by the colonnades near the fountain and came to the passenger's side.

After he opened the door for her, Claire asked, "When can I see your Le Notre garden?"

"No better time than the present."

After they were inside the house, they went upstairs to reach the terrace by way of the library. From their outside vantage point, Claire had a panoramic view of the entire garden design. A central and a cross-axis pattern revealed the skeletal structure of La Notre's baroque design. Indeed, the stone terrace ran most of the length of the east wing of the chateau, leading the eye north to the Loire and beyond. "Amazing. Le Notre visualized this beauty and made it a reality."

"It is remarkable." Marc-Claude touched her elbow lightly and led her to the horseshoe-shaped staircase leading down to the garden. Water gurgled from the mouths of mythical beasts. Misty droplets of water mingled with the air. Cherub urns splashed down the front of the huge fountain between the wraparound stairs.

At the bottom of the stairs, Claire turned toward the chateau to find that evenly spaced, arched niches ran below the terrace floor. Each niche showcased a marble statue or a huge urn. At the far end of the garden, a mirror-image fountain balanced the formal design. "Let's walk down to the other fountain."

"As you please, Mademoiselle. "

The grand parterre contained hedge-enclosed rectangular flowerbeds and emerald areas of grass. The formality of the extensive ornamental gardens gave way to small shrubs and progressively larger ones leading into the forest.

Goodness knows when or if Michelle would be home anytime soon. Claire couldn't wait to clear the air with Marc-Claude—to hear in his own words why he hadn't mentioned they were going to Chateau Fleury. What better time than now to ask? She bit her lower lip, afraid of how he might interpret her question. "Why didn't you tell me we were going to Chateau Fleury tonight?"

There. The deed is done.

He shrugged. "I thought you knew."

"How *would* I know? No one told me." Breathing deeply, she stopped and faced him. "You know the extent of my interest in Chateau Fleury!"

He frowned. "During all the time you spent with Michelle, you're telling me she didn't mention it to you?"

"Michelle and your parents spoke of the fundraiser, but no one mentioned Chateau Fleury."

"*Désolé*. I'm sorry you weren't told."

She turned and walked on at a clipped pace. Could she believe him? Why not? He hadn't hesitated when Michelle asked him to take her to the event. He had talked freely about the restoration projects— perhaps, a bit too enthusiastically. No matter how much she wished otherwise, the fact remained that her interest and his interest in the place were in serious conflict.

He caught up with her and held her gaze. "Am I forgiven?"

What could she say? "Yes . . . only because you thought I knew." She wanted to believe him, and at that moment she was inclined to do so.

They continued to walk, stopping to look at the fountain before retracing their steps to the chateau. The moon journeyed toward the west, adding a little light in the sky. "You spent a lot of time in the gardens at Fleury. What suggestions do you have to beautify them?" Marc-Claude asked.

"For starters I'd say a French garden in the front yard is rather more desirable than anemic patches of grass and a gravel parking lot."

"I've often thought the same thing. As a matter of fact, an old etching of the chateau depicts a formal garden."

Why had he asked that question—because he cared about what she thought or because the next project would be funding for the gardens?

Marc-Claude cupped his hand around Claire's elbow when they started up the stairs to the chateau. "May I suggest a glass of liqueur before calling it a night?"

"Sounds good."

They stood for a moment on the terrace and looked out over the garden before going into the library. Claire sat on the leather sofa, laying her evening bag on the coffee table while Marc-Claude went to fetch their nightcap.

He returned, sat beside her, and handed her a tiny crystal glass filled with a golden-colored liqueur. "To many more beautiful evenings like this one."

Touched by his words, she set down her glass and tilted her face close to his. Marc-Claude brushed a gentle kiss across her forehead. It felt so right. She closed her eyes and waited for their lips to meet. Instead, he moved away, straightened, and pressed his back against the sofa.

Both grateful and disappointed, she appreciated his tactful response to her moment of vulnerability . . . and indulgence in fantasy. She did so want to get to know him better and hoped he was the man she wished him to be. "Apricot?" she said, sipping the smooth liqueur.

He nodded. "A specialty of Chateau Lamont-sur-Loire. Made from our own apricots."

"It's superb," she said with sincerity.

Marc-Claude set down his empty glass. "We better get started on our research project tomorrow or the next day at the latest. And before then I'd like to finish reading the memoir."

Dang! I so hoped he would forget.

"The memoir, yes. I'll . . . get it to you in the morning," Claire said with a twinge of concern. She knew she couldn't rest easy while it was out of her possession. "Where do you suggest we begin our research?"

Marc-Claude seemed agreeable to waiting for the book. He lounged comfortably on the sofa while he appeared to think about her question. "The July seventeen, seventeen-sixty-seven marriage in the cathedral should be easy to verify." As if thinking out loud, he added, "Usually, the civil marriage occurred a short time before and not necessarily in the same location."

"At least we should find something in Tours," Claire said hopefully.

"We'll be lucky to find the birth and death dates of the children in Tours' records. I don't suppose you have access to the family Bible."

Claire shook her head. "Maybe we can do some preliminary work on the Internet."

Marc-Claude frowned. "Information is only as good as its source."

"I know what you mean," she said.

"Information about the Marquis' service in the King's army and Marie's appointment as Lady of the Queen's Robe can be checked out in Paris." Marc-Claude glanced at his watch. "I've kept you up too late."

"Not at all . . . what time is it?"

"Eh . . . one-thirty."

"It's later than I thought. If we want to get an early start in the morning, I better call it a night." She stood and picked up her evening bag. "I'll see you in the morning."

"Bonne nuit," Marc-Claude said in a mellow voice.

The next morning Marc-Claude ambled into the breakfast room a few minutes after ten. Smiling when he saw Claire, he came to the table and sat down across from her. "Did you sleep well?" he asked, holding her gaze.

She swallowed the last of the grape she had been eating. Although Marc-Claude wore a casual black polo shirt and black denim pants, he retained an aura of sophistication. "I don't remember anything from the time my head hit the pillow until I awoke this morning."

He glanced at her large tote. "You brought the memoir for me?" he asked, holding out his hand.

She nodded, swallowed the last of her coffee, and slowly removed the book from her bag. She set it in the center of the table, halfway between them. "Guard it with your life. Give it back as soon as you're finished—*tonight*."

"You can count on me." He stood. "More coffee?"

"Please," she said as he left for the buffet. Indulging her desire to stare at him without his knowledge, she feasted her eyes on his devilishly tempting male physique.

He picked up a tray from the sideboard, placing two small plates and two mugs on it. After pouring coffee, he selected two flaky croissants and spooned a bit of old-fashioned rose-and-pear jelly onto each plate. Then he returned and set the tray on the table. "Is everything okay?" he asked, giving her an enigmatic look.

"Uh . . . yes." She averted her eyes and nodded. What had she revealed in her expression?

He passed a cup and plate to her before sitting down. "If you'd like, we can revisit Le Notre's garden this afternoon while it's daylight and see some of the other parts of the park as well."

"I'd love to."

"I'll meet you at three." Marc-Claude looked around at the sound of footsteps and lowered his voice. "In the library."

Michelle strolled to the table and pulled up a chair. "*Allo*. What are you two whispering about?"

Marc-Claude chuckled. "Now, little sister, you don't need to know all of our secrets."

"You exasperating tease! Claire will tell me later."

"You think so?" Claire said, heat stealing onto her face.

Focusing on Claire, Michelle said, "Did you get enough to eat?"

"More than enough. Everything's delicious."

"I have to leave you now," Marc-Claude said as he slid his chair from the table.

Michelle frowned. "Well, you don't have to go just because I'm here."

"Jacques and I have some things to go over."

"Right now? You haven't finished eating." Michelle held his gaze. "We would enjoy your company."

"Another time." Marc-Claude stood and picked up the memoir on his way out.

Michelle reached for his plate and pulled it forward. She broke off a piece of the croissant and covered the end with jelly while giving Claire a sly look. "Well, so much for male company for breakfast." Her attention shifted to another topic as smoothly as shifting gears in a new sports car. "So how'd you and Susan Fisher get along?"

"I like her. She reminds me of my Aunt Sarah . . . a patient listener."

"Are you going to see her in Paris?"

"I plan to," Claire said.

"It can't do any harm."

"That's how I see it," Claire replied.

"Great." Laying her napkin on the table, Michelle changed the subject yet again. "Felicity and the committee members are coming over at eleven to put together our summary report for the fundraiser. Is there anything I can do for you before then?"

"No. I'll read in the library. You'll know where to find me."

After Michelle left, Claire sat by herself, sipping coffee. She ran her fingertip around the blue and yellow swirls on the tablecloth and wondered whether Marc-Claude would have stayed longer if Michelle hadn't come in. He hadn't seemed in a hurry before there were three of them. Had he wanted to talk to Jacques without Michelle or . . .

On the way along the deserted corridor, Claire realized she had begun to think of the library as her retreat. Upon her arrival she sank onto the welcome comfort of the sofa, savoring the time alone. Hopefully, Marc-Claude would finish with the memoir and return it when they met at three. Meanwhile, she'd read as much of the hypnotherapy book as she could and have it finished before her first session with Susan.

Fewer than forty-five minutes had passed when Michelle broke into her sanctuary. "Claire, now's your chance to hear Marc-Claude's talk about our weapons collection."

"Now?"

"Yes. The museum curator and his new assistant are here, so Marc-Claude will make it interesting. Let's go."

Claire placed the bookmark at the page she'd last read and tucked the book into her canvas bag.

The massive door, constructed of heavy wood fortified with metal straps, stood ajar. Felicity and four other visitors, two men and two women, stood in front of a glass-topped weapons case. Just inside the door Michelle stopped and whispered, "The museum curator is on Felicity's right and his assistant is next to him."

Felicity acknowledged them with a tentative wave. Moving closer to the curator, she returned her attention to Marc-Claude, who motioned them in and continued talking about the collection. "In sixteen twenty-five or thereabouts," he pointed to an object in the case, "the Duc de Laval commissioned a well-known Dresden goldsmith to make that hunting *trousse*. A sheet of silver was used to make the scabbard."

The curator adjusted his glasses and leaned closer to the case. "A fine piece. Looks like Botza's work."

Felicity nodded at the plain-looking man of average height. "You're so knowledgeable—a goldmine of information. That knife is one of my favorite items in the de Laval collection."

The curator stood a little taller. "A valuable tool. The blade's designed for efficiency."

"Marc-Claude, I'll bet you could learn some things about your ancient arsenal from this man." Felicity patted the curator on the arm while keeping her eyes on Marc-Claude.

Claire failed to understand Felicity's fascination with the hunting knife with the long curved blade. Personally, she preferred looking at the lacey pattern of the silver sheath—a real work of art.

Marc-Claude directed their attention to an equally lethal weapon in the same case on the other side of the trousse. "Notice the tines on this military fork have been widened to form two cutting blades." He turned from the case and moved in front of two swords displayed side by side on the wall. "These two swords go back to the fourteenth century and the time of Guy the First. The one on the right accompanied him during raids along the river.

"The one on the left belonged to his arch rival." Raising his arm as if wielding a sword, Marc-Claude lunged at the curator. "The old warrior's luck ran out at age sixty-two when he was mortally wounded by that very sword."

The curator gasped and jumped away from the mock attack.

Had Marc-Claude acted out of jealousy? Claire wondered.

"You're outrageous." Felicity glared at Marc-Claude.

Ignoring her, he continued his animated presentation. "The victor's glory soon ended. Guy's men ran the villain through with his own sword before they returned the mortally-wounded Guy and the trophy sword to the fortress."

His composure restored, the curator said, "It's truly remarkable and ironic to have both these swords in your possession."

Marc-Claude nodded.

"Is it possible for the museum to show several of these items in our upcoming History of French Weaponry exhibition?" the curator asked.

"Prepare a list, and we'll discuss it and prepare an agreement."

"I'll act as the go-between." Felicity linked arms with each of them, drawing the men against her body. When Marc-Claude withdrew his arm, she led the curator to Michelle and Claire. "It's nice to see you again . . . so soon," she said to Claire. Felicity proceeded to introduce the curator to Claire, and when he excused himself to talk to Marc-Claude, she said to Claire, "We must set a time for our visit at Chateau Fleury."

Why not set a time now?

"Oui. I'll be returning to Paris soon," Claire said.

"I'll give you a call tomorrow."

Michelle stepped between them and gave Claire a beseeching look. "Would you mind terribly if I don't have lunch with you today? The committee members want to work through the lunch hour to complete the report."

Claire seized the moment to retreat. "No problem. Don't give it another thought." As she walked away, she thought, *There goes Marc-Claude's reading time.*

As he climbed the outside stairs to the library terrace, Marc-Claude whistled "Plaisir D'Amour," an old French ballad. It was a tune that always stirred feelings of contentment deep within him. The comparison between Claire and Felicity had a way of intruding into his thoughts. *Claire's like a breath of fresh air, though feisty.*

He felt a sense of freedom, enjoying her company, with no need to think of her as a potential marriage partner. Of course one of these days he would marry a suitable aristocratic woman—French, most likely. Duty! Shaking his head, he dismissed the thought. Today, he'd enjoy the challenge of *l'Americaine.*

When Marc-Claude came into the library, he knew where to look for her. He smiled at how well he already knew her preferences—she'd staked out her claim to the sofa by the fireplace on her first day at the chateau. "I'll bet you're ready to get outside for a while," he greeted her.

She turned, easing into a smile. "Not necessarily, unless you're suggesting a walk in the garden."

He reached for her hand as she stood and led her out to the shady terrace. His pulse quickened. His thoughts fragmented, leaving him shaken by the emotions he felt. Chastising himself, he let go of her hand. He must not give into his unwise attraction to her. They were on different sides: she, the plaintive, alleging a grievance against the de Fleury family, his family and he the defendants. She could well be encouraging his attentions to gain a competitive edge—to distract him. If he didn't watch out, things could easily spiral out of control.

Chapter 9

The next day Marc-Claude arrived at the library at three to meet Claire, as agreed at breakfast. "I'm here to show you more of the surrounding area." He and Claire left the library via the terrace and went down the stairs to the gardens. "Too cold out here?" he asked as she pulled her heavy sweater closer around her.

"No. I'm just adjusting after being inside." Claire looked up toward the puffy clouds. "Does it ever snow here?"

"Yes—in the winter."

"It must be beautiful then."

"It is . . . especially nice during the holidays."

They came to the intersecting north-south avenue and Claire stopped, pointing to the right, across an open area. "Wow. That niche is cut right into the hedge." She left the path, went to the arch-shaped opening in the yew hedge, and sat on the high-backed bench there. Lingering a moment, she turned to Marc-Claude with a self-conscious smile. "I didn't notice it last night."

Charmed by her fascination, he said, "Michelle and I used to play hide-and-seek here. Want to know the best hiding place?"

She smiled indulgently. "Where?"

"Behind any one of those benches in the niches. Granted, you'd have to squeeze by it."

He remained on the walkway while she gingerly explored among the tall hedges. Upon her return, she brushed a stray curl from her face. "I can see why."

The steady rhythm of their steps on the stone esplanade reminded Marc-Claude of the afternoon he'd run along this path to get away from his father. Only eight years old, Marc-Claude had spent an anxious night in the forest before his fear and hunger overcame his devastation. *You've shamed us all with such a dismal performance.* He recalled his father's words shouted in the heat of his son's loss in the ping-pong match with a neighbor. What had his father expected? He'd played against a fourteen-year-old boy. Humiliated, Marc-Claude had wondered how he could face his friends and their parents again.

"What other games did you play back then?" Claire's voice

interrupted his dismal memory.

"Hmmm. Football mostly," he smiled indulgently, "what you Americans call soccer. And later, tennis. Enough about me, though. What happy memories do you have of your childhood?"

"Every summer our family spent two weeks in California at our Laguna Beach timeshare. My parents relaxed while my brother and I explored the nooks and crannies along the Pacific shore."

"Nooks and crannies? What do you mean?"

"I'm sorry, let me explain. The coastline of Laguna Beach is high above the ocean on cliffs—kind of like Chateau Lamont. There are rugged rocks to climb, coves to investigate, and tide pools to examine. It's much different than the beaches farther north—and very different than along the Loire."

"Sounds like fun," Marc-Claude said.

"Oh, yes, it was. We also visited the Pageant of the Masters. It's spectacular. It recreates masterpiece paintings with live actors. It's amazing how they stay still so long."

"I've heard about the attractions there. It would be a nice place to spend a few weeks," he said as they approached the end of the hedge-lined path.

Claire motioned to a sunny bench and started to sit down just as a jay flew from the green wall of yews, scolding and flapping its black-and-white wings. "I guess not," she said and got up in a hurry.

"It should be safe to sit now, if you want to change your mind."

"No. There's more to see," she said.

"Okay."

After leaving the formal garden, they entered the park-like grounds in front of the chateau. The moss-covered path wound among white birch and green cypress to a point where it branched in two directions. One trail led into a heavily forested area and the other circled back to the lawn by the drawbridge. They took the one closest to the front of the chateau and rounded the corner to the side of the west wing.

"Now I know where we are—not far from where we started," Claire said.

"Right."

The gentle slope of the ground became steeper as they made their way along the solid walls of the house. Several small, narrow windows on the lower level of Lamont were about ten feet above the ground, with those on the second level larger and another ten feet higher.

The old Tour de Laval anchored the end corner of the fortress nearest the Loire. But before they reached the tower, Claire stopped in front of an arched doorway on the ground level. "The chapel? Let's go inside."

"How'd you know?" He spoke in a casual, jesting way.

"I could say the stained glass windows, but I won't."

"So?" Marc-Claude prompted.

"The high Gothic arch over the door."

Marc-Claude reached into his pocket for his key ring, selected one, and unlocked the tall, double, flame-shaped doors. "We rarely use this entrance," he said as he opened it. "We usually use the direct access from inside the house."

"How did you happen to have the key with you?" Claire asked.

"It's a master key."

They turned and faced the small altar at the front of the church. A plain, gray stone baptismal font stood near the corner. A west-facing rose window scattered rich jewel-colored patterns around them.

Claire sat and rested against the smooth slats of the wooden chairs. "It's so quiet here."

Marc-Claude sat down beside her. "Do you want to stay longer?"

"For a little while. I like it here."

"I do, too," he said.

"It's hard for me to imagine what it means to you," she said. "Your family history is here."

"Lamont is our family home, for better or worse. It's in my blood . . . so to speak. I am obliged to defend it. You do understand, I hope."

She looked at him for a long moment before she spoke. "Too few people have such continuity in their lives. I am one of the fortunate ones. I have the diary and locket that connects many generations of our family."

She doesn't let me forget our conflict for long. She hadn't commented on his loyalty to his family, rather she emphasized what she thought would support her connection to Chateau Fleury. Marc-

Claude stood. "Ready to go?"

"I guess so," she said as she got up and followed him outside.

"We still have plenty to see," he said as they continued on the esplanade, following along the side of the chateau past the tower. A short distance farther, the manicured lawns gave way to the forest, and the brick walkway met paths leading into the woods and two others descending toward the river. The view from the rocky cliff led the eye to a grassy plateau and beyond to the spectacular view of gold and green trees edging the pale yellow sands along the emerald water of the Loire.

An unexpected gust of wind whipped Claire's hair, and she brushed a wisp from her face. "The view is beautiful," she said. "It's like an Impressionist painting."

Marc-Claude stretched and filled his lungs with the crisp air. "Nice analogy, or is it a simile?"

"Analogy is okay . . . or simile, if you're feeling poetic."

"I'm not much of a poet," Marc-Claude said.

"You might surprise yourself."

He scoffed at the suggestion and dropped the subject.

The forest eclipsed their view to the northwest, but to the southwest the meandering river lay before them. A small motorboat came into view, appearing as no more than a child's toy, before it sped out of sight.

Claire glanced at Marc-Claude. "Which way now?"

"This way is pretty rugged." He motioned toward the forest side. "But it's almost directly in line with a sheltered cove along the river. The other way is steeper and farther." He hastened to add, "But there are stairs for easier access."

"Is this way cleared or overgrown?" Claire pointed straight ahead.

"Cleared."

"Okay. This way." She moved slowly, looking down as she made her way along the uneven path. They walked in silence until they came to several large rock formations. "This rocky area reminds me of home."

"Home . . . the American West? You don't seem like a girl from the 'wild west'."

"I'm not." She laughed. "I haven't spent a day on a ranch."

"There's so much I don't know about you."

"What would you like to know?"

"Begin with your family . . . brothers or sisters?"

"My only brother, John, is eighteen. No sisters."

"As I recall, you told me that your great grandfather settled in Boise, and your family has been there ever since. Is he your genealogical link to the French de Fleury family?"

"No, that's from my mother's side."

"Your parents met in Boise?"

"At college . . .Boise State, as a matter of fact."

"Your mother's family came directly to Idaho from Louisiana?" Marc-Claude asked.

"No. They went west by way of Colorado and California."

"And what about you? What do you want to be doing ten years from now?"

She seemed to ponder her response. "I want to be granted tenure and continue teaching at the university."

"What about having a family of your own? Do you see marriage in your future?"

"Yes, in a vague sort of way. I haven't had much time to think about it."

"Does that mean you're not seriously involved with someone at this time?"

"Exactly. What about you?" she asked.

Now what have I done? "Your story sounds like mine. I do want a family but don't have any specific prospects at the moment."

Claire cleared her throat. "I'm very demanding when it comes to marriage. I must have love, respect, and *trust* for, and from, any man I marry."

Mademoiselle, trust is a two-way requirement! He kept his retort to himself.

The trees thinned out as they neared the river, allowing the warmth of the sun to reach through the scattered white cumulus clouds. Low-growing grasses mingled with vines before surrendering to the golden sands along the water. Wild flowers gave off sweet floral scents. Bumblebees buzzed from flower to flower.

Glistening grains of sand covered the beach area of a crescent-shaped cove. Sandbars broke through the surface of blue-green water, forming random patterns of gold. Farther out in the river a tree-dotted island repeated the gold and green colors of the Loire Valley.

"Look. A boat's tied to that tree." Claire waved in its direction and made her way toward the small, faded blue craft.

Marc-Claude followed along a few steps behind. "It's been there for years."

"Does anyone use it?"

"I doubt it," he said. They stopped beside it. Areas of paint had peeled away, exposing gray patches of weathered wood. Marc-Claude pointed inside and moved his hand toward the back of the boat. "No oars . . . or motor. Probably no longer seaworthy."

A rogue gust of wind whipped Claire's hair and snatched at her sweater. Fluffy white clouds changed to angry, slate-gray. The sun hid behind a thick blanket of black clouds hovering overhead, and the clouds opened up, drenching them with huge, punishing raindrops.

Take her to the boathouse—yes.

"This way." Marc-Claude reached for Claire's hand and took off in a slow jog before sprinting along the sand. "There's a boathouse—not far."

They ran beyond the path they had come down and turned into the woods below the chateau. Nearly hidden among the trees was a small building, looking like a lost chapel in miniature. As they drew closer, details could be distinguished. The decorative lintel above the Gothic door displayed two elegantly carved warriors standing at attention. Above the door at the point of the arch, an angel looked down.

Marc-Claude reached for the handle and gave a determined push. "I'll light a fire when we get inside." The hinges scraped as the door opened. A damp chill filled the air inside the moss-covered stone structure. Not until their eyes adjusted to the change of light were the rectangular table and matching wooden chairs visible in the center of the room.

At the far end a long, oversized sofa dwarfed the small fireplace. A neat stack of firewood, a tin matchbox, old newspapers, and a pail of sand sat near the hearth.

"It won't be long before we're warm and dry," Marc-Claude said as he layered logs, kindling, and wads of old newspapers in the grate. He opened the damper in the chimney, struck a match, and lit the fire. Flames sputtered, threatening to die before growing brighter.

Still shivering, Claire hugged herself and moved closer to the fire. "Do you come here often?"

"Not really. Why?"

"Everything you needed for the fire was here."

"The gardeners see to that." Marc-Claude took off his damp jacket and pulled his shirt over his head. "You're cold and wet. We have to get you warm. Here, put this on while your blouse dries." After handing his knit shirt to her, he was left with only a thin undershirt on his upper torso.

Claire tilted her head and stared at him. "I . . . I . . . okay." Turning her back to him, she took off her sweater first, then slowly removed her blouse and pulled on his shirt. It hung loosely on her slender frame. As if to conserve its warmth, she clutched the surplus fabric and doubled it around her. Ignoring Marc-Claude's outstretched hand, she took her sweater and blouse to the fire and spread them out on two logs beside his jacket.

"You don't *trust* me to arrange your clothes by the fire?" He left her at the fireside and sat on the sofa, trying to decipher her expression.

She came to the sofa and stood in front of him. "It's not that. It's a habit of mine to be self-sufficient."

"You realize you've denied me the chance to perform my chivalrous deed for the day?"

Patting the cushion, he motioned for her to sit down.

She did so with no evident hesitation. "Sorry, I don't do well as a 'damsel in distress.'"

"That may be a good thing," he said.

"On a serious note," she asked, "How long before our clothes are dry?"

"An hour, if we keep turning them," he said.

Her demeanor changed from cautious stranger to flirtatious friend. With a twinkle in her golden-brown eyes, she smiled at him. "Am I to believe that you live by a code from the age of chivalry?" She shivered ever so slightly, slipped her hands inside the extra sleeve length, and moved closer to him.

She needs to get warmed in a hurry. He turned toward her, placed his hand on the small of her back, and drew her closer.

She slipped her arms around his neck and pressed against him. But then she moved away, turned, and stared into the fire. *Oh, my God, what must she think I'm doing?* "I'm sorry. I wasn't thinking clearly."

"It wasn't anything you did," Claire said, a faraway look in her eyes. She reached over and touched his arm with icy fingertips.

Marc-Claude folded back the long shirtsleeves, took her hands, and began to gently massage them. "Let's try to melt these icicles, shall we?"

"Oui, merci." Her voice was a hoarse whisper. She rested her head against his chest. "That feels good . . . how can your hands be so warm and mine so cold?" Her voice was odd—different somehow. Her French, although excellent, normally had a slight accent. There was none now!

Marc-Claude wondered why she'd lost her American accent. He had rather liked it. *Maybe it's just my imagination.*

She spoke so softly that he had to lean closer to hear. He couldn't resist nuzzling his face into her lavender-scented locks. Lifting her face to his, he brushed his lips across hers. An internal warning screamed, *Not now. Not here.* He raised his head and moved away, the sweet taste of her lips still a temptation.

Claire lifted her head and kissed him. Their warmth grew to a searing heat. His resolve faded. Responding to her passion, he crushed her to him, abandoning himself to the moment. Their kiss grew more demanding. She quivered ever so slightly. He wanted her.

Don't! This is insane.

Marc-Claude slipped his hand under the oversized shirt. Stroking her bare skin, he kissed the tip of her nose and cheeks before seeking her lips again. He caressed her throat and shoulders, and then his fingers fell slowly to her breasts. She arched her body toward him and moved to her side, coaxing him to her. His body ached for fulfillment, and his soul cried out not to give into the heat of the moment. Now at the precipice, he must stop or risk defeat.

Her fingertips crept along the bare skin of his stomach. Every nerve ending cried out in exquisite tension. Each beat of his heart thundered in his skull. A renegade moan escaped his lips. Was she . . . a sorceress? He pulled his hand back and sat up then reached for her hands and pulled her upright. In a husky voice, he said, "Not like this."

Marc-Claude hurried outside before she could stop him. The rain had stopped, but cold wind remained, lashing him again and again. The drastic change in temperature relieved his frustration but did little to clear his head. *"Mais je rêve!"* he muttered. *I don't believe it.* Things had gotten out of control lightning fast. What could he say to her or she to him? He had no doubt that she shared the blame.

Only after his passion ebbed did he dare go back inside. He found her sitting where he had left her, a stoic expression masking her emotions. Had she been in charge all along?

He sat down, taking her hand in his, and entwined his fingers through hers. Claire looked up at him, a tear poised to roll down her cheek. *How did she manage to make me so aware of her?*

Wiping it, she said, "I suppose you'll say you left in such a hurry because of some misguided sense of honor?"

"What if I did?"

"I'd question it."

"If I'd stayed here one second longer, we wouldn't be having this conversation."

"So?"

"I didn't want you to have regrets later."

She kissed him on the forehead. "I don't know what came over me. Thank you for being the sensible one."

The dying embers gave off a red glow around them. Marc-Claude went to the fireplace and tested each piece of clothing. "They're dry enough to wear. We'd better get out of here."

While she changed, he extinguished the fire with sand and poured water on it. He took his shirt from her, pressing it to his face to again experience her fragrance before pulling it on. "Your sweater is still a little damp," he said and wrapped his jacket around her shoulders. He was reluctant to leave, but all he said was, "Let's go. It's getting dark."

By the time they reached the chateau, the last vestige of the copper-colored setting sun had spread across the horizon. "At least we're back before dinner." Marc-Claude exchanged her sweater for his jacket and watched her disappear down the hall. *What if . . .?* He shook his head. *Non.*

He needed to clear his head before he tried to read the memoir. Marc-Claude headed for the anteroom where he kept his jogging clothes and changed. He would keep his run short to be back in time for dinner, but he would make up for lack of distance with increased speed along his short, three-mile trail. Questions swirled around in his head. What had come over Claire—and why that brief lapse into flawless French? Why had she seemed like another person and acted that way, too? Was it all an act to place him in a compromising position? He didn't think so; she had been as consumed with passion as he had.

As soon as he walked through the door after his run, his mother called, "Marc-Claude, I need to talk with you. Now." Madame de Laval hurried toward him. She'd obviously been waiting for him.

Irritated, he said, "Not now."

"I won't take long."

Reluctantly, he followed her into her study. He remained standing and glanced at his watch. "You have five minutes."

She stood before him, her eyes piercing. Lips pursed, she picked a long auburn hair from his shirt and walked to the wastebasket, flicking the hair into it with disdain. "Please sit down." She sat in a chair across from him.

He locked eyes with hers. "Get to the point."

"I looked everywhere for you this afternoon." Her voice raised an octave. "Where were you?"

"Calm down." His voice hardened as he struggled to show the woman who had given him life some respect. "Claire and I went for a walk around the grounds."

"All afternoon?"

"Not all afternoon."

"I'm concerned about decorum. The Americaine may misinterpret your intentions."

Marc-Claude moved to the door. "Your concerns are unfounded, Maman." He continued out.

She called after him, "We must talk more later."

Marc-Claude had run farther than first planned and had also been delayed by his mother's meddling, which left him just enough time to shower and dress for dinner. When he arrived in the dining room, the first thing he noticed was that his mother had set an unusually formal table for the small family dinner—no doubt to test Claire's knowledge of French formal table settings. Little did his mother know that her behavior ran counter to her purpose—it only garnered his sympathy for Claire.

Madame left her husband's side and approached Marc-Claude. "The girls are late. What can have delayed them?" She nodded at her son.

In no mood for her insinuation, he said, "I have no idea. Why don't you ask Père?"

"Don't be ridiculous."

"I concur. Let's not be ridiculous," Marc-Claude said with quiet emphasis.

"Dear, leave it be," General de Laval said. "Marc-Claude is right, non?"

His wife paced around the room muttering, "Punctuality is a virtue."

"I'm sorry, Maman." Michelle said as she and Claire came into the room. "We're only five minutes late."

"Let's be seated." Monsieur de Laval held the chair for his wife at the foot of the table before taking his place at the head. Marc-Claude assisted Claire and Michelle before he sat down across from them beside Jacques.

The seven-course meal progressed with little conversation. Marc-Claude noticed that on several occasions Claire glanced his way for a clue as to which spoon, fork, or knife to use—and that his mother kept a watchful eye on her.

Following custom, the de Laval family and guests gathered in the salon for after-dinner drinks and conversation. Marc-Claude would much rather retire to his apartment and finish reading the memoir but saw no polite way to forego the tradition. He sat across from Claire but slid his chair back from the conversation circle.

"Our fundraiser brought in donations and pledges of a hundred and fifty thousand euros. Isn't that fantastic?" Michelle ran her finger around the bottom of her glass.

Madame's expression changed from somber to pleased as she smiled at Michelle. "Special congratulations to you and Felicity."

"Merci, Maman."

Monsieur de Laval nodded. "Each of you is to be commended." Michelle beamed at the praise from her father, who turned to his son and said, "Marc-Claude, you make me proud."

"Merci, Père."

Claire set her glass down and leaned back in the chair. "Congratulations on a job well done."

Marc-Claude focused on Michelle. "I concur with Claire."

A brooding expression crossed Madame de Laval's face as she glared at Marc-Claude. After a long pause she said, "Felicity wanted to see you before she left this afternoon. She waited as long as she could before giving up at five."

"I'll give her a call," Marc-Claude said nonchalantly.

"This has been a frustrating day. I'm exhausted." Madame rose. "You'll have to excuse me for the evening."

Monsieur de Laval adjusted his chair, his expression serious, but said nothing as his wife turned her back and walked stiffly out of the room.

"It *has* been a long day. Bonne nuit." Marc-Claude stood, smiled at everyone, and departed. He must finish reading the memoir before morning. Taking the stairs rather than the elevator to his private apartment on the third floor of the west wing, he pushed the door shut behind him. The spacious suite of rooms, remodeled to his specifications, provided a respite from the events of the day.

He poured a snifter of brandy and sank into his favorite easy chair before he dialed Felicity's number. "It's Marc-Claude. What's up?" He cradled the phone to his ear and listened for a moment. He shook his head in exasperation, but all he said was, "Thanks. I'll give you a call if I think of anything you can do to help with the exhibit." After flipping his phone closed, he muttered, "Really? That's what you hung around for hours to tell me?"

After emptying his glass, Marc Claude stood and walked to the table to get started on the memoir. *Where is it?* He'd left the book right there on the table before Michelle called him to the weapons room. He picked up the legal pad and looked under it before giving it an impatient toss. No sign of the book. *Think! Where is it?* He had been in such a hurry to get dressed for dinner that he hadn't noticed whether the book had been there or not. He went from room to room, checking his desk and bedside tables. After searching frantically, he was back where he began.

He dashed down the one flight of stairs to his mother's room and tapped on the door.

She opened it and stood facing him in her dressing gown. "Did you come to apologize for being so inconsiderate this afternoon?"

He ignored her remark and came into the room. "A book has been taken from my apartment. Do you have any idea who may have been in my rooms?"

Vigorously shaking her head, she said, "A book? I have no idea."

"Merci." He dashed out of the door and returned to the salon. Michelle, Jacques, and Père turned and looked at him, dismay registering on their faces. "Has Claire left for the evening?"

Michelle nodded. "Yes, a few minutes ago."

"Good."

His father frowned. "Why?"

"I don't want her to hear about this yet. She loaned me a book, and now it's missing from my apartment. Do you know of anyone who may have taken it?"

With a puzzled expression, Monsieur de Laval shook his head. "Are you sure it's not there?"

"I'm sure. I've looked everywhere."

"No one has been up there that I know of."

Michelle and Jacques agreed they knew of no one either.

"If you think of anyone who could have taken the book, let me know right away." Marc-Claude moved out of the room. *Felicity had motive and opportunity. But does she know about the diary?* First thing in the morning, he would have to tell Claire that her book was missing. *Zut. All this right after the boathouse debacle!*

Chapter 10

Claire stepped out of the shower and grabbed one of the fluffy, butter-colored towels, still thinking about Marc-Claude and the boathouse the previous afternoon. As she dried her body, she wondered about her seductive behavior toward him—so out of character. Had her fantasizing that morning about his prowess in bed contributed to her actions? Or was she just rationalizing? Still, it was uncharacteristic. Claire considered herself a levelheaded woman who liked to take things slowly. In this case her head had been preempted as her heart melted with his tender caresses and delicious kisses. Now, in the quiet of the moment, her head told her she did not belong to his world—no matter what Marie whispered in her ear.

She hung the towel on the rack. Impatient to get started with the de Fleury research, she dashed to the closet to get dressed. One session with Marc-Claude should reveal whether he sought the truth or whether he wanted to obscure it.

She slipped into a conservative ecru pantsuit to avoid any hint of the temptress. Even so, the soft cashmere-blend against her body brought a flood of memories of their intimate encounter.

She took special care in applying her makeup and added a copper clip to her chestnut brown hair. She couldn't deny she wanted to look her best. After a final twist of loose tendrils around her face, she took one last look in the mirror. A smile of satisfaction crossed her lips as she closed the door and headed toward the breakfast room.

Lost in thought, she followed the carpet-lined corridor to the stone staircase in the pavilion tower near the weapons room. Marc-Claude had shown remarkable control in turning away from the opportunity to make love to her. There could be no doubt that his passion matched her own. Did he really want to protect her from her wild abandon? Or was there some other reason? She prayed that at least he'd be waiting for her this morning with the memoir as he had promised. She wondered to what extent the boathouse experience would impact their working relationship.

"Hey, Claire, I wondered if you were skipping breakfast. Come on in." Michelle pulled out a chair for her, patting the seat.

Where is he? Marc-Claude wasn't there! It felt as if her heart dropped to her feet. "I slept in until the last minute."

Michelle stared at Claire. A knowing smile played upon her lips. "Don't you look nice this morning?"

More shaken than she cared to admit, Claire managed to say, "Thank you," as she nervously smoothed the navy-blue silk shell her mother had given her for her birthday. Jittery, she focused her thoughts on her mother and the cheerful kitchen at home. Right now she would like to confide in her about Marc-Claude and the turmoil she felt. She could almost hear her. *Don't get involved with him. He'll only hurt you.*

Michelle tapped the table. "I wouldn't say it if I didn't mean it."

Claire forced a smile. "Thanks. Marc-Claude offered to take me to the archives in Tours to do some genealogical research."

Michelle's animation gave way to a thin-lipped half smile. She stared into her cup and frowned before speaking. "You and Marc-Claude again, huh? Well, I don't know how to say this."

"Say what?"

"Uh, I know Marc-Claude can be charming when he puts his mind to it."

"It seems to come naturally." Claire said, wondering what Michelle was getting at.

"Oui. I don't want you to misinterpret its meaning."

"Michelle, I'm not naïve." *Oh, yeah!*

"Neither is my brother. He's done some pretty irresponsible things in the past."

"Haven't we all?"

"I know that you and he disappeared all afternoon yesterday. I just don't want you to get hurt. You understand what I mean? Maybe I can help you understand how it is with him. He's not always as together as he seems. When he went away to college he got mixed up with a wild crowd . . . about ten or so of them, both male and female, from some of the oldest noble families of France. They spent just about every weekend in Monte Carlo." Michelle sat quietly, watching her.

"So? That was a long time ago." Claire didn't want to listen to Michelle's exposé about Marc-Claude's past. Had Madame enlisted

Michelle's help? Claire shifted nervously in her chair. "Michelle, you really don't need to tell me tales about Marc-Claude."

"You need to know. Marc-Claude tried to befriend a shy girl in their group. It was a total disaster."

With a heavy heart Claire considered excusing herself and leaving. Michelle was badmouthing him and, indirectly, her too. Anyway, it seemed that Marc-Claude had thought better of having breakfast with her.

Startled, she sensed a touch on her cheek and heard Marie say, "Don't give up. You do belong with Marc-Claude."

"Our parents hope that Marc-Claude and Felicity marry soon and have a . . ." Michelle's face became expressionless as she looked toward the door. "Hi, Marc-Claude."

He nodded and gave his sister a dubious look. "*Salut.* Sorry I'm late." His golden eyes brightened, and a warm smile brought an immediate softening to his features as he looked at Claire.

Michelle's face continued to wear a deceptively composed look. "Claire says you two are going to Tours today."

With a tempered yet curt tone, he answered, "That's correct."

Spreading pale pink jelly across her croissant, Claire glanced at Marc-Claude and found him focused on her.

"Which family records do you want to look up today?" he asked in English with just a trace of his native French accent. Although a mundane question, each word rolled smoothly off his tongue.

"Why did you speak to me in English?" Claire asked, relieved to find him warm and friendly. "Don't you think I understand French?"

"Just wanted to get your attention." His mouth quirked with humor.

Michelle spluttered, hurrying to swallow the water in her mouth. "Come on, Marc-Claude. Be nice."

Claire leaned her head into the cup of her hand and tried to conceal her pleasure at the attention. "I'd like to begin looking for records such as marriage or maybe . . ." She stopped in mid-sentence at the chirping of his cell phone.

"Okay, okay," Marc-Claude muttered as he depressed the TALK button. "Allo. Laval here. Five items from our collection?"

Taking a small appointment book and a pen from his pocket, he began making notes.

Michelle reached for his pen and paper. "Let me."

"Which ones do you want?" For Michelle's benefit, he repeated the list as he listened to the speaker. "Seventeenth century trousse and scabbard, sixteenth century helmet—the Henry the Third burgonet—fourteenth century sword of the first Guy de Laval, seventeenth century bullet mold and early nineteenth century detonator—the small Belgian pistol. "I'll get started right away."

Right away? What about Tours and the archives? Claire wondered why the hurried change of plans.

Marc-Claude shook his head. "Pick them up tomorrow morning? I don't know. I'll do my best." He nodded. "An unscheduled pre-opening event tomorrow night. That's a tight schedule. Felicity's there? She offered to have her security man pick up and deliver the weapons?" Marc-Claude raised an eyebrow. "Put her on the line."

Tapping the table with his forefinger, he said, "Felicity, not so fast. Any time before mid-afternoon is out of the question."

Claire nodded. So Felicity was behind the sudden rush to keep Marc-Claude from their research project. What would he do?

"Okay, I'll stop by there today with an agreement for signature. Then we'll finalize arrangement for the transport." Marc-Claude said, concluding the call.

He's postponing our day in Tours. With that thought, Claire imagined her mother's sad expression.

"I'd estimate between twelve-thirty and one. Until then." Marc-Claude pressed the OFF button and flipped the phone cover down. He took the pen and notes from Michelle and said, "Sorry about the interruption. Eh . . . Mi, are you free to take Claire to the archives?" He placed his hand on Claire's arm. "I know it's important for you to get started today. I'll pick you up after I finish at the museum."

Claire couldn't look at him, her disappointment too great. He'd cast aside his promise to her in haste with little regard for her feelings—and he hadn't returned the memoir yet.

Michelle maneuvered through traffic on Rue Nationale, turned the car to the right onto a side street, and continued several blocks before parking in front of the Archives Departementales d'Indre-et-Loire.

Still smarting from Marc-Claude's abrupt change of plans, Claire gathered up her briefcase and came around the front of the car to wait for Michelle. They climbed the six steps leading to the entrance of the elegant limestone building. After entering a spacious room with a high ceiling, they stopped at the service counter.

Michelle introduced Claire to a matronly woman with obviously dyed black hair. After reserving one of the plain wooden worktables and explaining that Claire would be researching her family history, Michelle said, "Please take good care of our Américaine guest."

The woman smiled and said to Claire, "Just ask if you need anything. I'll be here the rest of the day."

Michelle led Claire to a small utilitarian table that appeared misplaced on the elegant, spacious, black-and-white marble floor. Claire set her briefcase on one of the honey-colored oak chairs at the table.

Michelle motioned for Claire to follow. "You'll find the marriage records directly ahead of us. You already know that the ceremony took place in Tours at the Cathédrale de St. Gatien, so my suggestion is to begin your search by date." After a brief review of the organization of the records, Michelle asked, "Do you have any questions before I leave?"

Claire shook her head. "Can't think of any."

"I promised Felicity I'd stop by this afternoon." Michelle glanced at her watch. "It's eleven twenty-five now. I'll be back by four if Marc-Claude can't pick you up."

"Okay. Hopefully, I can complete my preliminary search before the end of the afternoon," Claire replied.

By 3:30 she had looked—without success—though all the records that might have had the information. She resigned herself to the notion that she would not find anything today. With a sigh she slipped her pen into a portfolio pocket then pressed her hands to the sides of her head and closed her eyes

A wasted day!

She had found no records of the wedding—and in the

confusion of the morning, she hadn't asked Marc-Claude for the memoir.

Had she missed something? According to the diary, Marie's wedding took place on 5 July 1767 at La Cathédrale de St-Gatien in Tours. Where were the records? She had gone through all of the card files for 1767—twice—before reviewing records on microfiche. After that she had combed through all the entries for the de Fleury name, reviewing each one involving grooms of that name. But despite all her effort, she had nothing to show for her afternoon's work.

Claire picked up her briefcase and went outside to find a sunny spot to wait for Michelle or Marc-Claude. Trees along the street had begun to cast shadows on most of the benches in front of the building, and just as she walked by, a man sitting on one the benches folded his newspaper and left.

As she soaked in the warmth of the day, she relaxed her tense shoulders and stretched her arms like a cat in the warm afternoon sun. Her thoughts turned to Marc-Claude, and she wondered whether the museum had provided him with an excuse to avoid being with her. She hadn't waited long when she spotted the silver Peugeot. She watched as Marc-Claude parked and got out of the car. She had nothing to show for the time spent with the archives. Would the two of them together have had any better luck? Probably not.

"Ready?" he asked as he opened the car door for her. "I had hoped there would be time for us to stay in town for a while, but I have to be home by five thirty to meet the museum's delivery truck." He returned to the driver's seat and checked the rearview mirror before pulling away from the curb. "How'd your project go?"

"Not well."

"What *did* you find?" Marc-Claude's expression stilled and grew serious.

"Absolutely nothing. I can't find a single record of the wedding."

He glanced at her. "I'm not sure how many of the records have been transferred to databases. Some are still kept in card files."

"Why didn't you warn me that the records are in disarray? I'd expected to walk right in and find them today."

"And you well could have. I'll talk with the priest at the cathedral. He may have useful suggestions or information for us."

"Okay," she said. "Let me know what he says."

He nodded. "Some of the records were destroyed during the revolution. Let's hope that didn't happen to the ones you're looking for."

"I certainly hope not! Is there something you're not telling me?"

"Non. I'll talk to the staff at the archives and see what they say."

"Thank you." Did she unjustly blame him for her frustration? She decided to try to clear the air about her behavior the previous day. "About yesterday . . . I can't explain why I acted as I did in the boathouse."

"It happened. We both contributed."

"You have a terrible impression of me."

"Not at all," Marc-Claude said rather too quickly.

"Sometimes, I'm annoying when I insist on being self-sufficient. And then yesterday I came on to you."

"You *can* be rather abrupt in your responses."

"Right." They both laughed and Marc-Claude continued, "You seem to be on the defensive so often. It seems to me you don't want to ask for help."

"Oh . . . I don't know. Recently, I've been disappointed in some people—myself included."

"Your expectation of others can influence their responses to you."

"Perhaps. I noticed a change in myself after my father's business partner ruined our family business. Not only did we lose the business, but Dad lost his will to live."

"What happened?"

"He died of a massive heart attack less than two months after his partner betrayed him."

Marc-Claude reached for her hand and squeezed it. "I'm sorry."

The touch of his hand sent a wave of longing through her. "Surely, in your work, you see many self-serving people . . . the misuse of power . . . the corruption of corporate leaders."

"I see my share but remind myself that for each of those, there are two others working to make our world a better place."

"I like your optimism." She touched his arm for emphasis.

Laying his arm across the back of her seat, he said, "You did catch me off guard yesterday."

"I know."

"It seemed so natural . . . so free. I got caught up in the moment," he said.

"It was spontaneous. We weren't thinking, that is until you went outside."

"It wasn't easy, but I didn't believe you really wanted otherwise."

"Blame the seductive circumstances for my mixed signals," Claire said.

Marc-Claude glanced at her. "As it turns out, at least we aren't having next-day regrets."

She took a deep breath and exhaled slowly before speaking again. "May I ask you something . . . uh . . . personal?"

"What is it?"

"Your mother—and sometimes, Michelle—speak as if you and Felicity have an exclusive relationship. Do you?"

Marc-Claude shook his head. "Non."

"Just wondered. You don't give me that impression."

"There is another matter we need to discuss," he said with staid calmness.

Claire's heart thumped. Could it be that he wanted to reveal his innermost thoughts to her? No chance . . . most likely he wanted to change the subject.

"Of course," she said.

He rubbed his hand along his chin. "I have a confession to make."

"I'm listening." Did he want to hedge on his response about Felicity?

"About your book . . . the diary. I've misplaced it."

"Misplaced it! What do you mean?" she said in shocked disbelief.

"I left it on my desk yesterday morning. When I returned last night, it wasn't there."

Was he sincere? Without the memoir, she had no original records of her French family history. And he would have no need to fear her claim. She chose to say nothing rather than accuse him of blatant betrayal.

"Be assured, I'll find it."

Claire nodded, trying to take comfort in his assurance but to no avail. She linked her two index fingers together and pulled on them until they hurt.

As if reading her body language, he said, "Relax. I *will* find the memoir."

"How can you be sure?"

"The book has to be somewhere, now doesn't it?"

She gave a weak nod of acknowledgement. She had felt they'd reached an understanding and could work well together, but now her doubts about him threatened to make that impossible. One thing for sure, he kept her in a state of turmoil. She could not assume anything about him. She'd have to think of some way to test him further. The waning sun cast long shadows along the two-lane country road, mimicking her shadows of doubt.

Marc-Claude kept his eyes on the road and appeared preoccupied with his own thoughts. Rounding a curve, he tooted the horn and waved at two small boys riding bikes. "Who knows? Maybe they're training for the Tour de France."

Claire welcomed the break in the silence and the change in topic. Pointing at two riders farther ahead coming toward them, she said. "Perhaps they are, too. Did you ever dream of riding in competitions?" she asked as she recognized Michelle and Jacques on the bikes and waved at them.

His face brightened and a broad grin spoke volumes. "As a matter of fact, I did."

Aha, she had discovered something else about him. "Were you in any competitions?"

"I won the Prix des Jeunes at Chateauneuf-la-Forêt when I was ten."

"Impressive. Did you go on to win other competitions?"

Regret tinged his response. "I placed in a couple after that."

"I've never been in an official bike race, but I enjoy the benefits of cycling," Claire said. "It's like yoga on wheels to me."

"Interesting way to put it. After I went away to college and got my car, I didn't cycle for probably four or five years."

Too engaged in Monte Carlo?

"Going away to college changes many things."

Marc-Claude turned into the Lamont driveway. "Too bad there won't be time for riding while I'm here . . . afternoon appointments in Paris tomorrow."

"Will you be leaving in the morning?"

He nodded. "Before noon."

"Michelle and I went riding my first day here," Claire said. "Do you suppose there will be time to take a short ride yet this afternoon?"

"I doubt it. I don't know how long I'll be tied up with the museum pick up."

Disappointed, Claire asked, "Do you have a bike in Paris?"

"No. I don't often have time for it. Once in a while I rent a bike at the Bois de Boulogne."

Claire refrained from saying she'd like to ride or hike with him in the ancient royal hunting forest, now an expansive park. In her view such a suggestion should come from him. She had already made it clear that she was interested—and he had said nothing.

Chapter 11

Marc-Claude again scoured his rooms for the missing memoir. After a half hour or more, he sank into his recliner and swiped the back of his hand across his forehead. Where could it be? He sighed, stood—reluctantly admitting defeat for the time being—and locked the door behind him as he left for the library.

When he arrived, Jacques, Michelle, and Claire were already there, engaged in a lively conversation about Loire Valley bike trails. Two oversized logs hissed and crackled in the fireplace as if protesting their sacrifice to the dancing flames. Claire appeared relaxed, resting her head against the plump pillow-back of the leather sofa. She looked up expectantly at him as he entered the room. He knew what she wanted—her memoir! At a loss for words, he shook his head and sat down beside Jacques, noting her look of displeasure.

"Here he is now," Jacques said under his breath with a dubious look. "I suppose he'll want to talk about cultural communication."

"Do I detect an interest in the idea, Jacques?" Marc-Claude asked.

"I wouldn't go that far." With a nervous shrug, Jacques fingered the collar of his brown-and-white checked sport shirt.

"Well, you mentioned it," Marc-Claude pressed him, pleased with the diversion. Somehow, when he talked to clients, he didn't lack for words. "It's an opportunity if you're interested in a continuing dialog with the Americans."

Michelle glared at Marc-Claude and moved behind Jacques's chair, rubbing his shoulders. "You sound just like Père. I think Jacques is ready to change the subject."

"Okay . . . Marc-Claude, if you think it'll work." Jacques broke eye contact and turned his attention to Michelle. "Mmm, that feels good, *cherie*."

"Claire, can you be ready for a session by the end of the week?" Marc-Claude asked.

"I can . . . providing I get the printing done." Claire flashed him a doubtful look. "That is, if Jacques wants to go ahead with the plan."

"I have agreed to one," Jacques said with resignation.

"In that case I'll need to get started as soon as possible," Claire said. "Michelle, will you be able to return to Paris earlier than planned?"

"I can't leave until I've signed off on the committee report. Felicity is finishing it up and writing letters for signature."

"Claire, I can drop you off at Michelle's apartment tomorrow morning," Marc-Claude offered.

"Well," Michelle looked from Marc-Claude to Claire, "remind me to give you the key."

The clock, decorated with a sculpted hunting scene, chimed once, marking the half hour. As if on cue, the butler carried in a tray set with tea and coffee pots and cups.

Marc-Claude nodded at the man. "Merci. Set it on the table. We'll serve ourselves."

Michelle filled four cups with coffee and passed them to the others before sitting down. "Jacques, the coffee will warm you up for a walk in the garden."

"Chérie, I'm already warmed up when I'm near you."

She rubbed her hand down his back. "You're a sly one. You know how to *please* a lady."

Marc-Claude cleared his throat. "How far did you two ride this afternoon?"

Jacques looked at him as though he had forgotten he was there. "Oh . . . uh . . . about four miles, wouldn't you say, chérie?"

The chirping of Marc-Claude's cell phone broke into the conversation. "Excuse-moi." He turned his attention to the offending device and cradled it to his ear. "Gérard!" After a brief pause, he continued, "May I ask why the Procureur de la Republic is calling me at this hour?"

A knot formed in the pit of his stomach. "*Zut*. What do you have on it?" He frowned. "I'm on my way to the station. I'll need the report for insurance purposes. See you soon." Marc-Claude pressed the OFF button and closed the cover.

"What happened?" Jacques asked with furrowed brow.

"Unbelievable! There's been an accident and robbery involving the weapons transport." Marc-Claude spoke rapidly. "No injuries but three of our weapons are gone."

"Who knew the plans? Must have been an inside job," Jacques said.

"I don't want to think so." Marc-Claude's thoughts went to the missing memoir. What next? Could there be a connection? But who even knew about the book or the time of the shipment to the museum? "I'll get more information from the procureur and inspectors. But first I need to let Père know." His father didn't care about Claire's memoir, but he definitely cared about the weapons. Marc-Claude couldn't deny there might be a connection. If so, that suggested someone familiar with the household. He shook his head and rose to inform his father before he left for the police station. "Be ready to leave for Paris in the morning," he said to Claire on his way out.

Marc-Claude went past his mother's apartment on the way to his father's suite at the other end of the hall—he didn't want *both* his parents screaming for him to do something about the robbery. He tapped on his father's door, hoping he wouldn't find the older man's old war injury bothering him this evening. His news would bring down his father's wrath soon enough without pain exacerbating it.

General de Laval opened the door slowly, as if ready to slam it if he wanted to avoid his visitor. "I thought it was your mother come to grouse again. She's agitated about the attention you pay to Michelle's guest. Well, don't just stand there. Come in and talk to me."

Marc-Claude perched on a stool, the seat closest to the door. "Père, you had better sit down, too. I have bad news."

His father settled into his favorite recliner. "Get to the point."

Although he hadn't added *soldier*, Marc-Claude felt the thrust of the command.

"There's been a minor accident involving the delivery vehicle on the way to the museum."

"What the hell are you trying to tell me? Were any of our weapons damaged?"

"I don't know about that, but three of them are missing. I'm on my way to see Gérard as soon as I leave you. I'll know more then."

The general stood and glowered at his son. "You were in charge and you have failed. What the hell did you do to assure a safe delivery? Who arranged it? I don't want to hear from you again until you can give me some answers. *Comprenez-vous?*" his father shouted and then lowered his voice. "Now get out of here before I say something we both regret."

Marc-Claude was already at the door before his father had finished the sentence. He shook his head at the turn of events. His father always found fault. It was either perfection or rejection with him. To complicate matters, Marc-Claude had to be in Paris by one o'clock the next day for a meeting with the Turkish ambassador. The burning in his upper stomach confirmed his untenable situation—he couldn't please everyone. There was Claire and her research and lost memoir, his parents and the welfare of the family legacy, and Felicity hovering ad nauseam.

Claire experienced a mix of hope and anxiety as she slid into the seat of Marc-Claude's Peugeot for the return trip to Paris. She'd hit upon the perfect way to test him—blood tests. DNA proof of her claim! She needed answers—and soon—as to whether he sought to sabotage her research. Actually, there was some risk in it for her as well. Surely, he'd recognize that. However, she sensed that all was not well with him today. His shoulders were tight, she could see, and he'd been unusually quiet all morning, having spoken to her only when necessary. She knew no way to improve his mood. She had to smile at her observation that at least his olive-green polo shirt and khaki slacks should be more comfortable than his office attire.

She certainly wouldn't try to make small talk during the two-hour trip to the city. He'd have to be the one to do the talking. She understood that he had a lot on his mind—just as she did. She guessed the last thing he would want to talk about was her memoir.

Marc-Claude started the car and, with a restless flourish, backed it up, turning sharply into position to pass across the drawbridge. He didn't slow down or take his eyes from the winding road from Lamont until he reached the main highway.

Claire was relieved that at least he settled into a smooth pattern of driving—although rather too fast for her liking. He didn't take the road all the way into Tours, as Michelle had but rather took the roundabout directly to the D952 and stayed on it for about thirty minutes before he picked up the A10, the motorway to Paris, a timesaving route, no doubt.

At least she could look forward to her scheduled hypnotherapy appointment with Susan. Her whole future could depend on finding out what was happening to her. Was Marie a figment of her imagination, or could Marie be a guiding angel, supplying solutions to her dilemma? Added to doubts about her own good judgment was her growing fondness for Marc-Claude.

They drove in silence for a while, lost in their own thoughts, until they neared the Orléans Forest. Then, glancing at Claire, Marc-Claude asked tentatively, "Do you want to talk about it?"

His question brought her back to the moment. All the while he had seemed indifferent he must have been concerned about her. It didn't matter what he meant. "Yes, I do. Did you talk with the priest at the cathedral about our research?"

"Eh, not yet, there hasn't been time, but I will," he promised.

She felt the urge to share the great weight of her problem—at least a portion of it—so she continued. "I plan to meet with Susan Fisher, the psychologist, about my anxiety and bad dreams."

"Really?"

"That's the first thing I want to do when we get to Paris." She hastened to add, "That doesn't affect my meetings with you and Dr. LaMotte."

He nodded. "I think the training session may help restart Jacques' negotiations." With a shrug, he said, "Jacques and Michelle better return before the last minute."

It's only small talk for him. "I'll be ready. That's the best we can do." Claire peered out of the window and tried to imagine the royal hunts that might have taken place in the dense forest many years ago. "What kind of trees are those?" She pointed to the forest.

Marc-Claude glanced toward the woods. "Mostly oaks and Scots pines."

"I'm sure there are numerous stories to be told."

"Yes, a great many."

Claire sighed and closed her eyes, making a mental note to look up some of the forest's history.

"What sort of troublesome dreams are you having?" Marc-Claude's voice was gentle.

Claire straightened and chose her words with care, not wanting to reveal the extent of her problem. "Terrifying recurrent ones about the French Revolution."

"I hope Susan gets to the bottom of it."

Claire gave a little laugh. "I don't know what I'll do if she can't."

"I'm sure she will be of some help."

"Talking about it does help." The tension in her neck and shoulders eased. "I feel more hopeful already."

He reached for her hand and gave it a squeeze. "Good."

"What did you find out about the weapons theft?" Claire asked.

"Not much yet. The investigation is still underway." Marc-Claude seemed pensive. "Gérard will keep me informed."

"No rest for you until they're found."

"For sure. It's *my* personal nightmare. There should have been no hitch in the delivery. My father is livid. At times like this he has a closed mind."

Claire nodded and resisted the urge to say anything that could be construed as critical of his father.

One thing to be said for Marc-Claude's proclivity for speed was that they arrived in Paris in record time. Before she knew it, he was navigating the Étoile at the Arc de Triomphe, the point where multiple streets converged like a gigantic wheel with twelve spokes meeting at the hub. She marveled at Marc-Claude's skillful merge with the free-for-all traffic. Still, she couldn't help holding her breath until they reached the Avenue des Champs Élysées. "The Étoile makes my head spin. How do you get through here without any traffic signals?"

"The key is to be decisive, leave no doubt about your intentions." Marc-Claude added, "Experience helps, too."

"I'm not sure I'd survive long enough to get experience." As she watched the view along the expansive, tree-lined avenue, she questioned its showplace status. It lacked the charm of old Paris—too much modern commercialism, movie theaters, clubs, and fast food emporiums.

"Come to the office any time—at your convenience," Marc-Claude said.

"I'll be there this afternoon."

"I'll alert my assistant to expect you."

The commercial section of the avenue gave way to a park-like setting. As soon as the Champs Élysées met the Rue de Rivoli at the Place de Concorde, the familiar buzzing began in Claire's ears. It grew louder and louder until it morphed into the thundering sound of an angry crowd. She flinched and squeezed her eyes shut, trying to will away the nausea that threatened to overcome her. Fighting for control, she opened her eyes and looked away. *Concentrate! Focus. Marc-Claude.* She fixed her eyes on him until they passed the square and crossed the Seine.

He tapped her arm after turning the corner onto the Boulevard St. Germain and asked, "What's wrong?"

She lowered her eyes and moved her head to and fro, hoping to clear it. It worked; she felt less disoriented. "A touch of motion sickness, I guess. I'm better now."

"Do you often suffer from car sickness?" he said.

"Occasionally."

Marc-Claude rounded a corner. The tires squealed. "Hang on, we're almost there." With a quick maneuver he parked the car, got out, and came around to open the door for her. "I'll come back for your valise," he said as he offered her his hand. They walked side by side on the walkway until they reached the front gate of Michelle's apartment building. Inside a verdant courtyard the sweet perfume of flowers in bloom and flourishes of carved stonework provided an oasis from the Place de Concorde and the city.

By the time Claire finished fumbling around in the bottom of her purse for the apartment key, Marc-Claude had unlocked the door.

"Oh, you have a key, too," Claire said.

"Yes, Michelle and I exchanged keys. Just a little insurance should the need arise."

"That makes sense." She didn't feel at ease being alone in the apartment—after all, this was Paris, the site of disconcerting visions. "Will you have time for a cup of tea?" Claire asked, hoping he'd come in and stay a little while.

"Can't stay long . . . but I'll make a cup for you."

"Thanks. You probably know this kitchen better than I do," she said lamely and sat at the kitchen table.

Marc-Claude opened a cabinet and took out a teapot and canister labeled TEA. After he poured water from the kettle, he added fresh and stood while he waited for it to boil. "If you'd like me to pick you up when you're ready to come to the office, just give me a call."

"I don't think that will be necessary, but thank you for the offer."

"Okay."

They sat at the table in silence and waited for the water to boil.

Claire broke the silence. "I hope Jacques is happy with the results."

"I do, too. At least we'll give it a try," he said.

Steam flowed from the copper kettle and Claire watched Marc-Claude pour boiling water into the teapot.

"Sugar or cream?" He set the *faience* sugar bowl and pitcher, painted with folk art of blue and yellow flowers, on the table.

"Neither."

"Good. Michelle probably doesn't have any cream anyway." He brought the matching teapot to the table and poured a cup for her before going to the car for her suitcase. He soon returned, set her luggage by the stairs in the entry, and came into the kitchen. "I do have to go now." He placed a friendly kiss on each of her cheeks and said, "I'm sure things will go well with Susan. See you at the office afterward?"

"Yes, I'll stop by after my appointment." She walked with him to the door.

Marc-Claude looked into her eyes, his gaze as soft as a caress, before turning to leave.

She watched him walk along the stepping-stones until he disappeared through the wrought iron gate. Picking up her purse, she walked slowly back into the kitchen. The cheerful ambience of the predominately yellow kitchen and Michelle's jungle of green plants cheered her, as did the concern Marc-Claude showed—when he was of a mind to do so. She breathed deeply of the moist aroma of orchids and ferns in the air around her. After she finished her tea, she removed Susan's card and telephoned to confirm her 9 a.m. appointment the next morning.

Susan responded. "That will work, but my one-thirty appointment just cancelled. How about rescheduling for this afternoon at one thirty?"

"I'll be there."

"Do you need directions?"

"No, I have your address. I can find it." Just the anticipation of her first hypnotic regression within a few hours relaxed Claire enough for her to notice she was hungry. She opened the pantry door and looked for something to eat with a second cup of tea. A box of raisins and a somewhat dry *pain au chocolat* were the only appetizing things she found. She chose the pastry. After tidying the kitchen, she started for Susan's office.

When she came to a little arcade lined with shops, she stopped in front of a small antique shop long enough to read the price tag on a marble-top console. She shook her head and glanced at the number above the door of the adjacent bookshop. It suggested that Susan's office was on the second floor above it. Eager to get started, she climbed the stairs with the fervent desire that she would leave the psychologist's office with some clue about her odd experiences.

Susan was working at her computer and looked up as the door opened. "Hello, Claire. Come in," she said.

"This is charming. How do you get any work done with all these wonderful shops so near?"

"Sometimes, the temptation does get the best of me." Susan motioned toward a plush blue armchair. "We'll get started in just a moment."

A spent log glowed in the tiny fireplace across the room. Floor to ceiling bookshelves lined the wall on each side of it. Through an open door Claire glimpsed a small kitchen, and beyond it a closed door cut off the view.

How quaint. She lives here, too?

Susan's sparkling blue eyes engendered confidence, and Claire felt the residual apprehension dissolve.

"You've had a number of 'spontaneous regression' experiences . . . reliving past events, I believe." Susan said.

"Yes, and recurring dreams about them. I seem to have no control over them."

"I don't need to know more now. It's better to let things unfold during hypnosis."

"How many sessions do you think I'll need to get to the bottom of this?" Claire asked

"At least two or three, maybe more."

Claire nodded. "That will work."

Susan handed her a form. "Please fill it in the best you can. It'll give me enough information to begin."

Claire was relieved to see that none of the questions asked for information she'd be reluctant to disclose. She could be as brief as she wanted with her explanation of the reason for her visit. She completed the form and set it on Susan's desk.

Susan looked over the information and put the paper in a folder. "Do you have any questions or comments before we start?"

"No. I'm ready to get started." Claire followed her into a cozy room dominated by a big, green leather recliner. A small desk and ivy-print ottoman completed the furnishings. Facing the recliner, a wall shelf held trailing ivy and a large carriage clock. A pair of oil paintings, one of a tranquil ocean scene and the other of a snow-covered mountain, hung on the wall near her framed professional certificates.

Claire settled into the recliner while Susan sat by her side.

"Have you ever been hypnotized?" Susan began.

"No."

"Do you daydream—get lost in thought at times?"

"Well, yes, doesn't everyone?"

"During those times, you're actually in a hypnotic state."

"I'm fully aware when I daydream."

"During hypnosis, you are in control at all times. No hypnotist can persuade you to do anything you don't want to do."

"That's reassuring."

"When in a wakeful but relaxed state, our brainwaves slow so that the subconscious mind is much more accessible. Ready?"

"Yes."

Susan's voice took on a singsong rhythm. "Now just sit back and relax. Look at the clock on the shelf. Any time you want, simply allow your eyes to close. Take a deep, deep breath. That's it. Now let go while you exhale. You'll find yourself going deeper and deeper into relaxation."

In spite of her curiosity about the process, Claire allowed relaxation to flow over her like a refreshing spring breeze. Vaguely aware of the ticking clock, she let her eyelids close. A sense of peace surrounded her. Her rhythmic breathing and the sound of Susan's soft, droning voice seemed to recede into the distance. She continued to disengage from her surroundings.

She heard Susan ask her to imagine a stairway to a beautiful garden and then realized that Susan had been counting for a while.

". . . eight . . . seven . . . going deeper and deeper into relaxation with each step." Susan continued, "Moving back in time to the eighteenth century in France. Becoming aware of your body . . . receiving impressions. Good. What are you experiencing? Tell me, where are you? What do you see?"

Feeling as if someone spoke to her when she was groggy with sleep, Claire forced herself to speak. "In my bedroom."

"What is the date?"

"November eleven, seventeen sixty-eight."

"And what are you called?"

"I am called Marie."

"What are you wearing?"

"I . . . I'm . . ." Claire stirred.

"That's all right. Just relax. Yes, that's good. What are you feeling or seeing now?"

Chapter 12

Convent School, Paris - May 1767

"I'm leaving the convent school forever." Marie squared her shoulders and sat on the dormitory bed beside her roommate. "Helene, I'm to be a married lady."

"I think I shall die once you leave me here alone." Helene's chin dropped to her chest.

Marie wrapped her arms around her friend and gently rocked her. *Will I ever see her again? What can I say to ease her pain?* "You'll marry soon."

"How can you be sure?"

"I know your family will arrange it." Marie wished she could be certain. "Well, after all, you *are* their only daughter."

Her shoulders slumping, Helene pulled away and raised her eyes to the painting of the Holy Virgin above her bed. With a catch in her voice, she asked, "Has your marriage agreement been signed?"

"Well . . . no." Marie hastened to add, "There's a tentative agreement. In a few days our families will finalize the articles of the contract."

Helene stared in dismay. "What if he's old and ugly?" she asked with a glimmer of hope in her eyes. "What would you say?"

Marie paused to consider the possibility. "I'll still be a married lady with all the accompanying privileges. Anyway, my husband will go away in the king's army. I'll be able to go to the opera, theatre, and such . . . and I could take a lover like Duchesse de Roix."

Both girls broke into giggling fits, but after a few minutes a pensive look crossed Helene's face. "I want to be part of King Louis' court and dance the evenings away with handsome, charming courtiers."

Again, Marie hugged her friend. "When we're married ladies, we'll attend balls at Versailles and operas in Paris and . . . "

The *abbesse* stood at the door. "Marie, Madame de Condé has come for you." Instead of her usual stern manner, the schoolmistress' voice dripped with honey.

Marie obediently followed her to the reception area, wondering what her mother would say. She seldom saw her mother, a soft-spoken woman who wore elegant gowns at Versailles and served the queen. She had little time for her daughter—or her husband, so rumor had it.

"Hurry, child," Marie's mother took her hand. A honeysuckle scent surrounded her. "We have many hours of travel to reach Chateau Fleury."

"Chateau Fleury?"

Marie stood silent as her mother thanked the abbesse for caring for her daughter. By the time they went outside, Marie's trunk had already been loaded. The coachman stood by the door of the coach, waiting for them before he closed it and climbed up to his seat.

With a crack of the whip, the coach lurched forward and moved away from the convent and the heart of Paris. The sound of horses' hooves echoed as the carriage moved along the wet cobblestone streets of the city. Pedestrians scurried out of their way. Smoke filled the air and steadily curled from chimneys atop buildings around them, reminding her of chessmen burning on game boards. Along the Seine, seagulls shrieked, wings flapping, in pursuit of fishing boats dotted along the river.

After the carriage traveled some distance, Marie heard blood-curdling cries. "Maman, what's that?"

"Silly girl. Pig squeals from the slaughterhouses."

Marie grew silent and decided not to reveal her lack of worldliness.

In time the cobblestones gave way to dirt roads. The carriage slowed, but the ride remained rough along the rutted country road.

Marie stole a look at the stoic lady beside her. She'd closed her eyes. Had she done so to dream of her lover? Marie wished she could be as beautiful. "Maman, tell me about my future husband. Is he young . . . is he handsome?"

Madame de Condé answered without opening her eyes. "I've been assured that he is most satisfactory."

"You haven't seen him?"

"No."

"Is it permitted that I know his name?"

Her mother opened her eyes and looked at Marie as if seeing her for the first time. With satisfaction, she said, "Certainly. He is the Marquis de Fleury. Yours will be a brilliant alliance."

"In what way?" Marie longed for more information.

"His father is well placed at the Court of Versailles. He serves our king, Louis Quinze. One day the Marquis may continue in his father's post."

"Does that mean I'll live at Versailles?" Marie asked. Just the thought brought ripples of excitement through her body.

"Yes, during the time he is in active service to the king." Her mother continued, "Chateau Fleury will be his also."

"But what if he doesn't want me when he sees me?"

"He'll adore you. You're young, pure, and pretty—unspoiled."

Marie's hopes were dashed. He wanted a young virgin. Was the marquis a lecherous old man? How many wives had he buried?

Her mother added, "Besides, you bring a bountiful dowry and family connections to this union."

Loire Valley - 1767

With her hair poufed high and clusters of curls pulled to one side of her head, Marie felt like a true lady in her pink *peau-de-soie* gown. She began to believe that the Marquis *would* want to marry her.

The stark contrast between the magnificent, gilded, blue boiserie walls in the salon at Chateau Fleury and the cold, gray stone of the convent, where she had spent the last ten years of her life, awakened her senses. Dancing flames from hundreds of candles sparkled on the Bohemian glass chandeliers. Elegantly dressed men and women milled around and greeted one another. Voices blended into a steady hum. How could Versailles be more exciting?

At least two to three inches taller than most men in the room, her father stood out in the crowd. She saw him come in her direction with a young man, almost as tall as he. The Duc de Condé took her by the hand. "Marie, I wish to present the Marquis de Fleury."

She gulped in disbelief at her good fortune. The marquis had a generous mouth, an aquiline nose, and wore his military uniform well. His smile widened into approval as their eyes met.

He's gorgeous . . . not old . . . about my age.

She tried not to stare, but his chocolate-colored eyes held her spellbound. He lifted her hand to his warm lips and kissed it. Marie's heart skipped a beat.

"It's a pleasure, Mademoiselle de Condé," he said.

The touch of his cool fingers sent waves of anticipation through her. She offered a small, shy smile, and stammered, "Y … you are most kind, Monsieur."

The young marquis offered his arm and escorted her to her seat at the dining room table. She sat beside him, surrounded by de Condé and de Fleury family members.

Marie's body responded to the nearness of him. She quivered at the memory of his lips on her hand and imagined his mouth brushing her hand before seeking her lips—as she'd read in the taboo novels smuggled into the dormitory.

The authoritative voice of her father brought her out of her reverie. "If heaven is to have this marriage, say so, Marie."

She knew this would be the only time her father would ask about her wishes. "It shall be so," she said in a clear and calm voice.

Duc de Fleury rose from his chair and motioned toward the salon. "Best begin with the articles of the contract," he said in a level voice. "In the meantime, our young people shall converse and become acquainted."

To Marie's delight, the wedding date was set for one month hence.

Marie waited in the Cathedral of Tours for the marriage ceremony to begin. When the music sounded, she started down the aisle, her ivory silk and lace wedding dress swooshed around her with every step. The ribbon and lace headdress draping her hair would be the envy of any princess bride. She murmured a prayer of thanks that she was not encumbered with a heavy train on the back of her gown.

The officiating clergymen faced her—the Archbishop of Tours, the Archbishop of Paris, and Cardinal de Condé. Her stomach flip-flopped as though playful butterflies cavorted within. Exhilaration filled her—her wedding day! Averting her gaze from the assemblage of high-ranking church officials, Marie focused on her betrothed, who waited for her at the altar. Doubts clouded her joy. She'd grown up in a convent, and he was a worldly man. Could she please him?

Clothed in his Regiment-of-the-King uniform, the Marquis de Fleury presented a commanding presence for a boy-man of eighteen. His broad-shouldered, muscular but lanky frame fit perfectly into the red-trimmed blue coat. His aristocratic face concealed his emotions as she came to stand before him. He faced her and spoke in a clear, resonant voice. "I, Andre, take you, Marie, to be my wife. I espouse you."

She wiped a tear of joy tinged with uncertainty from her cheek. *Will God bless our union?*

Her happy moments faded. She sensed a malevolent presence among the guests. Looking over her shoulder, her eyes met the piercing ones of Louis-Philippe d'Orléans, Duc de Chartres. The powdered wig of the king's cousin bobbed in time with the swivel of his head. A Machiavellian smile crossed his lips.

Paris – 1767

The newly wed Marquis and Marquise de Fleury returned to Paris to begin married life. It was a happy time for them both, during which Marie put aside her misgivings and all but forgot about d'Orléans. During Andre's one-month leave from the military, they spent every moment together, getting to know each other—making love and sharing their dreams for the future, followed by more lovemaking.

One afternoon three weeks after their wedding they lay in bed. As Andre kissed his wife on the cheek, he murmured. "In one more week I have to return to the king's service."

She looked into his eyes. "I suppose. But I don't count the

days. I'm content just the way things are." She kissed him to silence him.

He turned his face away and put his hand over her mouth. "You try to distract me, but I need to say this. What will you do while I am away?"

"Wait for you, of course," she said, pressing her body against his and rubbing his back. "All the more reason not to waste the time we have."

"Marie, I worry that you live in a dream world. In life there are good times and bad ones. You must be strong, I beg of you."

What is he thinking—that he's not coming back from battle?

She shuddered and snuggled closer. "Hold me." She coaxed him with kisses.

The final days of their honeymoon flew by, regardless of Marie's wishes. After Andre returned to his post, Marie began preparations for presentation to the queen. Later, as the wife of the Marquis de Fleury, her mother assured her, she could expect an appointment to the queen's court.

Every afternoon for a week Marie practiced amongst the chairs and furnishings of her room with Monsieur La Clere, her private dance master, who took the role of the queen. He despaired of Marie's progress as he sought to coach her on the fine points of etiquette required at court.

"No, Marie, you appear to have two left feet." Monsieur La Clere threw up his hands after her attempt to curtsey and remove her glove with grace. "Now, let's begin again."

Finally, the day of presentation at Versailles arrived. Marie wore an uncomfortable and stiff-bodied gown with a skirt that extended to each side by four feet. She waited in a crowded room outside the queen's chamber with women in similar attire. A quick glance around the vast room startled her. She hadn't thought there would be so many women with their own *robe de cour* with *pantiers* measuring up to twelve feet across the body, and she'd have to navigate around them. At Versailles at last—but Marie could only rally enthusiasm for a successful end to the day.

Silent review of protocol for presentation to the queen offset her nervous anticipation. *Remove my glove, bow to kiss the hem of the queen's gown.* At least she felt regal in her attire while she stayed in one spot. Tiny, gold-embroidered forget-me-nots adorned the bodice and sleeves of her cornflower-blue gown. Blue chalcedony, set in dainty gold floral settings, mimicked the effect at her ears and neck. Her mother had selected the blue silk flowers and tiny gilt birds that balanced precariously atop her white powdered wig.

To look at her, no one would guess she came fresh from the convent. However, once they saw her move, there would be no doubt.

Sister Agnes would not be happy with her lack of poise. All of their court etiquette classes at the convent were for naught—seemingly so remote. Bowing to the hemline while wearing a novitiate's simple linen frock did not compare to the weight of the wide panniers, yards of fabric, and heavy peruke. *This hairpiece will be my undoing with one wrong move.* The weight of the large white wig, towering on top her head, upset her sense of balance.

"Come, Madame, it is time to meet the queen."

Moving slowly, Marie made her way toward the elderly queen, the wife of the unfaithful Louis XV. The kindly Queen Marie Leczinaka looked more than her sixty-six years, in spite of the powder and rouge on her sunken face.

Marie made three curtseys before the queen, managed to remove her glove, and began to bow to kiss the hem of her gown. Thankfully, the queen followed custom and held up her hand to stop.

"Madame, the king awaits your arrival," a courtier said to Marie at the conclusion of her time with the queen.

I have no time to settle my stomach and frayed nerves!

Chateau Fleury – One year later

"My . . . my baby is so ill." Marie's body shook with each heaving sob. "It's been five days now . . . the fever hasn't broken. The doctor said there's nothing more he can do and hasn't been here for two days." She held little Andre-Pierre on her lap and patted his head with a cool cloth. Suddenly, she jumped up and held him inside her robe against her skin. "I've chilled him. He's so quiet and hasn't coughed. I can't feel his little chest move. What am I going to do?" she wailed.

"Do you think his fever broke, and now he's able to rest?" She gently swayed with him in her arms.

Marie's maid, Zoë, came to her side and placed her hand to baby's forehead. "Madame, I'll take him. He is cold now."

"No! That's not true," Marie screamed and ran out of the room, sobbing and gasping for each breath until she met Nanny Cecile. "No! He is not dead!"

"Here, let me take him. Nanny reached for the baby, but Marie clung to him. Nanny touched his cheeks and then his forehead. "My dear, hold him as long as you want. Come, sit down with me." Marie did as she asked while Cecile gently brushed Marie's hair from her face, as she had done many times before she left for the convent. "There, there, dear. Go ahead and cry. You must let go of the pain."

"But, Cecile, what am I going to do? I shouldn't have taken him out with me to the garden. Two days later he was sick."

"He was bundled up. I don't know how that outing could have harmed him. Others here were sick too. I just don't understand why it happened."

"Nanny, how can I go on living without him?"

"Hush, child. Don't say such things. I know of your deep love for your baby, but life must go on. You're young and healthy. You'll have many more babies. Your husband loves you very much and needs you to be strong."

"Nothing can take the place of my little Andre-Pierre," Marie lamented. "He needed me and I failed him." Marie handed the baby to Cecile. "What did I do wrong?"

"Nothing. You did everything you could." Cecile stroked Marie's hair. "We all did."

Marie wiped away her tears. "Andre must be told."

Cecile nodded. "Yes. I'll notify the other family members. Duc de Fleury will send word to Andre to come as quickly as possible. I'll send Zoë in to sit with you while I'm downstairs, and then I'll be here with you the rest of the night."

The next morning when Marie awoke, Cecile said, "I'm happy you were able to sleep a little."

"I'm so tired. I just want to sleep." Marie pulled the sheet over her head.

"It will take a while to feel better. It's important that you eat something to keep strong and be ready for your husband. Andre should be here in a few days."

Marie didn't have the strength or the will to disagree. She allowed Cecile to help freshen her hair and apply a little makeup before going downstairs.

Duc de Fleury, Andre's father, laid his knife and fork across his plate and cleared his throat. "Andre should be here on Wednesday by nightfall. The funeral for *petit* Andre-Pierre is arranged for Friday morning at ten o'clock."

Marie pushed bits of gooey, yellow egg yolk around on her plate. She forced herself to take a couple of bites for the benefit of the others around the table.

My husband will be here soon. What will he say? Will he blame me for our son's death?

Her breath caught in her throat, and the knot in her stomach became unbearable. Marie stood and kissed her father-in-law on both cheeks. "Thank you, dear Père, for taking care of the arrangements. If you'll excuse me, I'm going to try to get some rest."

Weary, she climbed the stairs to her boudoir. The silence from the nursery hit her like an avalanche, threatening to smother her. She struggled to breathe, passed by the sitting area, and went straight to her bed. After tugging the heavy brocade curtain around the bed to assure privacy, she released her pent-up tears and gnawing fears.

Late Thursday afternoon Marie awoke from a fitful sleep when she heard the sound of thundering hooves growing louder by the minute. She ran to the window and saw three riders. *Yes, yes, thank God, Andre's here.* Her heart skipped a beat. She hurriedly slipped into her clothes. Arranging her skirt around her, she sat on the chaise and waited for what seemed like an eternity. The longer she waited the more nervous she became. *What will he say to me? Will he blame me?*

"Marie, Andre's here and has spoken to his father," Cecile called in a breathless voice. "He's on his way up to see you." Nanny went into her own room, adjacent to Marie's sitting area.

Marie forced herself to stand and go to her dressing table. Shocked by the pale reflection in the mirror, she hurriedly sought a solution. From among the array of jars and compacts of creams, rouges, paints, and powders, she selected rouge for her cheeks and powder for the dark circles under her eyes.

She paced while she waited. Why hadn't he come to her yet? She froze at the sound of a light tap on the door. Her heart thumped as though it would jump out of her chest.

Andre's classically handsome features remained evident beneath days of unshaven stubble and dust. He looked tired. His face revealed the effects of the strain and pain he endured. He stood for a moment looking at her before drawing her tightly against his body. Brushing her cheek with his lips, he whispered, "Père delayed me. Forgive me?" His touch, firm and urgent, conveyed his emotions.

She wanted to comfort him but had nothing left to give. She pushed him away. Eventually, they'd have to face their loss together before healing could begin. Just not yet. "I'm sorry. I just can't, not now." She began to cry. "Our precious Andre-Pierre is gone."

"I'm sorry, too. I just don't know what to do for you." A glazed look of despair spread across Andre's face. "I'll leave you to rest."

"I need you to grieve with me."

"I can't. You've shut me out," Andre spoke so quietly Marie had to struggle to hear him. Before she could retort, he left the room.

Desperation closed around her more quickly than the darkness of the approaching night. He didn't understand. She had failed him, too . . . the way she had little Andre-Pierre. The thought of sitting through the evening meal brought unbearable torment. Surely, he would return soon, and then she'd make it right with him. She called, "Cecile, I'll take my supper here in my boudoir. Please bring me a tray."

Although she had no appetite, she drank the hot chocolate, all the while wondering how she could go on. Restless, she went to her desk and began to write a letter to Helene. Thinking of Andre, who needed her now as she needed him, she couldn't keep her mind on letter writing. She felt numb and dropped her quill. *Where is Andre now?* She desperately needed him with her, but she hadn't conveyed her love for him. On the verge of tears, she watched a black-blue splotch of ink become an ugly blemish on the floor.

Marie left her desk and tried to clean up the stain before giving up and flopping down on the bed. Raucous male voices drifted through the open window from somewhere outside the chateau. Was that how a drunken party at a victorious army camp sounded? "Andre, you belong with me . . . come to me now," Marie whispered, sorry for her churlish behavior toward him.

She lay in bed for hours, unable to sleep, and wondered whether Andre would return to her. Sometime before dawn he fumbled with the door and stumbled into bed. At least he hadn't gone to another bedchamber.

She lay motionless and wide awake. Andre's even breathing suggested he had fallen asleep almost before his head hit the pillow. The smell of alcohol caught in her nostrils. Conflict raged within her and made sleep impossible. She studied the profile of the man she loved so much and reached to brush a stray lock of hair from his face. Moving closer to him, she wrapped her arms around him and kissed him but roused nothing more than a mumble and a grunt. She drifted to sleep for a couple of hours only to awaken at dawn. She got up and resolved to be strong at the funeral in spite of her anguish.

When she was ready to leave the bedroom, her husband still slept. She walked over to him and gently shook him. "It's nine-thirty in the morning. You have to get up."

Andre opened his eyes and looked at her. "All right."

Marie's nerve failed her when she had the chance to comfort her husband, the man who walked by her side and yet both were alone. She'd let him sleep right up to the last minute and now had no time to express her need and affection for him. Her mood matched the chilly, gloomy morning.

An overlay of gray covered her world on that dreadful day. Friends and relations gathered at the family cemetery. A somber, black wrought-iron fence separated the place of the dead from the world of the living. In this place generations of de Fleurys had united with their ancestors in eternal rest. Little Andre-Pierre would be buried in the cemetery plot outside the crypt reserved for illustrious de Fleurys who had made their mark in the world and who at least had had sufficient time to do so. It was not fair. Their baby would soon be forgotten.

Cold raindrops mingled with her hot tears. She pulled her black cloak snugly against her body but still felt chilled, an unquenchable freeze. Andre stepped closer and slipped his arm around her waist. She leaned against him like a rag doll, her energy drained by the relentless pain. Andre remained stony-faced, hiding his grief, but still his warmth comforted her.

Cecile reached over and pressed Marie's hand with her own. The priest kept his words to a minimum, allowing little Andre-Pierre to be relinquished to the earth as if he mattered so little.

Following the service, family and friends partook of a light lunch served in the salon. Andre moved around the room in a restless fashion, pausing now and then when someone spoke to him. Eventually, he made his way to Marie and slipped his arm around her waist as he spoke to his parents. "The battles rage. I must get back to my men right away." He kissed Marie on the cheek and whispered, "I love you."

"So soon? Surely your leave is for a week at least." With a knowing look in his eyes, his father added, "Your duty is to spend time with your wife."

"It's better this way. Marie needs time to grieve," Andre said.

Marie wanted to plead with him to stay but said nothing. Why beg when it would do no good. She'd have to be patient and pray that he truly did love her enough to forgive her. She sighed. Her troubled spirit quieted. *I'll make it up to him when I get the chance.*

Andre came to her and laid his head on her shoulder. "Our beautiful son is gone, but we must go on living. I'll return soon." He raised his head and his glistening eyes looked into hers before he departed with the other two soldiers.

"Be safe. I love you so. Hurry home," Marie whispered, although she knew he could not hear her.

Cecile came to Marie's side. "My dear, men express sorrow differently than women. That doesn't mean they don't care."

Marie watched her husband until he disappeared from view. *Mon amour, I promise I will never push you away again!*

Chapter 13

"When I count from one to five, you will be back in the present, feeling relaxed and refreshed." Susan began counting. "One . . . now letting go of that time and place . . . two . . . releasing those emotions. Three . . . feeling your body and the awareness of your being here. Four . . . eyes opening. Five . . . you're feeling good, wide awake and refreshed."

Claire moaned and her hands gripped the arms of the recliner as the gentle voice of the hypnotherapist drew her back to the present. She stretched and arched her back, adjusting her position in the chair. Although she'd just relived Marie's anguish at the loss of her son and estrangement from Andre, she was calm—unlike the way she often felt when she awakened in the mornings. Her body felt as light as if floating on a cloud, her mind quiet and yet alert.

Susan patted Claire's arm. "Good session. You're a good subject. How do you feel about it?"

"I was there. It's really amazing."

"As your sessions reveal conflicts in Marie's life, you should be released from the effect of those subconscious memories that have plagued you," Susan said.

Claire leaned back in the chair. "I don't know what to think. It's all so real . . . but reincarnation?"

"Your belief is not a prerequisite for hypnotherapy to work. Healing comes from your subconscious." Susan slid her chair back and stood. "How does two o' clock tomorrow work for you?"

Claire raised herself to sitting position then stood. "Fine." She went with Susan to the reception area. "See you tomorrow."

Claire stepped into the late afternoon sunlight outside the office door and wended her way down the stairs to the busy street where she hailed a cab to take her to Laval and Associates. She just didn't feel like walking the distance in her relaxed state—a wise decision in that she'd misjudged how many blocks separated the two establishments. After paying the fare, she left the cab and approached the entrance to the law office.

A look of recognition and welcome brightened the receptionist's face when Claire entered. "Bonjour, Mademoiselle Bennett. I'll buzz Monique. She's expecting you."

"Merci." Claire moved closer to the desk. "Is Monsieur Laval free to see me for a few minutes?"

"Desolé. He's tied up all morning on international conference calls." As the receptionist spoke, a tall, statuesque brunette approached, hand extended.

"Mademoiselle Bennett, I'm Monique." She wore a gray suit that did little to disguise her physical attributes. "Monsieur Laval asked that I make sure we're ready for the workshop. Come with me. We'll work in my office."

Claire followed her across the hall to a well-appointed office furnished with a walnut desk, credenza, and conference table.

"Please take a chair." Monique sat down at her desk and Claire selected a chair facing her. Monique's efficiency became evident as she gave a rundown on her plan to have things ready for the workshop.

After Monique completed her summary, Claire rose. "Thank you. It seems all you need from me are the handouts."

Monique looked toward the door. "Monsieur Laval, things went well? You've finished already?"

Claire turned toward the door and her eyes met Marc-Claude's gaze. A tingle like an electrical current rippled through her. Why did he have such a powerful effect on her?

Marc-Claude looked back at Monique and held up his hand. "No, I'm just on a short break. Claire, may I have a word with you?"

"Of course."

He led her to a room farther down the hall and closed the door. "Is Monique taking good care of you?"

"Yes. With her help, I'll be ready for the workshop."

"Good." He ran his hand along the top of the desk. "I'll be tied up here all afternoon, but if you'd like, we can have dinner at that little place in Montmartre that I mentioned to you."

"The one you pointed out when we were there?"

"Oui, Chez Antoine."

128

"I'd like that."

He gave her a quick kiss on each cheek and walked with her to the door. "I'll call when I'm leaving here. By the way, it's casual dress tonight."

As Claire passed Monique's office, she waved to her on the way out.

By the time Claire reached Michelle's apartment, she was in a mellow mood in anticipation of the evening out with Marc-Claude. She made a pot of tea and looked through Michelle's CDs for some music to match her mood. Humming while she searched, she selected *Romantic Piano*, a collection of classic love songs. After pouring a cup of tea, she sat in a swivel rocker and let her mind drift.

As the familiar classic songs played, her thoughts turned to Marie and Andre. They had been so right for each other when they married. How could things have changed so in a year? Of course they were both deeply scarred by the loss of their baby . . . but still, they had each other. Didn't that count for anything? How could they be so blind to each other's needs? Claire shuddered and felt tears sting her eyes. The poignant words of "Somewhere My Love" overcame her effort to control her emotions.

Her heart ached for Marie and Andre. What had happened to them through the years? They did have one more child—Janine—in 1778. No sons. There was still so much she didn't know about them, but she took comfort that portions of the diary recorded their love for one another.

As the song ended, Claire felt a touch on her cheek—by now the familiar sensation when Marie was near.

Be assured that Andre and I love each other. You must know by now you are a part of our saga. Marie impressed upon her.

"What do you mean?" Claire spoke softly.

I'll share no more for now. You must go within—as you did earlier today.

"And after that?"

Marie didn't answer. The music ended, leaving Claire alone in the eerily quiet room.

"All right, be that way," Claire muttered, just in case Marie was listening.

Claire roused herself and changed for dinner about five o' clock. She passed the time watching television while she waited for Marc-Claude. Shortly after the movie ended, she heard a tap at the door. She glanced at the clock—6:15—and hoped she wasn't overdressed in her blue knit sweater suit. She opened the apartment door for Marc-Claude and saw that he had changed into a black leather jacket and a casual shirt paired with gray jeans. When he said *casual*, he meant it.

"Nice outfit. You look great," he said, without any reference to whether he considered it casual enough.

"Is it okay for tonight?" Claire asked.

"*Perfaitement*. Shall we be on our way?"

She nodded, picked up her bag, and pulled the door shut behind them.

Marc-Claude took the Pont de Neuf across the Seine, passed the Louvre, and continued in a northerly direction until they reached Montmartre. He parked near the old St-Pierre church at the foot of the sharp incline to the Basilica of Sacre-Coeur. Before getting out of the car, he turned to her and said, "You'll like it here."

"How do you know?"

"It's unique—a place for free-spirited fun."

"Hmmm. Sounds great." She ran her fingers along his hand, stifling an urge to run them through his hair, as Marie had with Andre during their intimate times together.

"Let's go." He removed the keys from the ignition and they walked along the Place St. Pierre, holding hands until they reached the stairs leading up the incline. "Ride or walk?" Marc-Claude pointed with his free hand at the cable car platform.

"Walk." She tugged his hand and started racing, challenging him to keep up with her. She couldn't recall having been this playful since her dad died.

By the time they reached the first landing of several, they

needed to catch their breath, so they paused and relaxed in each other's arms for a few moments. The tree-lined stairs and soft light from the quaint streetlamps provided a sense of seclusion.

By the time they reached the terrace in front of the Basilica, all sense of seclusion vanished. They stopped for a to-go glass of wine and found a corner at the edge of the fence. Standing apart from the crowd, they sipped wine while they looked out over the city lights below. Soft guitar music wafted through the night air.

There's no place like this. He's right. Claire wished she could hold onto such contentment forever.

Marc-Claude's voice brought her back to the moment. "Ready to go to Chez Antoine?"

"I suppose, but I could stay right here and be happy."

"Until you got hungry," he said and reached for her hand.

As they started across the terrace, a little boy ran toward them. "Catch it," he shouted in English as he threw his red ball at them.

Marc-Claude nabbed it before it hit the ground.

The boy darted to him, holding out his hand. "Give it back." He stomped his foot.

"This isn't a good place to throw things," Marc-Claude said and put it into the outstretched hand. "You could lose your ball or hit someone."

Claire leaned forward and held the boy's gaze. "Where are your mommy and daddy?"

Concern replaced his bold stance. He looked around and called, "Mommy . . . Mommy."

Marc-Claude patted him on the back. "It's okay, stay here. She'll find you."

Claire straightened. "How old are you?"

"Four." He held up four fingers.

He looked from Marc-Claude to Claire. "Where are your kids?"

"We don't have any." Marc-Claude chuckled.

"Oh." Then the child saw his mother and ran to her, clutching his ball against his chest.

Claire and Marc-Claude continued across the square to the street, passing the stairs they'd come up. Claire slipped her arm through Marc-Claude's. "You're really good with children."

"He was a cute kid."

"Do you look forward to having your own?"

He nodded. "Someday. And you?" he asked.

Claire grimaced. Why did she have to bring up this subject? She liked children—when they belonged to someone else. The thought of her own always created a feeling of self-doubt and anxiety. Strange.

"Well?" Marc-Claude stopped walking and faced her.

"I . . . haven't thought much about it," she said.

Strolling arm in arm, they reached the Place du Tertre, which was filled with shops and cafes. As they drew near the Roberto Santoni Gallery, Claire said, "I'd like to stop in and see if Nadia is there. I'd like to chat a bit . . . let her know I'd like to talk more with her."

"Okay. If you promise not to take long."

"Promise." Claire intended to simply touch base with Nadia while in Marc-Claude's presence.

As luck would have it, as they came in Nadia was just finishing up with a customer. She glanced toward Marc-Claude and Claire. "Be right with you."

Claire paused when she felt a tap on her shoulder as they neared the vineyard painting. She turned and caught a glimpse of Marie.

You can trust Nadia.

What do you know about her? Claire fired back in thought.

She served me well.

Claire realized that she and Marie were quite adept at communication by mental telepathy or whatever. Claire ruefully shook her head. *This is getting out of hand.*

Marc-Claude drew up next to her. "I thought you wanted to see the painting again."

"I do." Claire peered at the cash register and saw Nadia start toward them.

"Monsieur Laval, it's still not for sale." Nadia turned to Claire. "But I expect you aren't shopping this evening. I understand that you and I share a mutual interest in helping abused women."

"Yes. Perhaps we can talk more about it over lunch."

"Of course. I'll give you my card. Call at your convenience." Nadia dashed off to the register and returned with a business card that read: Nadia Sala, Director for the Center for Abused Women.

After leaving the gallery, Marc-Claude stopped by the window of the wine and cheese shop next door and pointed at the poster in the window. "The *fete du vin* is on Saturday."

"What events will there be . . . wine tasting?" Claire asked.

"Of course, wine tasting is a featured event at the grape harvest festival."

"What else?"

"Parade with marching bands . . . street theaters. Later in the evening, a variety show . . . banquet and ball . . . and more wine tasting."

They followed the winding cobblestone street past quaint three-story buildings, far from the crowds of the square. A little café straddled the location where the street forked. A green awning hung above the door, and metal planters filled with red geraniums sat on ledges along the second-story windows. The sound of guitar and piano music flowed out the open, street-level door. Claire paused. "Let's listen."

"Want to go in?"

"No." She pivoted around to face him and put her arm on his shoulder. "Let's dance," she said, her voice not quite her own. Had Marie spoken for her?

Marc-Claude's eyebrows rose inquiringly. "Right here?"

"Yes. I want to dance here—just the two of us."

Marc-Claude drew her to him, twirling her around and softly repeating words to the music as they danced.

Her eyes kissed mine . . . love in them shine . . . such love divine.

Claire was no longer in Montmartre. Instead she and Andre danced the minuet to the music of violins, cello, and harpsichord in the Versailles Hall of Mirrors. She wore a royal blue gown and Andre a gentleman's court dress. She leaned close and whispered, "I can't stop loving you."

Marc-Claude's arm tightened around her waist.

And now she's gone . . . Like a dream that melts with the dawn.

Her memory stays locked in my heartstrings . . . she was ne'er mine.

After the music ended, Claire was back outside the little café in

Montmartre, clinging to Marc-Claude's hand. Had he experienced anything stranger than dancing on the street?

"So beautiful . . . what's the name of that piece?" she asked. She squeezed Marc-Claude's hand and cuddled against him, fully contented. Tonight it was just the two of them. *So, that's how love feels.*

"'Plaisir d'Amour.' I've always liked it."

Claire looked up at him. "I thought I heard a violin. Did you?"

"No. Just guitar and piano."

"Oh," she said.

"We won't be able to dance at Chez Antoine," Marc-Claude said. "Shall we have dinner another place where we can dance afterward?"

"No." Claire didn't want the magic to end. She wanted him to herself. "Let's walk a little longer." She pondered her unusual and happy experience with Marc-Claude on this quiet street in Montmartre as they danced together to the strains of "Plaisir d'Amour." She had been completely at ease with him. And it seemed like the air had cleared between them—as if an unspoken barrier had been swept away and lightness of spirit left in its place. What did Marie have to do with it?

Would her next regression reveal a connection between "Plaisir d'Amour" and Marie?

The next morning Marc-Claude sat in his office and stared at the stack of papers on his desk. He could no longer deny it—he was falling in love with Claire. He still couldn't believe that the night before he'd danced with her on the street outside a small café in Montmartre—and he'd been caught up in the magic of "Plaisir d'Amour," as had she. Claire had been free and affectionate, the two of them bound together in harmony like notes of a chord. It all felt so right. He shook his head and wondered why she had asked him if he'd heard a violin, when only a piano and guitar had played inside the nightspot?

The specter of his father's certain accusation thrust at him about shirking his responsibilities *again* struck a dissonant chord in his heart. How many times would he have to do battle with the general? Whether or not things worked out between Claire and him, now was the time to throw down the gauntlet and forbid his parents from intruding into his personal decisions—even if it meant he'd have to sever his relationship with them. Restless, he stood and paced while he evaluated the full import of his decision. Once done there would be no turning back.

Until the strange evening in Montmartre with Claire, he'd convinced himself that his head ruled over his heart. What exactly had changed him? He wondered about Claire's mercurial moods. Sometimes she was as celestial and distant as the North Star. Other times they seemed to be bound together as completely as Siamese twins in the womb. If he hoped to have a future with her, he'd have to win and hold her trust and confidence.

At the sound of soft footsteps outside his office, he looked up and saw her—a vision materialized. "I was just thinking about you." Tension drained from his shoulders. "How are the preparations going?" he asked as she entered.

Claire set her purse beside the coffee table and sat down, her sparkling eyes soft and tranquil. "Very well." She took a deep breath and said, "The conference room's reserved and the print shop promised a one-day turnaround on the handouts."

After closing the door, he eased into the brown leather chair next to hers. "Good." He tapped his fingers on the chair's arm and steeled himself to say what he must. "I really enjoyed myself last night. How about you?"

A slight smile curved her lips, soft as rose petals. "I did . . . very much."

"I'm glad." He averted his gaze for a moment to gain control of his emotions in preparation for asking questions—questions she might prefer left unasked. "I noticed on the way back from Tours you seemed troubled and tense." He glanced at her.

Claire's serious expression confirmed his need for tact. "I was . . . and so were you."

He nodded. "Eh . . . you appear preoccupied . . . bothered by something. Anything I can do to help?"

She kept her eyes softly upon him, but her silky voice held firm. "I'm not ready to talk about it yet."

"I'm a non-judgmental listener. Say as much or little as you like," he said, hoping to put her mind at ease.

"If I do, will you promise not to jump to conclusions about what I say?"

"I have already assured you of that."

"Do you recall when I told you as we passed by the Place de Concorde that I felt ill . . . like motion sickness?"

Marc-Claude nodded.

"Well, that wasn't all." Claire sighed, "I seemed to be in two places at the same time . . . the past and the present."

"Really? I can understand your concern."

"Since I've been here, I've had several similar experiences—more vivid than just déjà vu."

"There has to be a reasonable explanation," Marc-Claude said, worried it might be something he didn't want to admit.

"That's why I'm seeing a hypnotherapist."

He nodded. "Michelle's friend."

"I've had one hypnotic regression and I'll have another later today. I seem to be witnessing life experiences of Marquise de Fleury." Claire cast a furtive glance his way.

So what is she trying to do—make a case for her claim to Chateau Fleury? Or is she simply deluded? If that were the case, he wouldn't stand in her way, out of any loyalty to his family. He would help her find the truth. "So it could be . . ."

She raised hand. "Before you say anything, let me hasten to add that most of my experiences are of things not recorded in her diary," she said with a stubborn set of her jaw.

"Has the hypnotherapy helped?"

"I believe so."

"Any more unwanted visions?"

"I hope not. I'm less stressed than before I started with Susan. I haven't had any nightmares, either."

"What experiences have you had that were not mentioned in the Marquise's diary?"

"I've relived scenes between Marie and Andre—very specific, detailed, intimate scenes. I have a deep understanding of Marie's emotional state, her disagreements with her husband and her opinions about issues of her time. I worry for them because they're two strong-willed people."

"You sound as if their life is still unfolding," he said, keeping an even tone. "That's all in the past."

"Marie speaks of . . ." Claire stopped in mid-sentence. "You don't seem to understand what I'm telling you. Do you think it's impossible?"

"Honestly, I don't know what to think. I find it difficult to believe in reincarnation. Perhaps the diary has triggered your thoughts."

"No." Claire shook her head. "There's so much more than the diary," she said with passion.

"Be that as it may . . ." Marc-Claude paused. "You must know how I feel about misplacing the diary. I know important it is to you, and I won't rest until I find it." He leaned toward her and continued, "I haven't had much luck with records at the cathedral. But I think the possibility of testing for DNA evidence will be useful, whether it substantiates your claim or not. You and I must put the question to rest, if at all possible."

Claire's face brightened. "Do you think it's possible?"

"We won't know if we don't give it a try. Your locket contains a sample of Marie's hair. If it hasn't deteriorated too much from age, it can be compared with yours and also Felicity's—that is, if she's agreeable." Marc-Claude gently touched Claire's arm. "I don't want doubts, yours or mine, to stand between us."

"I don't either." Claire reached for his hand and squeezed it. "Why not just test my blood and Felicity's? But if she won't, wouldn't yours or Michelle's do? I don't want to chance damage to the hair in the locket."

"My blood won't work. It has to be through the female line." Marc-Claude glanced at his watch after a distant church bell rang the hour. "A client is due here any moment now. We can pick up where we left off later. Perhaps over dinner?"

"Tell you what. I'll fix dinner at Michelle's apartment." Claire stood. "We can talk undisturbed."

Encouraged by Claire's calm demeanor and openness, he said, "Perfect" and rose.

"Say six o'clock? I hope you like Cajun chicken salad," she said as she went to the door, ready to leave.

"I'll be there." He walked back to his desk and sat. His life had already taken a new direction. He'd see it through, come what may.

With time to spare, Claire walked to Susan's office, mulling over Marc-Claude's suggestion of DNA testing to determine her claim. He'd done so without knowing of her desire for the tests and despite its challenge to his de Fleury cousins. Why would he risk an unfavorable outcome? Warm feelings for him flowed in contrast to the chill of the outside air. Claire climbed the stairs to Susan's cozy office and went in. She stood before the crackling fire in the little fireplace and waited.

"How does this fast-track schedule work for you?" Susan asked.

"All things considered, I'm keeping up. Fortunately, I have time to come each day. That's not to say I wouldn't prefer more time to digest each session before moving to the next one."

"Normally, we'd take about a month to cover the ground you're doing in a week."

"I do have some questions that I need answered," Claire said.

"Tell me about them."

"Marie and I look so much alike that it's easy for me to think I did live her life in the past. Is it true in every case that the person being regressed finds a past life personality that looks like their twin?"

"No, not necessarily. It is believed they share common collective or subconscious memories. Other than that, they may be of the opposite sex, another race, even a different personality type, to mention just a few possibilities. In your case perhaps your and Marie's genetic link contributes to similarity in appearance. There are recorded cases of lookalikes who are not genetically related. But more often than not they don't look strikingly similar."

"What else carries forward from a past life?"

"As I mentioned earlier, suppressed memories of traumatic experiences may produce unexplained phobias and fears. There may be preferences to certain activities or locations that are unusual. Talents may carry forward or, perhaps, just a keen interest without the accompanying ability to express them. Odd as it may seem, cell memories may be present. For example, someone who suffered a crushed leg in a past life may have an unexplained weakness in the same leg in the present life."

"I see. So if Andre is alive today and if we meet, can I expect to recognize him in some way?"

"I've read of cases where the subconscious mind seemed to recognize and respond to someone with a shared past life. Of course, it's unlikely those memories would rise to conscious awareness. And now, with you, it appears I'm working on a case myself. So you'd be drawn to him, no doubt, and feel as though you've known him all your life. The past bond would still exist between the two of you."

"Fascinating."

"Your question is a good one. It has been suggested that whole groups of people reincarnate at the same time to continue work on unresolved issues from their past life—or lives—together. Some of these souls may have been dear to one another . . . or mortal enemies. If enemies, the feeling toward them could be one of apparent, unjustified dislike.

"I'll be on the lookout for Andre and try to avoid any former foes," Claire said in an off-hand manner.

"Just be sure to take into account that all sorts of relationships are possible. Roles may be exchanged, such as a husband and wife returning as a daughter and father perhaps. So you see, if Andre is alive, he may be your mother . . . or your best friend in this lifetime."

"Okay, so I'd have an affinity for him or her but wouldn't realize there is a past life connection. Correct?"

"That's true, unless your subconscious mind reveals it."

"Enough questions for now. I'm ready to start." Easing into the recliner elicited anticipation of the next chapter in Marie's life.

"As you relax, let your subconscious mind take you to a time in Marie's life that will help resolve conflicts carried over from that life to the present one."

The expected flow of relaxation coursed through her body while her mind floated back to the eighteenth century.

Chapter 14

Versailles – 1768

Marie arranged her multicolored silk gown with care before she sat down at her satinwood desk. After she opened her diary and dipped her pink feather quill in ink, she wrote in the fine script taught to her at the convent.

> The masked ball is on everyone's tongue. Plans are in full swing. Excitement at the palace builds with each passing day. I welcome the diversion. This way I have little time to dwell on Andre's continuing distant behavior. I can't bear to think of losing his affection.
>
> Helene, my dear friend from the convent school, and I spend our free hours planning our costumes for the ball. We have chosen to represent Les Deux Pigeons from one of La Fontaine's beloved fables .The moral of the tale holds a special appeal. 'Do not wander from your true love or you may never find the way to love's path again!' It reminds me to keep my marriage vows uppermost in my mind.
>
> Thank God for Helene. We talk for hours. I best stop writing for now—she is to be here any moment.

Marie blotted the page and closed her green, leather-bound diary in anticipation of Helene's signature knock at the door. "Come in." Marie rose, opened the door, and welcomed the exuberant young woman, who tapped her foot on the parquet floor.

"I can't think of anything except the ball. We have to decide on fanciful costumes," Helene greeted her.

"You should dress as a lady because you're shorter than I am,"

Marie said, rushing to keep pace with Helene on the way to their favorite chairs by the fireplace. "I'll be a gentleman to lessen my chances of unwanted propositions from roving libertines . . . I hope."

Helene didn't sit right away but stood by the fireplace, peering and preening at her reflection in the mirror above the mantle. She glanced back at Marie as she made final adjustments to her gown. "And maybe my being a lady will garner welcome attentions from some of those marauders you reject." With a final flourish of her hand to her hair, Helene thrust her ample breasts forward, exposing a greater depth of cleavage. She tilted her head from side to side and took one last look at herself.

Marie watched in disapproval and scolded, "For shame, a married lady shouldn't be thinking about dashing gentlemen who are not her husband. Sit down this instant."

With feigned reluctance Helene sat. "Oh, Marie, you need to come out into society more often and sip the sweet nectars of life." She fastened her mischievous blue eyes on her friend. "You never know, a little sport may stoke the home fires."

"Stop such talk." Marie scowled. "Poor, poor Helene, you don't know what it's like to love a man—really love him." Marie's voice softened. "I'll always love Andre and be true to him."

"You'll always love him, and he'll love his mistress," Helene sneered. "You better get out and make a life for yourself, or you'll grow old alone."

"I have a good life here. I stay busy and enjoy the intimate suppers with the elderly queen and her friends. She's a gentle soul. There's good music, conversation, and card games. It's most satisfactory."

Helene rose and put her hands on her hips. "Paris pulsates with new ideas." She paused and looked Marie in the eye. "With your inquisitive mind, you would be challenged by the new philosophic ideas and scientific achievements of the day. The world changes as we speak." She came close to Marie and leaned forward, her face near Marie's. "I know of your thirst for knowledge."

Marie nodded. "Yes, I have read the works of Voltaire and the philosopher Rousseau. I agree with much of what they say."

"Promise me you'll come with me to Madame du Pont's salon next week. I've heard Rousseau may be there," Helene's tone was conciliatory as she returned to her own chair.

"All right, I'll think about it." *Andre would forbid association with such malcontents.* "Tomorrow is the revel. Remember, get here early. We must allow plenty of time to get into our costumes."

Helene stood. "I will, and I'll expect your answer then."

"No promises," Marie said, standing to see her out.

The next evening when Marie and Helene arrived at the ball, they encountered an odd assortment of characters represented among the guests overflowing from the Hall of Mirrors into surrounding salons. Marie managed to wedge herself into a space by the wall to enable the two of them to move the length of the arcade, past the seventeen large arched windows that looked onto the gardens and fountains. Light from thousands of candles flickered in the crystal and silver chandeliers and reflected in the seventeen Venetian mirrors on the opposite side of the room.

A gentleman, dressed as a tree, offered one of his branches to Helene and bowed before her. "Mademoiselle, may I escort you to the garden for a breath of fresh air . . . and whatever the evening may bring?"

Helene disengaged her arm from his grasp. "I'm not feeling botanical tonight," she said emphatically and turned away from him to Marie. "So it's all arranged. You'll come with me to Madame du Pont's on Monday."

Before Marie could answer, a petite facsimile of a Roman slave girl, exuding seduction, jostled and pressed her breasts against her, running her hand up and down Marie's gray silk vest. The scantily attired maiden cupped her other hand on Marie's white culottes-clad derriere. Apparently convinced she'd found a master for the evening, the girl made a motion toward the front of Marie's fitted breeches.

Marie grabbed her hand before it reached its non-existent target and quickly pushed her aside.

Helene offered her arm to Marie and giggled. "Men do have their own challenges at an event like this." To her credit, she stayed with Marie until eleven thirty, affording some protection. "I won't make any conquests this way. I only have thirty minutes before we all take off our masks," Helene lamented. "Do you mind if we go our separate ways now?"

Of course Marie minded, but she said, "Go ahead. I'll be fine."

When the sit-down supper was served shortly after midnight, Marie was surprised to see Helene approach—alone. "I didn't expect you'd still be here."

"I had so little time to make the acquaintance of a knight in armor. When he took off his mask, I made my escape. Or maybe your lecture on virtue tickled my conscience," she said with a laugh.

On a misty afternoon two days after the masked ball, Marie's coach drew to a stop in front of a modest house on Rue Saint-Honoré. Marie and Helene left the coach and made their way to the front door. To her great relief, Helene hadn't taken this opportunity to complain about her lack of a conquest the night of the ball.

"Oh, Marie, this evening is just the beginning of an unimaginable journey into the world of ideas." Helene emphasized each phrase as the butler welcomed them into the house.

Madame du Pont's salon easily accommodated the twenty-five or so guests congregated in groups of four or five. They bantered back and forth, apparently oblivious to conversations and activities around them.

Two King Charles spaniels barked excitedly when they spotted the newcomers. Marie reached down to pet one of the chestnut-and-white pups and murmured, "Thank you for the warm welcome."

A plain-looking, gray-haired woman with piercing, intelligent brown eyes came toward them. She wore a white lace cap and a black dress with a lace collar and matching lace-trimmed sleeves. No doubt she was the *Salonnière,* the hostess for the evening. In a gracious manner, she said, "Come in and join us. Supper will be served at nine. I believe Philosopher Rousseau will honor us with a visit tonight."

Rather than join Helene at the card game, Marie continued to the next table, where a heated discussion of Voltaire's novella *Candide* threatened to explode like a pyrotechnics show on the lawn of

Versailles.

A corpulent, red-faced man slammed his fist on the table. "Science, not the church, will provide the answers for our salvation here on Earth."

Marie watched the twisted features of his face and worried about the intensity of feelings that these writings generated. Perhaps Andre was right to be concerned about ideas espoused at some of the salons.

Compelled to speak up, she said, "The church encourages its members to be charitable and care for the poor. Science and the church should be partners in a better world."

"Madame, open your eyes to the truth about the church. If you do, you'll see greed and power-hungry leadership. The church suppresses the human spirit by fostering superstitions on its followers."

Marie disagreed and felt empowered at the thought of participation in such a debate, but she'd let it go, at least until she'd calmed down. She had always defended her beliefs and sense of right and wrong—but she also kept in mind there were usually two sides to every story. Her ire rose whenever people made sweeping statements about issues. The man had failed to acknowledge the good deeds performed by the church—but a troubling grain of truth lay in his words.

When supper was announced, the ruddy-faced man followed Marie to the table and took the chair next to her, continuing his tirade.

She felt her face burn with irritation. She tried to ignore him as much as possible. He was not interested in any views contradictory to his own opinions. No, she would not waste her breath on him. Many people at the salons sought answers to serious injustices. She felt a responsibility to be a voice of reason, to counter the radicals among them—when the time was right.

At eleven o'clock Marie and Helene took their leave, having given up all hope of meeting Rousseau.

On the way back to Versailles, Helene rested her head on the back of the seat. "At least there is nothing boring about these provocative suppers, wouldn't you agree?"

"I do," Marie said and wondered how she would reconcile her long-held views with the questions raised by the philosophers; many of them condemned the use of power by the church and monarchy. "We've accepted things the way they are without critical thought, I'm afraid."

Helene had been correct in her assessment that Marie's inquiring mind would be at home with the philosophers. Torn between loyalty to her husband, who accepted the current state of affairs, and her desire to keep an open mind to the merits of the ideas discussed at the gatherings, Marie struggled to stay away from the salons. But at the last minute, she couldn't resist the pull of them like a moth to light—unless Andre was home. She and Helene became regulars at the suppers.

Versailles - Ten years later, May 1778

Marie sat near a gold and blue table in their spacious apartment, admiring the elegant appointments of the room. *Andre will be here soon.* If only he stayed with her this time, she would be forced to give up the salons and keep silent about the ideas explored there—ideas that threatened their way of life. But he wasn't likely to save her from her unwise visits. Andre seldom came to Paris; he seemed to prefer short military leaves. Marie took out her diary and wrote of the pain in her heart until she had filled the blank page.

> *Ever since we lost baby Andre-Pierre, my husband spends little time with me, saying that he must serve the king. I don't know if he has a mistress or not—or if he is celibate throughout these long absences.*
>
> *During our eleven years of marriage, I have lost three infant sons—maybe this time will be successful. I won't tell Andre about the baby yet. I know that it broke his heart each time death claimed one of our little ones. He says he*

worries for my health and seems to stay away for longer
and longer periods of time. And now he tells me he is going
to fight the English in America. I'm frightened that he'll
be lost to us in that faraway land.

At times I'm so lonely here. Since Marie Antoinette
has been queen, she has become bitter and quarrelsome.
She no longer includes me in her small circle of friends.
She doesn't trust me because I go to Paris salons. She
doesn't agree with me that I can be of service at those
events by countering some of the outrageous opinions voiced.

If only Andre were here, I wouldn't displease everyone
so. I don't seem to be strong enough within myself to stay
away from those gatherings. I know I have useful insights
to add to the evolving opinions at such events. I can make
a difference. Yet, I'm risking the queen's displeasure. My
husband may suffer because of my actions—be disgraced,
lose his military commission, or even be banned from court.
If it gets to that, Andre might disavow me and send me to
a convent to live out the rest of my days—if I'm not
already imprisoned by Royal decree. God help me, I have
to follow my conscience.

Two months later, in early July, Andre whacked a large envelope on the table. "After all this, I'm kept here to fight the English at sea . . . on a ship with Philippe de Chartres, of all men, before I leave for America."

Marie looked up, leaving her needlepoint stitch unfinished. "Why are you so upset?"

"Why?" Andre's dark brown eyes hardened. "You know very well that Chartres is an irresponsible hothead who seeks to undermine the king."

The news lessened Marie's fears. At least Andre would be off the coast of France—not across the ocean on another continent. "Surely, it won't be for long," she said in a soothing tone.

"Long? One day is too long!"

This turn of events bought them a little bit of precious time together. But Andre squandered most of it in planning for his delayed assignment in America.

Marie fretted that a mistress would be a less formidable opponent. *He fails to admit the dangers*. "Andre, please ask for a reassignment," Marie implored.

"You jest! This is an opportunity of a lifetime. Those people seek their freedom from a tyrant."

So he had the fever in his blood. She wanted to scream, "I'm pregnant," but she lamely countered, "I don't think it's in your best interest." She couldn't even be sure she'd birth a living child or not disgrace him at court.

Andre tossed the papers on the table. "England is power hungry and aspires to dominate France and all the world. She must be stopped."

"There are many capable French military officers to go and help the Americans fight. It doesn't have to be you," Marie consoled.

"You of all people, a disciple of Enlightenment, should want me to go and help the struggling American revolutionaries in their fight against tyranny."

"France has signed a treaty of alliance with the Americans. They're assured of our help," Marie said.

"There's nothing more to discuss. The King's order is that I am to go right after this wild goose chase on the ship." With a restless stride, Andre left the room.

Three weeks later, on a sweltering afternoon, Marie answered the door and threw her arms around Helene, sobbing softly.

"Oh, no, not the baby," Helene said, as she patted Marie's back.

"Andre's wounded," Marie gulped. "I have to get to him before . . . God have mercy. Why?"

"Where is he?" Helene asked and hugged Marie. "Don't think the worst."

"At the naval camp hospital . . . at Brest. The ship's surgeon can do no more. It'll take me almost a week to get to him."

"Oh, my dear, I'm so sorry. Of course, you must leave right away."

Brest, France – July 1778

One look at the wound, the size and color of a tomato, and Marie knew the serious nature of Andre's injury without even studying the gaunt man in the bed. Thankfully, Andre's eyes were closed, so he wouldn't see the fear that surely registered on her face. His skin felt clammy and cold to her touch although he perspired profusely. "Andre, I'm here. I'm with you now," Marie spoke softly.

Delirious from the fever that raged throughout his body, Andre rambled incoherently when she spoke to him. "Off the deck. Stop the bleeding."

Although non-responsive to her presence, she refused to leave him. She prayed in silence while she talked to him, held his hand, wiped his fevered brow, and protested when the doctors bled him in the name of healing. The day after her arrival a small cot was brought into his room for her use. At least he clung to life, allowing her to cling to hope.

After a touch-and-go week, his fever miraculously broke, and he spoke her name. "Marie," he whispered in a raspy voice, heralding his slow but steady recovery.

Each day she asked the doctor when he would be strong enough to go home to Chateau Fleury. After three weeks the doctor gave her the news she'd waited to hear. "You may take him home." The surgeon handed her an envelope. "You must follow these instructions to the letter, consistently, until he recovers. If you do not, all the progress he's made may be lost. He is not out of danger yet."

"I will care for him myself. Thank you, doctor."

The following morning Marie, Andre, and a nurse climbed into a coach and began the slow, arduous journey home. They stopped daily along the way to tend Andre's wound, eat, and sleep. The nurse taught Marie how to dress his injury and change the bandages.

Loire Valley – August 1778

After they reached the chateau, the family physician came daily to monitor Andre's progress, but Marie forbade that her husband be bled anymore. Finally, after several days of constant care at Andre's bedside, she asked, "What do you remember about the battle the day you were wounded?"

An agitated look clouded his handsome features. "Men fell all around because of Chartres' negligence. He should be shot."

She placed her hand on his furrowed brow and said, "The king knows what he did."

Andre's convalescence progressed well under Marie's watchful eye. By the end of his first month home, he began to sit in a chair for an hour each day and gradually increased the length of time. His strength continued to build until he was able to go for short walks with her around the grounds. Surprisingly, he had allowed her to help him reach the next level of healing rather than being uncooperative.

One day after he awoke from a nap, he took Marie's hand in his and kissed it. "You know today's an anniversary, and I think it's time we celebrate."

She smiled at him. He looked so much better. "Anniversary?"

He reached for her and pulled her down beside him on the bed. "Two months in your capable care." He kissed her with a passion that startled her. His hands explored her body and hesitated when he reached her swollen belly. "What's this?" Andre flattened his hand on her stomach. "I think I just got kicked."

"I've been meaning to tell you . . . when the time was right." Marie placed her hand beside his. "But I've been so afraid that something would go wrong again. I didn't want you to go through that."

Andre cradled her in his arms. "When is our baby due?"

"Late October." Marie nuzzled against his chest.

"Ma chérie Marie, you worry about me when all the while you have endured so much. You should have told me."

Some days later while they took their daily walk in the garden, he said, "I've given a lot of thought to what is really important in life, especially, our life together. I now know what I've been missing." He grinned. "I really like sharing time with you and the little one with the powerful foot." Andre paused and drew her to him, kissing her gently.

"Andre, I love you so." Tears stung Marie's eyes. "I feared I'd lost you." She slipped her arm through his as they resumed their stroll; her heart sang with joy.

"I realize that personal glory and selfishness had a lot to do with my desire to go to America." Andre grew silent, his expression pensive. "Can you ever forgive me for thinking only of myself?"

"I'm sure at the time you thought it was the thing to do," she said. "Come on, or we'll still be here when it gets dark."

"All right, let's go," he said and reached for her hand. "I want our baby to grow up knowing his father, and I want to be an important part of your life."

"You can't imagine how often I've longed to hear you say those words."

Andre squeezed her hand and reached over to pat her stomach. "I'll request an assignment with the Royal Guard at Versailles so that our family can be together."

Marie flung her arms around him and quickly moved to his right side to spare his wound.

During the months before the birth of the baby, Andre requested and received an appointment to serve the king at Versailles, starting after the New Year.

Thankful that her labor was uncomplicated and mercifully short—as much for Andre as for herself—Marie took the noisy child from the midwife's arms. "You are much like your father," she cooed fondly to her daughter, looking at the child's puckered, red face.

"She is?" Andre asked as he came into the room at the

midwife's behest. He kissed Marie, looked at the baby, and then shook his head. "She's beautiful—just like her mother. What shall we call her?"

"Janine Marie . . . just as you suggested for a girl."

"I can't decide which of the two of you I love more. Maybe that's because there's no limit to my affection for each of you." Andre lifted his daughter from Marie's outstretched arms, kissed the baby's forehead, and said, "My precious, I will always be here for you." He gently rocked baby Janine until she quieted, seemingly transfixed by the sound of his voice.

Chapter 15

Claire dried her hands on a gold-checkered towel, leaving the dinner ingredients on Michelle's kitchen counter to answer the front door. *"Bienvenue*. Please come in," she said to Marc-Claude. "What beautiful flowers."

He handed pale yellow and burnished gold roses to her and kissed her on each cheek.

She held the bouquet for a moment, breathing in its fragrance, and was reminded of the significance of yellow roses—joy and friendship. "May I get you a glass of wine while I get the flowers in water and start dinner?"

"Only if you'll join me. I'll help you fix dinner afterward."

"Good idea." She tried to suppress a giggle. "That is, if you know your way around a kitchen."

"I learn quickly." He smiled, his eyes full of mischief.

"I'll be right back." She picked up the flowers and went to the kitchen. After she placed them in a vase, she added water and set them on the kitchen table. Satisfied, she glanced toward the salon and caught Marc-Claude watching her. Her pulse quickened. "What are you doing in here?" Their eyes met for a moment before she turned back to the counter.

"Watching you," Marc-Claude said as he came up behind her and looked over her shoulder. "Better get some of these things back in the fridge."

Claire turned toward him and laid her head on his shoulder. His receptive hand pressed her closer. She murmured, "Right," and felt a contentment that she didn't want interrupted.

Too soon, Marc-Claude stepped back and picked up the head of lettuce and dressing, taking them to the refrigerator. "I'll be in the salon."

After storing the other perishable items, she left the kitchen with the wine tray and joined Marc-Claude. "What are you looking for over there?"

"Michelle's CDs."

Claire filled two wine glasses and set them on the coffee table before joining him at the stereo. "I've already found one I like."

"Which one?"

"*Romantic Classics*." She removed the case from the shelf and handed it to him.

He took the disc from its sleeve and placed it on the turntable, adjusting the volume. He caressed her arm and guided her to the sofa. Sentimental piano music played softly in the background while they talked and sipped wine.

"I hope the workshop doesn't interfere with your therapy sessions," Marc-Claude said.

"There hasn't been any problem." Claire wondered why he mentioned her time with Susan. She had better things to talk about and decided to change the subject as quickly as she could.

"The Americans have extended their stay here until early next week," he said. "We could postpone the workshop for a few days."

"Well, I suppose that would work," she said, "Friday maybe?"

"Next week would be better. I leave for Ankara on Friday."

So that was it. "How long will you be gone?" She didn't want him to go.

"Until Sunday . . . if all goes well."

"Okay. Let's plan the workshop for Monday afternoon then."

"I'll have Monique reschedule."

Claire kept the wine flowing and pondered how she could make their time together more intimate. She almost upset her glass when Marie whispered in her ear, *You have to fight for the man you love. Don't waste these precious moments.*

Claire raised her left hand to her head and tightened her grip on her glass. *What?*

The evening news had reported on Kurdish insurgent riots in the Turkish capital city. Claire pushed away her vague, nagging uneasiness for Marc-Claude's safety. She couldn't allow it to interfere with their evening. She put her arms around him. "No more business talk tonight. Let's just enjoy the evening."

Whether it was the wine, or whether he'd been cautious about being too forward, Marc-Claude seemed to welcome her suggestion. He slid his hand down her arm and tightened it around her waist, placing his other hand under her chin and turning her face toward him.

His gaze was as soft as a caress.

Being close to him eased concerns about yesterday or tomorrow—only the present mattered. She indulged in visualizing lovemaking images. She had a feeling he'd be there for her and give her strength in difficult times ahead. *Take it easy.* She straightened and breathed in deeply. "Let's start dinner."

"Later . . . there's no rush."

Was he aware of her vulnerability to the seductive power of his magnetism? "We may not get dinner if I don't get started now," she said in a husky whisper. She rose and took his hands in hers.

Marc-Claude sighed. "I'm in no hurry for dinner."

Claire sat back and snuggled closer to him. "To tell the truth, I'm not either."

"So far this has been an unusual evening," he said and squeezed her hand.

Claire cuddled against him. "You surprised me in the kitchen. You know your way around in there."

He shrugged and brushed his fingers across her forehead. In response she pressed her lips into the pulsing hollow at the base of his throat. His lips touched hers with a slow and delicious kiss—so very familiar to her—and she abandoned herself to the tingle coursing through her body.

He kissed the tip of her nose, then her eyelids, and finally, his lips feather-touched hers with tantalizing persuasion. Waves of delight washed over her.

"Are you sure?" he asked, his mellow voice as soft as velvet.

No doubt he was deferring to her, giving her a chance to change the course they were on. She had a burning desire, an aching need for another kiss. She drew his face to hers in a renewed invitation. His lips parted hers and she gave into the rhythmic progression of the passionate language of love—the spark between them had ignited into an inferno of desperate need.

Aching for the fulfillment of his lovemaking, she slipped her hand inside his shirt and trailed her fingers lightly up and down his back. This time there seemed no hesitation on his part. He didn't resist as he had in the boathouse. When she pressed her body against him, his breathing slowed, but she could feel his heart beating more rapidly. As he unbuttoned her blouse, his hand lightly caressing her breasts, she moaned.

Marc-Claude took her hands in his and stood, leading her into the bedroom. The moon cast a gossamer light across the bed. He undressed her and then himself, his profile dark against the moonlight. There was no turning back. There seemed to be no sense of strangeness or self-consciousness between them. They gave into the need to touch each other, to embrace and to love. Responding in sublime union each step of the way, Marc-Claude lead her to unknown heights of delight while showing a tender reverence toward her.

A harmony united them in explosive fulfillment. Her body melded with his. At that moment she knew she existed to be with him.

An hour later they still lay entwined, basking in blissful completion. Claire pushed up on her elbows and looked into Marc-Claude's eyes. The intensity of her feelings defied words. Silently, she devoured every detail of his face—his nose, his mouth, his chin, and then onto his chest and abdomen. She froze when she saw the jagged, round, scar-like birthmark, about an inch in diameter on his left side just below his ribs. Marie's diary had described Andre's life-threatening gunshot wound as being on his left side below the rib cage. Marie had bandaged, dressed, and cared for it, nursing Andre back to health. Claire sat transfixed, staring.

Marc-Claude's guarded courtroom expression surfaced, demanding an explanation. He waited for her to speak.

A state of confusion gave way to the counsel he'd given her a week or so earlier—*trust your intuition.* "It's your birthmark," she said. "It looks like a scar from a gunshot wound."

"Gunshot? Well, I suppose it may. But it's not," he replied without inflection.

Her uncensored words flowed freely. "And that's not all. Andre de Fleury suffered an injury in the same location on his left side. Marie stayed with him until he was out of danger."

"You're joking?"

"I've never been more serious. Marie wrote about it in her diary, too. Didn't you read it?"

He gave a tentative nod. "Now that you mention it. What an odd coincidence." He drew her closer.

She didn't want to talk but desperately needed more of him. Long past thinking, she yearned to merge with him.

For a long while, the sated lovers lay together. Finally, Marc-Claude turned and gazed into her eyes. "I'm not sure about reincarnation, but I do love you."

Claire shook her head. "Believe what you will. It's enough that you love me."

When Marc-Claude started to get up, she asked with a catch in her voice, "Where are you going?"

He pressed her hand and kissed her lightly on the cheek. "I don't want to overstay my welcome. Besides, it's two a.m."

An irrational fear swept over her. "No, don't go. Stay with me."

He lay back down and held her against him. "For you, anything, ma chérie."

Claire lay awake, savoring the nearness of him, the scent of him, and the reality of him. Somehow, his rhythmic breathing reassured her of . . . what, safety? His or hers? She'd lost herself in a passion for him not unlike what Marie had had for Andre. How could Marc-Claude's birthmark, in the same location as Andre's wound, be a mere coincidence? *Marc-Claude isn't Andre . . . he doesn't even have chocolate brown eyes.*

Claire felt the familiar touch sensation on her left cheek. *Marie, what are you doing in here?*

Claire heard the response in her mind. *Don't worry, I just got here. When you went into the bedroom, I didn't follow. I gave you privacy—that's more than you did for Andre and me on our honeymoon. But it really doesn't matter, because you and I are one soul just passing through different time periods.*

Marc-Claude and Claire dressed and grabbed a cup of coffee before they got into his car to start their day—Claire to Susan's for her appointment and he to his office.

After Marc-Claude pulled up to the curb to let Claire out, he glanced at his watch. "Sorry. We're ten minutes late."

"I knew I'd be late when I suggested we have a cup of coffee." She leaned over to him and kissed him. She had her priorities! When she opened the car door to get out, a relentless wind whipped her scarf. She waved at Marc-Claude and walked briskly up the stairs for her appointment.

Susan looked up from her desk when Claire came in. "I'll be with you in five. You can go in and be seated."

Claire settled herself on the familiar recliner. As soon as Susan came in, Claire asked her burning question. "Remember our discussion about cell memories and suppressed memories of traumatic experiences? For example, a birthmark in the same location as a past-life injury?"

"Yes," Susan said.

"If I think Andre is alive today, how could I be sure?"

"Your subconscious mind knows the answer."

"It does? I need those answers." *Is it possible that Marc-Claude and I are caught up in the love mystery of Marie and Andre?*

"Yes. While you're under hypnosis, before we get started on the regression, we'll ask."

Claire shifted in the recliner and smiled. With eager anticipation she allowed her conscious mind to rest.

"Tell me, subconscious mind, is Andre here in this lifetime?" Susan said.

"Yes."

"Have he and Claire met?"

"Yes."

"What is he called today?"

Claire stirred, hesitated, and remained silent.

Susan rephrased the question. "What is his name in this life?"

Claire blurted out the answer just as she had received it. "Marc-Claude Laval. He's Andre returned. We've been given this chance to get it right this time." Luckily, Susan seemed to take her answer at face value. Claire couldn't mention Marc-Claude's scar without revealing that she'd seen him undressed.

Mercifully, Susan didn't question her further and brought her out of hypnosis. "You seemed ambivalent about answering questions about Andre's reincarnation, although you said you wanted to know."

"Were you surprised by what I said about Marc-Claude?"

"No. I wasn't really," Susan said. "At the fundraiser I couldn't help noticing how you and he looked at each other. He couldn't take his eyes off you. I'd never seen him like that with any other woman. I had a feeling you'd be together sooner rather than later." Susan patted Claire's hand. "Do you have more questions? If not, we best leave a visit with Marie until your next appointment."

"No more questions I can think of now. But who knows what I'll want to ask tomorrow."

"Real progress was made today. Perhaps the next sessions will explain the purpose of your meeting again and the lessons to be learned from this life experience."

Chapter 16

Paris - February 1782

After an extended time at Chateau Fleury, Marie arrived at Versailles with three-year-old Janine and Nanny Cecile. She spent the first few days getting them settled into a daily routine, much of which centered on reserving time for a late dinner with Andre. He kept busy with his responsibilities at the palace, a real contrast to the free time he'd enjoyed at Chateau Fleury.

One morning, after a particularly enjoyable evening spent with Andre, Marie glanced up from her embroidery as Janine, her hand held by Cecile, entered Marie's boudoir. The child broke free and ran to her mother. "Maman, come with us."

Marie hugged her and then raised her daughter's face close to her own. "Maman has a luncheon to go to today. Tomorrow I'll walk with you."

"You look pretty," Janine called as she ran back to Cecile. "I want to see the birds today." Her childish voice conveyed excitement.

Filled with mixed emotions, Marie recalled how often Andre told Janine she'd be the belle of the ball. She smiled inwardly at the image of father and daughter together. She also felt remiss about resuming her social engagements at the palace which, by their very nature, excluded Janine.

Her lady-in-waiting added the finishing touches to Marie's *toilette* and busied herself tidying the cosmetics, brushes, and other grooming paraphernalia. "Is there anything more, Madame?"

Marie rose and stood before the full-length mirror. "Non, merci." Satisfied with her appearance, she left for Helene's apartment a half-hour early so they could visit before the other guests arrived.

When Marie knocked on her friend's door, Helene opened the door wide. "I've missed you so much." She took Marie's hand and drew her into the salon. "It just hasn't been the same around here without you."

"Believe me, your absence has been noticed too," Marie said, happy to be with her carefree friend again. Things had been dull without her bursts of enthusiasm to spice up the days. She treasured her family, and Helene was like a potent spice, good in small doses.

"Louise-Marie d'Orléans inquired about you. She wants you to come to supper at the Palais-Royal," Helene said, lowering her voice in a conspiratorial tone. "They're entertaining philosophers. It'll be a family affair with only a few guests."

"How did she know I was back in Paris?"

Her friend laughed. "Word travels fast around here. You know that."

Marie nodded. "Who do you suppose told her?"

"I saw her whispering with Marie-Antoinette."

"That would explain it. Those two love to gossip."

"Well, how will you respond to your invitation?" Helene locked eyes with Marie.

Marie shook her head. "I don't know. When is the supper?"

"A week from Monday. It is said that young Louis Philippe will be there too as part of his education."

Marie pursed her lips. "I don't know. Andre will be displeased if he hears of it." She sighed. "I want to go but must keep the peace!"

"Why does he object?"

"He is convinced that d'Orléans is a troublemaker, one who advocates change to gain power for himself."

"In that case we can help keep the king informed of what goes on there."

"I've always liked Louise-Marie," Marie took a deep breath. "And Andre will be gone at least two weeks to Spain on a special mission for the king."

A week later, when Marie arrived at the Palais-Royal, sweet, timid Louise-Marie gave her a warm greeting and seemed genuinely pleased to see her. "It's delightful to see you again. How are your daughter and husband?"

"Very well, thank you."

"Isn't motherhood wonderful? My children are my life." Marie-Louise motioned toward her son who sat beside his *gouverneur*, Madame de Genlis.

"Oui. Andre and I cherish our little Janine." Marie's heartfelt sympathy went out to her hostess. Everyone knew of the affair between the tutor and d'Orléans. He'd been so bold as to appoint her as the one to groom his son for his role in life rather than entrusting him to a man as was the aristocratic custom.

The evening began without the host. Philosopher Rousseau gave a review of his latest writings and called for discussion. The nine-year-old d'Orléans boy listened with a disciplined interest to the debate on the merits of liberty for all.

Shortly after nine o'clock, the wayward husband made his belated entry, full of bogus contrition. Philippe d'Orléans' red face and boisterous voice gave evidence that, rather than having been at the scene of a carriage accident as he proclaimed, he had been detained in a bar—likely a bordello. The rouge smudge on his shirt suggested so.

He and five other men gathered around the table after making crude remarks about the attire of one of the women. With a swagger d'Orléans moved to the front of the room and addressed the guests in a gruff voice. "Honored guests, you're about to hear an amazing revelation. This revered palace of the d'Orléans family is in change. No longer will it be for the privileged few. It is to become a public pleasure park for the people of Paris, right here in the heart of the city, not removed from the common folks as is Versailles."

Obviously appalled, a matronly woman said, "Monsieur le Duc, you can't be serious."

"Can't I, Madame? We'll have something for everyone—even you. There'll be boutiques, clubs, billiard parlors, exhibitions, puppet shows, cafes, gardens, and bordellos. Yes, bordellos, for those who seek such pleasures."

The hum of voices rose to a deafening buzz. Small groups of people chattered among themselves while the libertine duke mingled with the guests. When he reached Marie, he leaned forward with his lips puckered. She moved so quickly that the unwelcome kiss missed its mark, brushing her cheek instead.

He jerked his head to the side as if slapped. With an arrogant glare, he said, "Madame, are you still angry about your husband's unfortunate injury while aboard my ship?"

Nausea swept over her at the thought of him and his filthy mind. "Monsieur, I'm sure you were unable to alter the course of events after the battle began."

When he spotted Madame de Genlis, he proclaimed over the din around them, "Now here is a *real* lady."

His wife slipped away like a whipped puppy, her usual defense when humiliated by him.

Disgusted by the turn of events of the evening, Marie departed as soon as good manners allowed. Philippe d'Orléans had surrounded himself with propaganda specialists and those who preached rebellion to further their radical views. The open discussions of contemporary writings seemed to be a thing of the past. The debates had become vicious. What a change had taken place in less than a year.

Paris – 1789

Andre paced in an agitated manner. "I'm astounded at the brazen nerve of d'Orléans. In the session today, the king proposed that the Estates General be convened, after one hundred and seventy-five years of inactivity, in exchange for an immediate one hundred twenty million *livre* of new taxation. Can you imagine what d'Orléans did?"

"Nothing would surprise me," Marie said. "He's an arrogant, immoral man."

"He stood up right there in the Court of Peers and said, 'Sire, this is against the law.'"

Incensed, Marie gasped, "No, no, that's impossible!"

"It is so." Andre continued. "Stunned silence swept across the entire chamber. Never before has a prince of the blood been so bold as to challenge the king and suggest there are constitutional limits to his power."

"He's openly challenging the king's power! He's gone mad," Marie remarked. "He publicly attacked the authority of the King of

France!"

Two days later Marie received a formal, written invitation to the Palais-Royal. *I must respond with my regrets.* She realized that Helene would try to change her mind but there was no way Marie could rationalize that the salon dinners were strictly intellectual pursuits. *Andre is right. These meetings foment discontent and danger of revolution.* She rushed out to look for Helene and met her in the corridor. "Helene, I am deeply distressed by the tone of discussions at Madame duPont's salons and the goings-on at the Palais-Royal. I will no longer attend any of those events."

Marie's friend put her arm around her. "Those people are all talk. Each one tries to say something more outrageous than the other."

"They are vicious and frenzied. They will stop at nothing! I don't want to be around them."

"Then I will not go, either."

Marie's eyebrows rose. "You are concerned too?"

Helene shrugged. "I'm going to Bordeaux with an unnamed gentleman. Ask no more."

"Can't you be serious for once?" Marie shook her head at Helene's lack of judgment in both social and political matters. "Think about what I've said."

"I always do and then make up my own mind."

"I have to go. Janine is waiting for me," Marie murmured as Helene turned and sauntered down the hall. On her way back to her apartment, Marie came to a group of courtiers. She slowed her pace when she heard the topic of conversation.

"d'Orléans is called Philippe Égalité by some, and the Palais-Royal is referred to as the Garden of the Revolution."

Some months later, on the evening of October 5, the low-slung sun cast a blood-red glow across the autumn landscape around Versailles. Marie had planned a quiet evening with several of her close friends. Now the ladies sat around the table with coffee and cakes while they watched eleven-year-old Janine rehearse her part in one of Marie-Antoinette's theatrical productions.

Although life seemed to be normal, an underlying uneasiness had plagued Marie since July, when Andre had told her about his concerns for the safety of the king and queen after the vicious attack and destruction of the Bastille. The royal couple steadfastly refused to consider increasing the number of guards on duty at Versailles, insisting there was no danger.

While Marie sat inside with her friends, Andre fulfilled his duty to the king. A small detachment from the *Gardes-du-Corps de Roi* stood watch in the courtyard and inside the palace.

Marie's guests departed earlier than usual that evening. Had her mood somehow affected them? While she pondered the possibility, she heard voices in the distance. They became louder and angry as they drew closer. Frenzied calls sounded around the palace. She ran to the window.

Throngs of women and men drew closer and closer to the palace. They carried torches, pitchforks, knives, axes, pikes, and old muskets. Now she could see the women wore the red dresses and white hats of fishwives. They shouted venomous threats at Marie-Antoinette.

"Kill them! Kill the guards! Kill the queen!" the crowd shouted.

Marie almost fainted when she saw bloody heads on some of the pikes. She ran to Janine's room, grabbed her daughter's clothes, and awakened her. "Hurry! Get dressed now! We're under attack."

Cecile rushed in and began throwing a few of their possessions into satchels. While they dressed and packed, Andre dashed in. "The palace is under siege. The queen has escaped to the king's chamber— for now. On my way to sound the alarm, I passed d'Orléans on horseback behind the mob," Andre said, a catch in his voice. "As he moved among them, the wretches chanted, "Long live our King d'Orléans."

Andre gulped and continued, "You must leave here. I've arranged an escort for you to get to Madame Rugh's house . . . not far from here. You'll be out of harm's way until I can come for you."

Marie reached for his arm. "What has happened?"

"The mob killed the sentry on duty and overcame other guards along the way. A gate that should have been locked was not. They entered the unlocked gate and stampeded the staircase. Apparently guided by someone who knew the way, they barged into the queen's guardroom without hesitation."

Hurrying around the room, Andre first helped Marie and then Janine. "The solitary guard on duty rushed to the locked door of the queen's bedroom. Pounding frantically on the door, he shouted, 'Madame, you must leave now. There are those who have come to kill you.' With his back to the door, he fought them off . . . until his last breath." Andre picked up the bags. "Go! Now! Your escort is waiting."

Chapter 17

Marc-Claude . . . reincarnated Andre! Claire ignored the slushy raindrops and, as she drew her wool scarf around her neck, she struggled to wrap her mind around how Marc-Claude's and her lives connected. The last two days had altered her reality. It was one of those pinch-yourself-to-see-if-you-are-awake times—joyful, combined with fear that it wasn't true. In spite of their efforts to resist, the force of their attraction had compelled them to express their passion. Now they faced myriad challenges. How would they respond to problems they faced because of the Laval family loyalty to Felicity, let alone ones carried forward from their past life together?

Maybe there's another explanation . . . not reincarnation.

Claire tilted and lowered her wet umbrella before she entered the Laval and Associates office. The thrill of being with Marc-Claude again was the one thing of which she could be sure.

Everything else has changed between us.

As she unbuttoned her navy-blue jacket, she recalled how her feelings for Marc-Claude had changed her best-laid plans; her guarded independence was no longer relevant. In past relationships with men, she had been able to be levelheaded and keep focused on her goals. A silent alarm always went off in her head at the slightest hint of temptation to deviate from her course. She'd remained within her comfort zone—until now.

"Bonjour, Monique," she greeted Marc-Claude's legal assistant. "Do you have a copy of the workshop checklist that I can take with me today?"

"Oui." Monique reached for a folder on the side of her desk and gave it to Claire. "Monsieur Laval asked that you stop by his office."

"Thank you." Claire took the folder and walked down the long hallway to Marc-Claude's office, but his door was closed. *He must be preparing for his meeting in Ankara.* She tapped anyway—he *had* asked to see her—so, expecting him, it came as a surprise when Michelle opened the door.

"Bonjour, Claire," Michelle greeted her. "Come on in."

Inside the office, Felicity sat in a chair as close to Marc-Claude's desk as she could—short of sitting on top of it. Turning toward Claire, Felicity smiled, contrary to her usual manner whenever they met. "So glad you're here."

"Bonjour," Claire replied and wondered why Felicity was there. *Pursuing Marc-Claude, no doubt.*

Marc-Claude looked up from a voluminous folder on his desk. His expression softened as their eyes met. "We've been waiting for you."

"Oh?" Claire's eyebrows furrowed as she held his gaze.

"We stopped by to help with your workshop preparations," Michelle said as she drew a chair forward for Claire.

Claire nodded and sat. "That's thoughtful, but it wasn't necessary."

"I'm in the city for the Wine Festival this weekend," Felicity said. "My chauffeur is on call to shuttle you about town today. I'm sure you have a million things to get done."

After Claire recovered from the shock, she said, "Thank you."

Marc-Claude closed the folder and stacked it on top of several others. "Ladies, please excuse us. Claire and I have a scheduled appointment."

"Felicity, we better get to work ourselves and leave Marc-Claude to his," Michelle said as she stood.

Marc-Claude rose and accompanied them to the door, closing it after them. "You've been on my mind all morning. I know how important it is to you to prove the authenticity of Marie's diary entries. I don't want that to remain a barrier between us."

Claire reached for his hand. "I don't either. I can't explain why I place so much emphasis on it—but I do." Her voice slipped into a hushed whisper.

Marc-Claude guided her to the loveseat and sat down beside her. He slipped his arm around her shoulder and kissed her gently. "I haven't had much luck locating your family records in Tours. I think our best hope is to pursue DNA evidence. I've spoken to Dr. Sartre, a leading authority in the field. He suggests mitochondrial DNA since it is inherited only from the mother and is passed unchanged along the maternal line, allowing genes to be traced over generations. Marie's lock of hair in the locket is our best bet for comparison to your blood sample."

Everything he said made sense, but it put at risk the hair sample in the locket, her last direct tie to Marquise Marie de Fleury—since the diary was still missing. Could she take the chance? Her shoulders slumped. "I . . . I'm afraid to risk ruining the lock of hair."

"I understand your concern. You don't have to sacrifice all of the hair. Just a few strands would be sufficient, leaving most of it undisturbed. And stringent laboratory protocol is followed to avoid any damage to the sample or contamination during the entire procedure."

Claire laid her head on Marc-Claude's shoulder, her stomach churning. "Do you suppose Felicity will agree to have her blood sampled for the DNA test?"

"I doubt it." Marc-Claude frowned. "She has nothing to be gained by doing so."

"I'm going to have to think about this," Claire said.

"I know." Marc-Claude turned her face toward him and kissed her. "There's no rush. Take your time. Consider whether it's something you want to do."

"I will. I better go now." She stood.

"Of course. Michelle and Felicity are waiting for you." Marc-Claude rose and handed her his mobile phone. "Take this with you."

"Won't you need it?"

"Non, it's my personal phone. I'll use my business one."

"I doubt I'll need it," she protested, but she tucked the phone into her purse anyway.

"I'll call you about dinner." Marc-Claude said as he walked her to the door. "There'll be time before I leave for the airport."

By the time Claire arrived at Monique's office, she found Michelle and Felicity at work in the adjoining conference room. Folders and several stacks of printed handouts sat on the table. Chairs rested against the wall.

Felicity was leafing through the stacks of paper. "Michelle and I will put these together."

Claire nodded her agreement.

"Now you're free to pick up the order from the printers," Felicity said. "Don't forget to go by the deli to select a special treat for the American clients."

"Naturellement," Claire said, wondering whether she could trust Felicity. She concluded she shouldn't and planned to check on their work upon her return.

Michelle glanced around the room and asked, "Does this arrangement work for you?"

"Perfect. Thank you," Claire assured her.

Felicity reached into her green Hermes croc-skin purse and pulled out her mobile phone. "I'll call Yasin to bring the car around. Okay?"

"Good. I'll be on my way." When Claire retraced her steps to Marc-Claude's office to pick up the folder she'd left—on purpose—on the coffee table, the open door revealed he'd momentarily stepped out. Her heart sank. Where was he? When she turned to leave, she almost collided with him. "I forgot this," she said, waving the folder.

He stepped back and closed the door. "I know," he said with a smile. "I started to bring it to you but had second thoughts."

Claire frowned. "And why is that?"

He reached for her hand and kissed it. "I wanted to see you alone."

Without reservation she moved closer and tilted her head toward him. "You were very much a part of my session this morning. Your name came up several times."

"Ummm," he mumbled without interest. Drawing her to him, he stroked her hair before his demanding lips hushed hers.

She wrapped her arms around him without a second thought. She'd almost forgotten where she was until the phone buzzer intruded.

It sounded several times before he picked it up. "The car's ready. They'll come looking for you if I keep you longer."

She sighed. "I wouldn't want that."

The chauffeur, dressed in the blue and gold de Fleury livery uniform, held the door while Claire slipped into the back seat. She cringed when she realized that he was the security guard who had been brusque at Chateau Fleury the night of the fundraiser. So much for friendly chitchat. She adjusted her skirt after she settled into the well-worn leather seat. The car, an older model, had aged reasonably well. The scent of new-leather air freshener hung heavy around her.

"Where to?" he asked in a solicitous tone while moving the lumbering hunk into the heavy city traffic.

Claire handed him the printer's business card. "Let's go to the printer's first."

He lowered the volume of the radio and glanced at her in the rearview mirror, his voice carefully modulated. "Do you mind if I make a stop on the way? I need to pick up wine for Mademoiselle de Fleury for the Wine Festival."

Claire hesitated. "All right." She hoped he didn't have a long list of stops.

He nodded. "She's given specific instructions that you are to select some of their best wine for your event."

Now that Claire understood the stop related to her event, she regretted her hasty judgment.

They entered a rundown area of old warehouses and other industrial buildings, and after several twists and turns, Yasin parked the car in front of an aged building with a faded sign. "Here we are."

Claire strained to make out the words but could only make out Les Pas...Brasserie. "Is this a brewery?"

"Not since the last century. Now it's used as a distribution warehouse for Chateau Fleury wines."

"In an old brewery building?"

"That's right. Not much has changed outside or inside, since it's just used for storage."

"Interesting," Claire said without conviction.

"The interior takes you back in time." He came around the car and opened the door. "Come in and make your wine selection."

"All right." She stepped out of the car, feeling relief at not being left alone. She didn't like the looks of the two scruffy-looking men in a van parked across the street. She wondered whether the chauffeur avoided using the front door because of them. He led her around to the side of the building and, with a large, tarnished key, unlocked a shabby door.

With a flick of the light switch, a vastly under-utilized storage area came into view. The room held no more than a couple hundred cases of Chateau Fleury wine and champagne of another label. If fully utilized, Claire figured the warehouse could accommodate ten times as many cases.

Before she could comment on the sparse offerings, Yasin gestured to the far side of the room. "The best offerings are kept in a special vault. Come with me and you'll see the perfectly matured vintage wines from which you are to make your selection," he said as he unlocked a door at the back of the room.

Pushing aside several cases of wine and rolling back a flimsy sisal rug, he flipped on a light switch and lifted a movable portion of the floor. He motioned her to the narrow, winding staircase and replaced the floor piece as they prepared to climb down. At the bottom of the stairs they came into a stone cellar, its low ceiling supported by chubby masonry piers. A few scattered cases sat on the rough stone floor.

Unsure of her footing, Claire edged along the wall of the dimly lit, dank room. While moving past niches filled with wine bottles stacked on their sides, she noticed dust and cobwebs on some of them, while others looked freshly placed. "Amazing—a perfect wine cellar."

"Isn't it?" he said with a grin.

Yasin pushed aside a large beer container, removed iron bars from across a thick wooden door, and pulled a flashlight from his pocket. "Before you make your selection, you must see these."

"More wine?" Claire asked as she watched the flashlight beam illuminate several boxes on the floor near the door. The light carried down a long, narrow corridor before it diminished into darkness. "How far does this cellar extend?"

"This is one of the tunnels from the old limestone quarries." With a casual wave of his hand, he studied her face. "They honeycomb the city."

Claire didn't move. "I've read about them."

"It's okay. Come in." He squinted and turned his attention to a stack of small, wood-slatted boxes. "These crates hold a collection of some of the finest Merlot money can buy."

Claire noticed a corkscrew on top of one. *Odd. Has someone been sampling the Merlot?* With a quick estimate of four to a box, she concluded the collection contained no more than fifty or so bottles.

Yasin took one of the bottles from a crate and ran his hands along it before handing it to Claire. "These quarries have figured in the history of Paris over the centuries. Several hundred years ago, bones from filled-up cemeteries were moved into some of the tunnels."

She returned the bottle to him and stepped around several larger cases. "Are we near the Catacombs?"

"Not far. During World Two, the French Resistance ran their operations from them."

"Yes, I've heard accounts of . . ."

He interrupted before she could finish her sentence, holding his finger to his lips. "Shhh! What's that? Did you hear that noise?"

"I didn't hear anything."

Still whispering, he said, "You wait here." He thrust the flashlight into her hand and made his way to the open door.

Claire followed, tiptoeing so as not to make a sound.

Clang! Bang!

The violent slam of the heavy door reverberated around her, followed by the raspy scrape of the iron-bars barricade locking the door.

Another moment and I would have been crushed!

Chapter 18

Claire's head spun in a dizzying frenzy. Angry waves of terror battered her normally rational mind like an island hit by a category-five hurricane. A full-fledged panic attack threatened—if she didn't die of heart failure first. Locked in the endless catacombs beneath Paris, her phobia of dark, musty enclosures jeopardized her survival. She'd thought her sessions with Susan had freed her from fears carried forward from Marie's memories of imprisonment in La Conciergerie while she awaited the guillotine. Now she knew better.

Where was the flashlight? Why couldn't she see its beam? She must have dropped it in her fright during the terrifying moment she'd almost been crushed in the warehouse door. She clawed at the cold stone floor, snapping a fingernail in her desperate search. Darkness seemed to squeeze icy tentacles around her brain, providing no respite for her thundering heart. *Yasin will come back for me—if he's able. But what if he's hurt or killed?* Fear within taunted. The enormity of her predicament hit her full force. *Oh, my God, I'm trapped like an animal.* What if he couldn't help her? She fought to control her wild emotions.

Her grandfather had been in Paris during the German occupation in the early 1940s. He'd told her about the old quarries, so she understood the dangers they posed. An unsuspecting soul could easily get lost in the miles of passageways. The walls might cave-in at any time or floors could suddenly drop into deep wells. Should she risk seeking another way out or stay put?

She resumed her search for the flashlight until the side of her hand struck a long, metal object next to a wine crate. Frantic, she grasped it, sliding the light switch back and forth while she shook it. Momentarily, the loose batteries rattled and reconnected, the beam illuminating the stash of priceless wines.

She leaned against the forbidding wall and waited until her nervous hands steadied. After anxious moments she calmed down and picked up the corkscrew and a bottle of Merlot. She put them in her purse and started to leave but turned back and took the other three bottles from the case. She concluded that although her large purse now weighed a ton, she'd have to manage. There was no way to know how long she'd be trapped. The wide over-body strap of her purse was a godsend.

She moved slowly as she followed the light beam. It reflected around the rim of a precipice, revealing a sharp turn in the tunnel ahead. Unexpected danger lurked in these caves. The curve in the tunnel might lead her to escape, and then again it could *dead-end*—in more than one sense. She must control her emotions while seeking her freedom and not think too far ahead. Was there a Metro exit nearby— or just a solid wall of skeletons to welcome her to their ranks? She dug around in her purse for the corkscrew until she found it and removed a bottle of wine. *Thank goodness*. The cork came out on the first try. She tipped the bottle and took a swig.

Ever cautious, she started out again and followed the beam along the corridor, dribbling wine to mark her steps in case she had to retreat the way she'd come. With great care she moved around the bend—still no end in sight. The light flickered for an instant before its normal illumination returned.

Continuing on, she came to a fork in the tunnel and decided to bear to the left, a direction that seemed to go on forever. She tensed. Had the flashlight dimmed again? Were the batteries about to give out? Surely not. She weighed the risk and rejected the thought of turning around and retracing her steps along the Merlot-stained stones back to the locked door of the warehouse. Who knew how long it might be before anyone found her. She leaned against the wall and waited for the waves of nausea to pass.

Splat. Splat.

She looked up and saw that a liquid seeped from the roof and had dripped on her head. She shuddered. "Yuck! What's that?" Instinctively, she shook her head to free herself of whatever had splashed. Droplets spread into the stale air around her. She dug around in her handbag and found a handkerchief. After patting her face, she shone the light on the cloth. Relieved to see that the moisture was colorless, she breathed a little easier.

As she glanced up, another liquid bead formed and threatened to hit her in the face. She had to get away from there; inching forward, she came within two steps of falling into what appeared to be a bottomless pit. "Ahhhh!" she screamed and clutched her chest. In her state of panic, she dropped the wine she'd used to mark her way. The bottle bounced and rolled into the gaping hole and disappeared from view. She didn't hear it hit bottom.

That could have been me!

She slipped to the floor when her left leg began to cramp. When her liquid legs would obey her again, she stood and inched backward, retreating to the fork in the tunnel by following the wine stains. She paused long enough to open another bottle of Merlot and formed a red X by the dead-end passageway. She started in another direction and continued to track her steps with wine drops. Again, it seemed the flashlight dimmed, or had she imagined it?

The sound of her heels striking the limestone broke the sinister silence in the narrow, stale passageway. The temptation to take a sip of the precious red liquid must be resisted. She needed to remain alert in this abominable place. She hadn't gone far when her foot brushed against a solid object. It went skittering across the stone floor. A rat? She might die of heart failure if confronted by a large rodent. She gulped and turned the light in the direction of the noise. A metal box lay in front of her. She set the bottle down and picked up the container, noting that scratches marred the abstract design on the lid. She held her breath and slowly opened it, afraid of what she might find. Three small candles and a few matches rolled around inside. Who could have left them there?

Claire swung the flashlight around in every direction. To her horror, straight ahead a fully clothed human lay face down in a rust-colored puddle. She wanted to run but her legs wouldn't move. Her eyes riveted on the body until the light flickered and almost went out, obscuring her view of the gruesome scene. Her foot hit the wine bottle. Frenzied, she grabbed it and held it to her chest.

"Calm down," she chastised herself. She took a deep breath and edged forward. A foul odor came from the corpse, a man who had been dead for some time, she surmised. Who was he? Had he entered from a place of possible escape for her?

To complicate matters, she had no idea what part of Paris lay above ground. She looked, but saw no wine marks at her feet. She lifted the bottle to her lips and tipped it up. Nothing! How could this bottle be empty already? With reluctance, she uncorked another one. A portal in the hard, cold wall on her right side beckoned her to leave her path again. An utterly confusing maze lay ahead, with tunnels branching off like limbs on a tree. She shook her head and dismissed any thought of going that way. Staying in the same tunnel lessened the risk of confusion as to where she had been.

Again the light faltered; this time it didn't return to its usual brightness. She opened the tinderbox, took out one of the matches, and struck it. Its head crumbled. She moaned and tried again. The second try almost succeeded, but the candlewick sparked, faded, and died. After two more tries the candle gave forth a tentative light that sputtered and threatened to go out.

Confusion and fatigue gripped her as she looked for a dry spot to sit—or to give up and lie down in her dismal tomb. She let a few drops of wax drip onto the box top, pressed the candle into the wax, and held it in place to harden to a makeshift candleholder. Afterward, she indulged in a couple swallows of Merlot—celebrating a small victory of sorts. After sipping the wine, she sighed. *Ummm . . . that's better.* Her overwrought body sank onto the hard floor as though the floor were a goose-down cushion.

She didn't have the energy to think about her predicament at the moment. She'd rest; there seemed to be no shortage of time. While she waited, her mind drifted to thoughts of Marc-Claude . . . and of Andre and Marie, who had endured crisis after crisis. Why must she have this crisis? She imagined Marie's presence, her abiding strength, and relaxed into an internal dialogue with Marie. *Things will be okay.*

Her head fell forward as she watched behind closed eyelids.

Marie gestured to Claire's purse.

Claire's eyes flew open and her entire body stiffened when the persisted jingle of her cell phone sounded. *Marc-Claude's phone! How could I forget?* She grabbed her handbag and fumbled for it. "Marc-Claude, Marc-Claude?" she whimpered, tears streaming down her cheeks.

"What's wrong?" Marc-Claude asked.

"Marc-Claude, thank God!"

"Claire . . . what's . . . wrong? Where are . . . ?"

"Help me. The phone signal is breaking up. Help me."

"What happened?"

"I'm locked in the catacombs."

"What?"

"I'm in the old quarry. There's a dead body in here."

"Catacombs . . . speak with Yasin?"

"He's not here." She slapped at a salty tear on her cheek. "I . . . I don't know what happened to the chauffeur. Just before the door slammed shut and locked, I heard angry voices, a scuffle, and breaking glass."

". . . chauffeur's . . . there?"

"I can't hear you. The signal is breaking up. He brought me to Chateau Fleury's warehouse to pick up wine for the workshop."

"Where's . . . located? Location?"

"I'm not sure of the address. It's an old brewery that accesses the underground quarry."

". . . nearby landmarks?"

"We turned toward the Seine before we reached the Arc de Triomphe and crossed the river. We went no more than two or three blocks farther."

". . . anything else . . . think of?"

"There's a faded sign on the building. Les Pas and Brasserie."

"Good."

"Can't think of anything else."

"Okay. Leave . . . phone on. I'll . . . police . . . way."

"Please hurry."

"I will."

Claire's hands felt like ice against her burning cheeks. A queasy sensation gripped her. She feared she might hyperventilate and tried to take slow, deep breaths to relax. The stagnant air clung to her nostrils.

The next twenty-five minutes seemed like an eternity while she sat huddled with her back against the wall. She jumped at the sound of the phone as it bounced around the abysmal space. With a shaky hand, she brought it to her ear.

"Hello? Marc-Claude, I'm okay. A little jumpy though."

"I'm at the police station with Inspector LaBeau. We've identified the location and are on our way."

"Thank goodness." Claire sighed.

"What can you tell me about the layout of the warehouse?"

"We entered a side door into a large room. Then we went into a smaller room. A rug covered a removable portion of the floor near the back that led to stairs down to a stone cellar."

"Side door, stairs to cellar, and then?"

"Oui. A wooden door with iron bars across it opens into the catacombs."

"Okay, we'll contact the Superintendent of the Catacombs and get a map, if possible."

"I've walked a long way in here and haven't found an exit. But I did think to mark my route by leaving drops of Merlot along the way," she said, her hope rising.

"Smart move. That'll help. Follow it back."

"I will." She thought better of distracting him by again mentioning the body that lay between them. She shuddered at the thought of it.

"Hang in there a little longer."

After lighting another candle and following the drops, she began to retrace her steps toward the warehouse. She walked slowly and focused on the faded red splashes on the floor of the dimly lit corridor. When she came close to where she thought the corpse lay, she slowed, taking care to keep her eyes fastened on the drops on the floor.

In a short time, she heard voices in the distance and began to run. *Slow down! What if the echoes play tricks?* She must keep a lookout for the marked path. As she moved along, she called out every so often, "Over here. This way." As the voice grew clearer, she relaxed—they were inside the tunnel that led to her. A beam of light outlined three silhouettes coming her way. She started to run and called, "Marc-Claude."

"Claire, I'm here. It's going to be okay." Marc-Claude's footsteps thundered toward her until he reached her and held her in his arms. "It's okay now." He drew her close to his side as they went back to meet the other two men, whom he introduced as Inspector LaBeau and the Superintendent of the Catacombs.

The inspector gave her a somber look. "Mademoiselle, I know you are anxious to leave. But I need to ask you a few questions. What is your estimate of the distance from here to the place where you saw the body?"

"Umm, that's hard to say—half-mile or more."

He handed her a map that looked like the circulatory system of the human body multiplied many times and pointed to an X on it. "We're here. Are the remains in this main tunnel or in another one?"

Claire placed her finger on her best-guess location. "Here. This one. At the fork, going to the right." She bit her lip "The other way drops into a pit."

"Merci, Mademoiselle."

The inspector's alert eyes settled on the Merlot bottle before he reached for it. He caressed it and whistled through his teeth. "It breaks my heart to see this precious liquid on the floor."

Looking at the improvised candleholder in her other hand, he asked, "What's that?"

Crime scene evidence. "A box of candles and matches I found . . . near the body."

LaBeau handed the bottle to Marc-Claude and took the box from Claire. He opened it, peered inside, and sniffed the fine, white-powder residue. Turning abruptly toward the warehouse, he said, "*On y va?* Shall we go?"

Marc-Claude put the cork in the bottle and placed it in Claire's handbag. "Let's get out of here," he said and slipped his arm around her shoulders. They left the dismal space and walked in silence to the wine cellar.

Claire trembled at the sight of the warehouse door. Had the chauffeur been harmed by the intruders? Was he lying dead in there? Could she remain calm if faced with another corpse?

As if sensitive to her anxiety, Marc-Claude squeezed her tense shoulder in a reassuring way. "Everything is okay in here . . . other than broken glass and spilt wine."

The first thing Claire saw when she entered was two police officers waiting for them—not much evidence of a crime committed there.

Inspector LaBeau motioned to them. "There's a body in the tunnel. Approximately in this location," he said, pointing to the map and summarizing what Claire had relayed. "Continue with the investigation and bring your report to me. I'll accompany these people to the station and take Mademoiselle Bennett's full statement."

"Oui, Monsieur," one of the officers said.

"The superintendent has agreed to stay and guide you through the tunnel."

Although she had been rescued more than two hours earlier, Claire remained shaken after she and Marc-Claude left the police station. She'd made an effort to answer the inspector's questions as best she could, and even though she knew she was safe now, the events in the catacombs continued to haunt her.

The strained look around Marc-Claude's golden eyes revealed his concern. "None of this makes sense. The sooner Yasin is located the better. He's our best bet for getting answers."

"Who'd have known we were there?" Claire asked.

"Good question. Who knew the chauffeur planned to stop there?" Marc-Claude squeezed her hand. "We'll get to the bottom of this."

She tightened her hold on his hand.

"I wonder if there's anything I have missed," Marc-Claude said.

"How could you have known?"

He shook his head. "That's what bothers me."

"I hope the inspector finds useful evidence."

"The important thing now is that you're safe. I'm going to see you stay that way."

"Where are you taking me?" she asked as they passed the Luxembourg palace, the seat of the French Senate, and its surrounding park and gardens.

"To my place, where I can keep an eye on you," Marc-Claude said while he continued on Saint Michel Boulevard in the historic St-Germain-des-Pres district.

"But you leave for Ankara tonight."

"No, I've sent one of my associates ahead. I'll go tomorrow, after you're settled in the apartment."

"That's not necessary. I'll stay with Michelle."

"Non. Not until we have a better idea who's behind this. I don't want you exposed to unnecessary danger."

"You don't think I'll be safe at Michelle's?"

"Not tonight, Claire. We can't be sure."

Chapter 19

After Marc-Claude drove past the Luxembourg, he continued on until he reached the Rue Notre Dame des Champs. "We're almost there," he said to Claire as he slowed and pulled the car to the security gate in front of a stately limestone mansion, one of the famous Parisian seventeenth-century *hotel particuleirs.* Lowering the window, he said to the attendant, "How's it going, Leo?"

It didn't surprise Claire that his apartment was in such an elegant building.

With curious eyes on Claire, Leo said, "Great, Monsieur Laval."

As Marc-Claude closed the window and moved forward into the garage, Claire looked around and wondered why there were so few vehicles in the huge garage. It appeared to occupy the entire subterranean level. "This *is* more secure than Michelle's," she said, counting only seventeen vehicles, mostly luxury ones at that. Marc-Claude's silver Peugeot seemed modest compared to most of the others, including a black Mercedes with tinted windows and an apple-green Lamborghini.

"That it is." Marc-Claude expertly maneuvered the car into parking space number one, next to a Cadillac, got out, and came around to open the door for Claire. "This way," he said, gently guiding her to one of three elevators and entering a code on the keypad. He stood to the side and held the door open, then followed closely behind and pressed the number-three button. The doors closed and the elevator soon glided to a smooth stop at the upper level.

To Claire's astonishment the elevator opened into a large room that reminded her of a ballroom. Seating areas along the wall left an expanse of open space in the rest of the room. "How many apartments are here?"

"Three . . . one on each floor."

"With a private elevator to your penthouse?" she said.

"You could put it that way," he replied.

"Why all the security precautions?"

"Primarily for my tenants . . . who value their privacy."

"Oh. Are they pursued by the paparazzi?"

"It has happened," he said.

"They're celebrities?"

"One is a well-known fashion designer, and the other is an acclaimed actress."

"How long have the apartments been in here?"

"Four years."

"And before that?" she asked.

"It's been our family Paris residence since sixteen eighty-seven."

Mega-rich!

"Wow. Chateau Lamont . . . and this, too?"

"Not anymore. I took it off my father's hands and converted it into the three luxury apartments."

"Does the family regret giving it up?"

"Actually, it works very well this way. It's now self-supporting, so to speak, and I live here rent-free."

Claire stood by the floor-to-ceiling arched French doors and gazed at the breathtaking view of the Seine with the lights of Paris reflected in the water. "What a spectacular view." She turned her head to the west and saw the lighted Eiffel Tower, its metal skeleton outlined against the dark sky. She looked back at Marc-Claude. "It's beautiful."

He smiled and nodded as he pressed the intercom button. "Please arrange a simple dinner for two on the balcony in an hour." Marc-Claude motioned for Claire to come with him. "I'll show you to your room. You probably want to freshen up a bit after the day you've had."

The intricately patterned walnut-and-cherry parquet of the reception hall gave way to plush, honey-colored carpet in the wide corridor. "In the guest room you'll find a selection of lounging robes." He hesitated as they went into a bedroom. "Desolé, that's all I can offer in the way of comfortable clothing," he said as he opened the closet door.

"I need to get some of my things from Michelle's to wear for dinner."

He shook his head. "Lounging attire is acceptable at dinner tonight."

"If you say so."

"Meet me in the reception hall when you're ready," he said on his way out.

Anticipating a leisurely warm bath, Claire went toward the bathroom but stopped at the doorway to admire it. *Wow, elegant simplicity.* An expanse of rose-beige surrounded her. The monotone room was sheathed in large, marbled, rose-beige tiles on the walls and floors. Three large arched windows looked into a private balcony garden.

Oh, yes! A whirlpool tub. The tub, a deeper shade of rose-beige, reposed between two matching columns adorned with carved wall sconces on each side. Two bronze sculptures stood on short columns. Three orchid plants—a pale yellow, a light pink, and a rose-pink shade—each with several stems of blossoms—sat on the counter between the two sinks.

Claire was beginning to come down from the effects of the afternoon, but she wasn't ready to think about the terrible events of the day. Watching the water flow into the tub, she was grateful to be alive and safe. An Eiffel Tower-shaped container held rose-lavender bath salts. Wondering whether it had been a gift, she sprinkled some of its contents into the water. As she closed the bottle, she thought it seemed out of place—too whimsical for Marc-Claude's taste. She shrugged and climbed into the tub.

Eager to get started, she turned on the jets and applied a green tea mask on her face. She lay back against the headrest and closed her eyes, cautioning herself to stay awake. It was pure heaven after being in the catacombs most of the afternoon.

I owe my life to Marc-Claude.

She eased into the sensory experience of the water pulsating against her tense muscles. Her shoulders and neck relaxed more and more as she drifted with the luxury and she lost track of time. She didn't know how long she spent in the tub, but finally, the thought of food encouraged her to get dressed. She stepped onto the warm floor tiles, bending down to test them. *Heated tiles!* She took a bath towel from the selection on a warmer rack and patted her body dry.

Only the best for the prima-donna-for-a-day.

Claire thumbed through the array of loungewear in the closet: feminine robes and masculine ones of all colors and styles. *What to wear?* She'd take a more leisurely look in the morning. For now she removed a luscious apricot garment from its polished walnut hanger and she slipped into it. She gazed at her reflection in the floor-to-ceiling, gold-framed mirror and nodded a satisfied approval.

At the sound of footsteps, Marc-Claude folded his newspaper and rose to meet Claire. He marveled at her beauty in the soft, apricot-colored lounging robe. The woman he loved—and as of today knew he wanted as his wife. The apricot complemented the reddish-gold highlights in her brown hair and the peach tones of her skin—a precious vision he'd almost lost. The soft fabric caressed the curves of her body, adding to her allure. "Feeling refreshed?" he asked.

"Much better." Their eyes locked for a moment before they glided into a silent embrace. "When I first saw you, I thought I had floated back in time again," she said, running her fingers along his robe, a gentleman's robe de chamber, the red-purple color of claret.

"Because of this robe? It's a copy of an eighteenth-century dressing gown."

"It suits you well."

"Merci. Shall we?" he said, lightly touching the back of her arm and leading her outside to the terrace and a table set for two. "If it's too cool we can come back inside."

Radiant heaters offset the chill of the autumn air. "I'm fine," she said, "It's wonderful to be able to be out here this time of year."

The valet served small glasses of orange liqueur before the main course of chicken, rice, and asparagus tips with white wine. They ate in silence for a few minutes, then Claire laid down her fork and picked up her wine. She ran a fingertip around the top of her glass and looked up at Marc-Claude, a crease in her forehead. "I need to let Michelle know that I won't be back tonight."

"No hurry. She'll just think we're having dinner together. I'll call her later and fill her in on what's happened."

Claire nodded. "That's good."

"More wine?"

Claire raised her hand in a "stop" gesture. "No more for me

tonight."

He poured half a glass for himself and put the bottle into the ice bucket. "I wish I didn't have to take this trip, with all that's happened today."

"I'll be safe here." Claire set her fork on her plate. "Is your client French or Turkish?"

"This trip is on behalf of the EU Commission. The Turkish government encourages companies to expand into the European market. It's an effort to strengthen their bid for membership in the EU."

"It sounds important."

"It is," he said, deeply troubled by the turmoil within himself. He would sacrifice almost anything to stay with Claire. "I don't like leaving you alone here."

"You don't think I'm safe, do you?"

"No, I don't. I think Yasin holds the answers we need. Until he's found and questioned, we won't know."

"That could be a long time—if ever?"

"I don't think so." Marc-Claude shook his head. "I have great confidence in Inspector LaBeau. He's tenacious. As we speak he's following up on a couple of leads."

"What sort of leads?"

He returned her gaze. "Was there a plan to abduct you and demand a ransom from Felicity? If so, was Yasin double-crossed or will there be a payoff demanded tomorrow? Is there a connection with the weapons heist?"

Claire nodded, her eyes misty. "I'm not really safe yet, am I?"

"I don't want to alarm you, but you have to understand the gravity of the situation. Let's hope we have answers in the morning." Rising, Marc-Claude came around and stood behind her, stalling for time to gain control of his emotions. He wrapped his arms around her shoulders and nuzzled his face in her hair. "You must know that I'd do anything for you." He moved to her side, taking her hand and entwining their fingers. "You *are* safe here."

She rose, went inside with him, and kissed him goodnight. As she moved toward her room, she trembled and turned back to face him. "I want you beside me while I sleep tonight. Please come to me when you're ready for bed."

After more than an hour and a half on the phone with Michelle, Felicity, and others, Marc-Claude returned to the balcony and poured another glass of wine, then took it inside and sat on the sofa.

No ransom note had been delivered yet. Before morning he must make the decision of a lifetime. No matter what he chose, his life would never be the same. He had a commitment to his clients in Ankara, but he also felt an overwhelming necessity to stay with Claire. To leave her seemed to abandon her—the way she'd told him Andre had when he left Marie at Versailles to escape while he protected the king. Neither he nor Andre could be in two places at once. Time challenged him to affirm his top priority.

If he severed his relationship with his family and risked his professional credibility, he might lose everything. What would he have left to offer Claire other than his devotion? More immediately, if he stayed in Paris, Laval and Associates' reputation with the Turks and the EU administration in Brussels could be irreparably damaged. He had always put his responsibility to his country and the Laval family before his personal wishes. But as important as those things were, this time the need to protect Claire was paramount.

In the boathouse he'd resisted the temptation to make love to Claire. He had known that once he tasted her sweetness, he would no longer be free to turn away. He had intended to return to Paris and leave her to Michelle, but the missing memoir, the weapons theft, and the workshop schedule had conspired against him. Now there was no turning back.

He closed his eyes and laid his head against the back of the sofa, pounding his fist into the palm of his left hand. *Without Claire all the rest is meaningless. I'm not going to Ankara.* Relieved that his decision was made, he got up and went to the guest room and climbed into bed with her. He slipped his arm around her and whispered, "Sleep well, my sweet."

She murmured, "I will," and snuggled against him.

Claire awoke alone, the bed still warm where Marc-Claude had slept beside her. Daylight brought renewed hope. She crawled out and donned a green robe before going to look for him. She didn't see him until she stepped through the French doors onto the balcony. She felt a surge of desire as she looked at his sleek profile, outlined against the brushstroke pink and mauve Parisian morning sky. Much rested and feeling playful, she slipped up behind him and pressed her body against his back.

He whirled around and pulled her against his warm body. "*Ma bien-aimee.*" He lowered his head and met her lips for a slow and thoughtful kiss.

"Wait." She pushed away and held him at arms' length. "What time is your flight?"

He laughed. "What flight?"

"Don't tease me."

"I'm not going anywhere."

A pang of fear ran through her. *What happened?* Staring at him, she asked, "Why not?"

"I've made other arrangements. Please come inside. We need to talk."

After they'd settled themselves on the sofa, he took her hand in his and said, "I belong here with you."

"No. You have business obligations."

"I know what I'm doing. Yesterday forced me to acknowledge what the most important thing in the world is to me. Claire, I can't imagine life without you by my side."

She put her arms around him and kissed him. "I love you, too . . . too much . . . I can't do anything to harm you."

"Claire, I'm asking you to marry me."

"I . . . I don't know what to say. I want you to go to Ankara. All this is happening too fast. You mustn't jeopardize this job because of me. I can't bear that responsibility. I promise I'll give you my answer when you return."

"I'll go on two conditions. One, you promise to stay here at my apartment while I'm gone. Two, you will seriously consider answering yes."

"I promise," Claire said quietly.

Chapter 20

Claire sat alone on Marc-Claude's balcony, soaking up the warmth of the morning sun and being lulled into an easy stream of consciousness. In her reverie Marc-Claude slipped a band of intricately woven yellow and white gold on the fourth finger of her left hand, a symbol of his eternal love. The ring was the same as Marie's! She stirred, and the image dissolved into the Parisian skyline as she opened her eyes.

Fewer than fifteen minutes had passed since Marc-Claude had left for the airport and she already missed him. When they were together, she drew strength from his presence. She wanted him in her life. What had prompted her to hesitate when he proposed to her? Fear? Doubt? Disbelief? Would he misinterpret her reticence and have second thoughts of his own?

She shook her head but deep down knew the answer. A successful marriage must be based on mutual love, respect, and *trust*. Confident about the first two, she still couldn't dismiss a nagging doubt about trust. Although she owed her life to him, she harbored fears about whether he'd deliberately *misplaced* Marie's diary because of conflicting loyalties about her claim to Chateau Fleury.

I have to be certain.

Tightening her grip on the glass in her hand, she gazed into it without registering the puddle of orange juice in its crystal bottom.

She almost dropped it when the valet's voice jarred her from her thoughts. "Mademoiselle de Laval is here to see you."

"Merci," Claire said. "Please have her join me."

Michelle stepped through the door onto the balcony. "I'm so glad you're okay." She reached for Claire's hands and drew her to a standing position, giving her a hug. "How are you holding up?"

Claire clung to Michelle without speaking while she sought to suppress her memory of the close call she'd had in the Catacombs. "I'm okay, I hope. If . . . if Marc-Claude hadn't given me his mobile phone . . . I don't want to think about what might have happened."

Patting her on the back, Michelle soothed, "But he did. You're safe here with him."

"I know I am." Claire's legs weakened, forcing her to slide

back down onto the padded seat of the wrought-iron chair. "He left for Ankara this morning."

Michelle sat across from her. "Bon. Last night he said he wasn't going." She poured coffee into an empty mug and offered Claire a refill.

Placing her hand over her cup, Claire said in a firm voice, "I insisted he go."

"Good for you. If he hadn't, there could have been irreparable damage to his career."

"I know."

"I brought your luggage. It seems you'll be here a while."

"Thank you. As much as I like this robe, I'm ready to get dressed for the day."

"I wish I could take you shopping or to lunch." Michelle broke eye contact. "But I can't. I promised to take Felicity home."

Claire frowned. "Her chauffeur hasn't turned up yet?"

"No. And she's heard nothing new from the police today. Have you?"

Claire shook her head. Anxious about being alone in Paris, she asked, "How long will you be gone?"

"A couple of days."

"Mind if I come along? I really want to finish up my family research in Tours."

Giving her a dubious look, Michelle placed her palm on the side of her face. "But Marc-Claude . . . oh, all right. After all, it's up to you. I'll have to leave my little car and take the Cadillac so we have enough room."

A twinge of guilt prompted Claire to pause a moment, but she pushed back thoughts of her promise to stay at the apartment. "I'll get dressed and let the valet know where I can be reached." Claire picked up her luggage and started for her room. She appreciated the opportunity to return to Chateau Laval and search for the diary, but she regretted going back on her word to Marc-Claude.

Better do it before I change my mind!

Claire opened the suitcase and grabbed the first outfit she saw. She slipped on the brown, cotton knit pantsuit and ran a comb through her hair. Crossing her fingers at her reflection in the mirror, she concentrated on her wish.

At least let me solve the memoir mystery.

She closed her still unpacked bag, picked it up, and went to meet Michelle.

"While I waited I called Felicity," Michelle said as she clutched her phone. "She's a bundle of nerves and so upset by what happened to you. And she's terribly worried about Yasin and the missing car."

Claire stared at her friend. "The limo is missing, too?" she asked as she finished a note to the valet.

"Yes. Let's go. Felicity is waiting at my place." Michelle nodded toward the door. "She's supposed to meet us outside by the curb."

Claire grabbed her gear and followed her to the Cadillac.

Michelle started the car and drove to the gatehouse. "*A bientôt.*" Michelle locked eyes with the guard and greeted him.

He regarded her for a moment before he found his voice, clearly smitten, "Au revoir. "

With a smug look Michelle edged forward and announced, "Tours ETA, noon."

The short drive to pick up Felicity was uneventful. Claire welcomed Michelle's silence as she sought a plan for her short time in Tours. Upon their approach to Michelle's place, Claire saw Felicity pacing on the sidewalk in front of the secluded apartment, circling her Longchamp-brand luggage like a big cat around its prey. As soon as the car stopped, Claire got out of the front seat. "I'll sit in the back."

"S'il vous plait, non, I prefer to sit in the back." Felicity gave her a stiff smile.

"You're sure?"

"Oui." After giving Claire a half-hearted hug and climbing into the back seat, Felicity said, "I'm sorry you were caught in that robbery at the warehouse. In some way I feel responsible."

Claire questioned Felicity's sincerity, but there was no doubt the woman was stressed. Did the strain of recent events and her father's stroke account for the dark circles under her eyes and her worried expression? She looked as though she hadn't slept for days.

Michelle slipped a CD onto the turntable and remained strangely silent during the duration of the trip. Apparently, the previous day's events had had a sobering effect on each of them.

At one point Claire glanced back at Felicity and noticed she'd curled up on the back seat with her face toward the rear of the car. Claire returned to watching the scenery as it passed, lost in her own thoughts.

Light traffic on the highway allowed Michelle to speed along the road to Tours and they made the trip in record time.

When the Cadillac slowed and came to a stop in Tours, Felicity sat up, looked around, and stretched. "Where are we?"

Michelle laughed. "You're almost home. You must have slept most of the way."

Nervously, Felicity rubbed her fingers back and forth on her cell phone. She keyed in a number then spoke into the phone. "I'm with Michelle. Meet me outside . . . out front in fifteen minutes."

When they reached Chateau Fleury, Claire recognized the de Fleury butler poised by the front door, ready to greet them. He walked out to the car and unloaded Felicity's two pieces of luggage then he and she started toward the house. "I'll call you later," Felicity called over her shoulder as she continued walking.

Michelle started the motor and sped away, a trail of dust following them along the gravel road toward the highway. "What's going on with you and Marc-Claude?" she asked, giving Claire a sideways look.

"What do you mean?"

"I've never, ever known him to be so emotionally caught up with another person, any person . . . as he is with you." A wistful expression crossed her face. "I doubt Jacques is as devoted to me."

"Marc-Claude is an exceptional man. We enjoy being together." Claire remained deliberately noncommittal.

"Enjoy being together . . . indeed. He couldn't be more vigilant about your safety if you were the Mona Lisa and he the head of security at the Louvre."

"I know, I'm very lucky," Claire said, a lump in her throat threatening to unmask her nonchalant pretense.

"I still can't believe he planned to cancel his trip to Ankara," Michelle's voice betrayed disbelief. "That would have been professional suicide for his future advancement in the EU."

"Why is that?"

"He's a member of the European Economic and Social

Committee. How well he works with the Turkish government is being watched by people in important positions."

"I didn't know. He doesn't talk much about his work."

Michelle mumbled, "At least he's in Ankara now."

Claire felt the sting of Michelle's protective concerns about her brother's future.

I know so little about what's expected of him.

As they drove across the Lamont drawbridge and into the courtyard, Claire viewed it differently—strange as it may seem, she felt a small sense of ownership. If Marc-Claude and she married, this fortress castle would be her home, too. Their children would continue the line of Lavals. *I must learn more about the Laval family line while I'm at the archives.*

Michelle lost no time getting out of the car and opening the trunk, but Claire took her time. After what Michelle had told her, she wondered how she could doubt Marc-Claude. She chastised herself for dwelling on a couple of storm clouds in an otherwise remarkably pristine blue sky. Life wasn't perfect. Yet she was driven to resolve her nagging doubts about Marc-Claude.

"Here's your bag," Michelle said and set it down by the open car door. "I'll let Maman know we're here."

Claire followed Michelle into the house into Madame de Laval's study.

"Maman." Michelle hugged her mother.

Claire stood a couple of paces behind them. "Bonjour, Madame de Laval."

Madame de Laval actually looked at Claire with a modicum of interest rather than with simple disdain. "Bonjour, Claire."

Why the sudden change? Surely, neither Marc-Claude nor Michelle could have told her anything to pique her interest yet.

"Will you be here for lunch, Michelle?" Madame asked.

"No, we're going to Tours. Claire wants to do some genealogical research."

"I'll expect you for dinner," Madame said with emphasis.

On the way to their rooms, Michelle said, "Meet me in the library at eleven fifteen. We'll stop at a little restaurant in town before you spend the rest of the afternoon at the archives."

Claire set her small case on a chair and opened it, selecting a blue wool pantsuit and black sweater to wear to town. After dressing, she stood by the window, facing the courtyard. An involuntary sigh escaped her lips as she visualized Marc-Claude's silver Peugeot parked in its usual place directly below her window. How she wished he were here with her. Leaving the window, she sat in the armchair by the bed, her hands pressed to her throbbing head. The ring tone of her cell phone amplified her pain. Irritated, she muttered, "Really, Michelle?"

But when she answered it, she heard music to her ears, the sound of Marc-Claude's voice. "Marc-Claude. I'm so glad you called." Pause. "Of course. I missed you the minute you walked out of the door." Claire hesitated and went on. "I'm at Lamont with Michelle. I know I promised. I'm sorry . . . but it's a perfect time for me to work at the archives."

She'd already disappointed him but had no choice other than to broach the next subject. "You'll be back Sunday?" she asked and took a deep breath, stalling for time. "While I'm here, I'd like to look for the memoir. Do you mind? Oh, thank you. It must be here somewhere." She paused. "Be safe. I miss you."

Marc-Claude had remained calm on the phone but had insisted on coming directly to Lamont on Sunday to take her back to his apartment, shortening his trip a day or so. She could tell that he thought she was in danger.

I better be extra cautious.

Within the hour Michelle and Claire had traveled to town, finished their lunch, and reached the archives. "Good luck on your search," Michelle said as she let Claire off in front of the building. "I'll be back around five."

Claire closed the car door and turned to climb the steep steps to the limestone building. Thankfully, her head no longer ached; she would be able to work efficiently to gather as much information as possible on this visit.

The guilt and pain of breaking her promise to Marc-Claude was eased a bit when, after several hours of research, she found the birth record of little Andre-Pierre de Fleury. Eagerly, she continued her search for Janine's birth record and found it as well. She decided to spend the rest of the afternoon tracing the Laval family line.

She sketched a crude genealogical diagram for the family tree, going back four generations. Working from Marc-Claude's birth, she went to marriage records of his parents. After that she continued with his grandparents on both sides and his great grandparents.

Noting that she had another hour and a half before Michelle was due back, she decided to start a search on the Maille Family. Marc-Claude's mother had been born to Jacques Maille and Aline de Fleury.

Aline de Fleury. Aline, the daughter of Count de Fleury, had one brother, Louis. A further search confirmed Claire's worst fears. Aline was the sister of Louis de Fleury, the current Count de Fleury. *Felicity's father!* Marc-Claude and Felicity's ancestor was the rogue count, the murderer of Janine's uncle. *The scoundrel who stole Chateau Fleury!*

Sitting in stunned silence, she pulled a tissue from her purse and dried her eyes. She relived the sense of betrayal she experienced every time she read Janine's memoir—this time she was the betrayed one.

Marc-Claude, why . . . why didn't you tell me? What else haven't you told me?

She cleaned her workspace and packed up to leave. Her headache had returned with a vengeance. Although she had another thirty minutes before Michelle would pick her up, she walked outside in a daze and sat down on a polished wooden bench to wait. Michelle, too, was a descendent of the interloper, and Claire would have to guard against treating her any differently from now on. To her knowledge Michelle hadn't deceived her, and she needed her help to search for the memoir. For Claire, finding the diary took on an immediate urgency.

In her heart she knew she shouldn't think less of Marc-Claude because of his forefathers; nevertheless, it bothered her. It was ironic—Andre reincarnated as Marc-Claude, the descendant of the man who stole Chateau Fleury.

Why hadn't Marc-Claude been forthcoming about the family relationship? Had he chosen not to upset her? Or was his loyalty stronger to his current family than to his past one? What were his motivations.

Michelle arrived ten minutes early. "How'd your search go?"

"Very well. How about your afternoon?"

"*Pal mal*—not bad." She motioned to the packages and bags on the back seat. "Take a peek at what I found . . . in the pink and black bag."

Claire reached back and pulled a pink bag toward her. Reaching inside, she lifted a perfumed, tissue-wrapped item. A risqué silk camisole and matching thong panties dropped onto her lap.

"Non, non," Michelle laughed at Claire's startled reaction. "Not that one . . . the large black one with pink flowers."

Rewrapping the tiny pieces of pink, lavender, and blue silk in the tissue and placing them in the bag, Claire exchanged it for the larger bag that contained a long, fuchsia-colored nightgown with tiny spaghetti straps. Black lace crisscrossed the bodice and trimmed the bottom and the hip level slit. Its companion peignoir coordinated with black lace around the collar and down the sides to the hips. The price tag dangled from the sleeve: €450! "Yipes! What's the special occasion?"

"A few days in St.Tropez. With Jacques."

"Always thinking ahead."

"Not always. I should have taken you shopping with me."

Claire gulped. *Not on my budget.* "Maybe another time." *Michelle can teach me a thing or two, I'll bet.* "I spoke with Marc-Claude on the phone this morning. He said it was okay for us to look for the memoir. Will you help me?"

"What makes you think we can find it if Marc-Claude couldn't?"

"He's had a lot on his mind and may have overlooked it. I have to satisfy myself. Where else can they be?"

"No one except the housekeeper would have been in there other than Marc-Claude. Maybe she threw it away by mistake."

Horrified, Claire asked, "She wouldn't throw away Marc-Claude's things would she?"

"Not intentionally."

"Will you help me look for it?"

"Well, if . . . Marc-Claude agrees to it."

"He did. I know he wants find the diary as much as I do."

"Whatever you think." Michelle seemed less than enthusiastic. "Let me drop off my yum-yums, and we'll go from there," she said as she pulled the car in the space next to Marc-Claude's and got out.

After stopping by Michelle's room, they climbed another flight of stairs to Marc-Claude's third floor apartment. Michelle said, "Marc-Claude's avocation is architecture. He must have inherited that from Grand-mère Maille. This apartment was remodeled to his specifications."

Inherited traits from Aline de Fleury . . . oh, no.

"And the house in Paris, too?"

"Yes. His apartment here includes a salon, dining room, kitchenette, study, and two bedrooms with private baths."

"His apartment in Paris is gorgeous."

Upon entering the salon, Claire saw the same level of attention to detail evident there. "This is the room. Marc-Claude said he left the memoir on the coffee table in his salon." Claire looked through the books and magazines on the lower shelf of the table.

"We'll start here then." Michelle looked under the pillows on the sofa and ran her hand around the sides of it before peeking in the flowerpots and systematically moving around the room.

Claire started on the other side of the room. She looked under the pillows of the armchair and opened the drawer in an end table. She blinked in disbelief, quickly followed by elation. There lay the diary—inside the drawer! A flood of relief swept over her. Clutching the book, she exclaimed, "It's here. I found it."

Michelle whirled around in her direction. "*You* found it? He searched everywhere. What's going on?" Doubt tinged her voice.

Claire heard the subtext: You found it? Why couldn't Marc-Claude? *Michelle doesn't believe me!* What could she say? Worse yet, Marc-Claude must have known where it was all the time. Shock and dismay paralyzed her. Now it was not just his lineage, but he had most likely lied to her as well. Surely, the housekeeper would not have removed the book from the coffee table. Regardless, he said he had done a *thorough* search.

Claire went limp and flopped down in the nearest chair. "I don't know. I didn't think it would be this easy." She'd looked for clouds and now she'd found a stormy one that threatened to destroy her happiness. How could it be?

Frowning, Michelle said, "Oh, God, I had no idea he was that distracted." She went to the door and opened it. "I've got to get out of here."

Chapter 21

Claire closed the door to Marc-Claude's private quarters before following Michelle down the narrow stairs. Distressed by the turn of events, she clutched the memoir and worried how she'd convince Michelle that she hadn't known where to look for the diary. She never wanted to suggest Marc-Claude had done anything wrong. Thinking back to their college days, Claire decided to give her friend time to reflect on her impulsive conclusions. Surely, she'd realize Claire hadn't been to the third floor of Lamont and so couldn't have hidden the diary.

Michelle waited for Claire at the bottom of the stairs. "I'm sure you can use this time to unpack," she said, an edge to her voice. "And I need to call Jacques about our trip. I'll meet you in the library in a little while."

"All right," Claire said and went into her room. She sat down in the feather-soft armchair and inspected the memoir, her heart thumping. *Is it damaged?* She hated harboring such thoughts, but for peace of mind she examined it page by page. To her profound relief, the only thing she found amiss was a tiny fold on the page that contained Janine's account of the fake count's fraudulent claim to Chateau Fleury after the revolution.

No wonder Marc-Claude flagged it!

Claire clutched the diary and walked to the window. Her eyes went to the courtyard fountain, her mind on the Lavals. Just because Marc-Claude had a special interest in the page didn't mean he had hidden the book from her. During his search, could he simply have overlooked it or not opened one of the drawers?

First things first. She had to make things right with Michelle in order to meet Aline de Fleury. In spite of how awkward it might be, she couldn't afford to ignore any piece of the puzzle.

In two days, I'll give Marc-Claude my answer. What will it be? Her heart ached whenever she thought about turning away from him for any reason. During her regression, she had felt Marie's desolation when Andre left her to grieve alone for their dead son. Again, Claire experienced the same lost-soul feelings. Was she just a pawn in some sort of cosmic justice? Were she and Marc-Claude destined to go through the same alienation as Marie and Andre had endured—without reconciliation?

She reminded herself that neither was she above reproach. Her promise to stay at the Paris apartment until Marc-Claude returned had already been broken. It wasn't really a lie, because she had intended to do so. But try as she might to rationalize, there was no denying she'd failed to keep her word to him. When he returned, she would honor her promise to immediately answer his marriage proposal. Such a dilemma—she loved him and wanted to marry him, but there remained ghosts from the past that might doom their happiness. Her heart would not allow her to refuse, but she could not ignore the threatening red flags. A glimmer of hope lay with meeting Aline de Fleury. Her mood brightened. Perhaps Aline would reveal some useful information about the chateau—or Marc-Claude.

Claire rushed to the library. There was no better time than the present to mend fences with Michelle. She slowed at the door when she found Michelle curled up by the fire, a cup in her hand. *A good sign.*

"I'm sorry I jumped to conclusions about the memoir," Michelle said when Claire took a seat next to her. "I realize it's not your doing, but it's not fair of you to blame my brother. We're all on edge about the diary fiasco."

"I know. A lot of unexplained things have happened in the past week."

"You *are* a dear friend. It's not your fault." Michelle appeared deep in thought, a telltale far-away look in her eyes.

Claire sat quietly for a few moments before speaking. "During my research, I found marriage records for your grandmother . . . Aline de Fleury."

Michelle's eyes shifted to Claire. "Oh? Grand-mère de Maille?"

"Yes. Her maiden name was de Fleury."

Michelle frowned. "Ah, I'm not sure." She shook her head. "I know it's strange, but I don't know much about her. There's some tension between Maman and her."

"Where does she live?"

"Near Tours."

"Don't you ever visit her?"

"Not often. The last time was about a year ago. Maman is always angry when she finds out. It's easier to stay away. Aline always sends birthday cards and Christmas gifts but leaves it to us to make the overtures."

"I'd like to meet her. Is that possible?"

"Eh, she's a bit nonconformist. You know, like I am."

"I'd like to tell Marc-Claude that I met her."

"Why? Did he tell you about her?"

"No."

Michelle shrugged. "Ummm, I guess it's okay . . . since it's important to you."

"How about tomorrow?"

"We can try."

The ring tone of the phone in Claire's pocket interrupted their conversation. She snatched the mobile and flipped it open.

"Hello?" Her heart leapt when she heard Marc-Claude's voice.

"Is everything okay?" he asked.

"Oui, but I miss you. How's Ankara?" Claire stalled for time, wanting to keep him talking to her as long as possible.

"Are you and Michelle settled in at Lamont? "

"Oui. I plan to use this time for my research. And I found the birth records of Pierre-Andre and Janine." Claire hoped that would help validate her actions in some small way.

"Better keep a low profile while you're out and about," Marc-Claude said with staid calmness. "We'll talk more when I return on Sunday." His voice mellowed, "You know that I love you."

"I love you, too."

After the call, Michelle gazed at her with a bland half smile. "For someone in love, you don't look very happy."

"Being apart isn't easy."

"Why didn't you tell him we found the memoir?"

"He needs to focus on Ankara for now. Anyway, it's much better to tell him face to face."

Michelle toyed with her cell phone and stood. "I have a couple of things to do. See you in the morning."

With warm thoughts of Marc-Claude, Claire continued sitting in her favorite spot on the Italian leather sofa, staring at the glowing embers, praying that her suspicions were unfounded. He must have put the book in the drawer. *It is possible he did it without thought.* Now was not the time to question his motives. There'd be time enough when they were together to evaluate his body language and his reaction to the news. Hopefully, after meeting Aline, she'd have a better sense of his family dynamics. Ready to return to her room and unpack, she stood and exhaled an anxious breath.

As Claire walked down the hall, Madame de Laval came up behind her. "Claire, I'd like a word with you."

What now? Swallowing a sigh, Claire turned and faced the woman. "Certainly, Madame."

Madame de Laval led the way back into the library. She sat in one of the brown leather chairs and motioned for Claire to join her. "I'm going to speak frankly. It's apparent that you have unrealistic ambitions to be part of this family." For a moment she studied Claire and shook her head. "You're taking advantage of Marc-Claude's temporary infatuation and playing upon his sympathies."

"Really? Infatuation! I can assure you that Marc-Claude is capable of making his own decisions!"

The other woman went on as if she hadn't heard a word Claire said. "You may have studied in France, but you don't—and never will—understand French men. Oh, yes, you may distract him; but I know my son. He will honor his heritage. No matter how much you'd like to be one of us, you never can be. He will keep with his own people."

The two women locked eyes until Claire could find the right words. "I wonder why you're worried about it." Claire rose and made her way to the exit. Madame de Laval's silence suggested she lacked a good response.

As Claire looked in the bathroom mirror while removing her makeup, she had second thoughts about confronting the phony count's daughter, mother of the hostile Madame de Laval. Could she stand another rude, sarcastic woman? Assuming Aline was like her daughter, of course. Had she gone too far with Madame de Laval? Would her confidence in Marc-Claude sustain her? There was no turning back. She straightened her shoulders. This meeting was necessary. She'd have to get through it, somehow. After all, she'd pressed Michelle to arrange it. If it turned out that Marc-Claude had deceived her and was as shallow as his mother suggested, she'd have to pick up the pieces of her broken heart and leave France as soon as possible.

Just before ten o'clock the next morning, Claire and Michelle arrived in Tours for their visit with Aline. Michelle parked in front of a symmetrical, traditional, one-story house that was partially concealed behind the heavy, drooping branches of a huge fir tree. They got out of the car and walked along an arbor-covered path bordered by a Monet-style flower garden of brilliant rainbow colors.

Claire looked up and stopped, shading her eyes to get a better look at a streak of black and orange. "A monarch, this time of year?"

Michelle looked around. "I don't see anything." The butterfly looped up and down, passing over their heads. "Oh, there it is." Michelle pointed upward.

The sweet scent of lavender and carnations lured bees for a feeding frenzy. Claire stopped walking as the monarch came back and briefly perched on a lavender branch. "Wait! Don't move," she said to Michelle as they both watched. And then the beautiful creature soared and was gone.

No longer distracted, Claire took her first real look at Aline de Fleury's home. The beige walls of the house were covered with red-leafed vines, precision-cut around the white trim of the French doors and matching windows. Four, white-trimmed dormer windows interrupted the uniformity of the steep, gray slate roofline. Michelle lifted the brass ring from the man-of-the-forest knocker and tapped lightly on the blue door.

It was opened by an animated, silver-haired woman wearing a long, botanical print dress. "*Mon petit chou*," Aline de Fleury greeted them. She wrapped one outstretched arm around Michelle and the other around Claire while directing them to the salon. "Please sit and make yourselves comfortable." She addressed her remark to both Michelle and Claire, but her eyes were fastened on Claire. "So this is Claire, your *amie de college*."

"Oui, Grand-mère."

Madame de Maille nodded to Claire. "Bienvenu. You are

welcome in my home."

Aline had Marc-Claude's golden eyes and mannerisms and Claire felt an instant connection to this older, female version of the man she had come to love. She liked Aline without reservation.

"Now Marc-Claude wants your college friend for himself, eh?" Aline bubbled along.

Michelle puckered her lips. "It seems that way."

"He should follow his heart, wherever it leads. Make yourselves at home while I get some coffee."

As they waited for Aline to return, Claire walked around the room, looking at the gallery-style display of colorful paintings on the walls. She stopped in front of one of the Montmartre café where she and Marc-Claude had danced to "Plaisir d'Amour." Drawn into it, she still couldn't put her finger on why the painting seemed so familiar.

Aline returned with a coffee service tray and paused beside Claire. "Do you like it?"

"Very much. It's beautiful."

"I painted it many years ago when I lived there."

"Really?"

"I don't need to tell you that Grand-mère is an artist," Michelle said with a smile.

The painting in the gallery at Montmartre signed Aline. That was it. "Did you also paint one of two lovers standing by the Montmartre vineyards?"

"Oui. How did you know?"

"I admired it in a gallery there."

Michelle turned to Claire. "You did? When?"

"When Marc-Claude took me to Roberto Santoni's gallery."

"Oh."

A thoughtful smile curved Aline's lips. "The Montmartre lifestyle allows one the freedom to be true to oneself . . . so necessary for the creative process." She set the tray on a small table and poured coffee before sitting beside Michelle. "Are your mother and father well?"

"Oui," Michelle said.

"Bon. Michelle, will you run a package to the post office for me? I'll use the time to get better acquainted with Claire."

"All right, Grand-mère, I get it. You want to have a heart-to-heart talk with Claire." Michelle stood. "Where's the package?"

"What did you expect after your phone call yesterday?" Aline rose and went to a drop front desk in the corner and returned with a package. She handed it to Michelle and returned to sit beside Claire on the love seat. After Michelle left for the post office, she said, "You and Marc-Claude are happy together?"

Claire nodded and wondered what she'd been told. "I can see Michelle filled you in."

"Not much. Marc-Claude told me about you."

About Chateau Fleury or just us? "I hope it was all good."

"Yes, my dear. All good."

I have to change the subject and ask her about the de Fleurys.

"It must have been exciting to grow up at Chateau Fleury."

Regarding her for a moment, Aline looked upward. "Non. It is a beautiful place and I love it. But for me there are too many unhappy memories. My parents didn't approve of my Bohemian outlook and made my life miserable. They were extremely rigid in their thinking."

"I'm sorry."

"They refused to allow me to study art. So what did I do? When I turned sixteen, I ran away to Paris and lived in Montmartre for two years before they found me, brought me home, and married me off to the old Marquis de Maille—a man almost three times my age."

"You opposed the marriage?"

"I wasn't consulted about it. Much to my relief, he returned to the arms of his mistress in Paris. All he left me with was a baby girl."

"Where did you live?"

"In his rundown chateau near Lyon. My daughter grew up to be just like him, status conscious and intolerant of anyone who doesn't fit into their mold."

"How difficult for you."

"My daughter and I were like oil and water together. I tried to give her direction in life. She'd have none of it. She tried to tell me how to live my life, and I'd have none of it. So I suppose it was inevitable that we parted ways when she married."

"You each have a good life . . . from what I can see."

"Oui. At least I can say that her father and I cooperated on two things all the years we were married—her conception and her marriage to Monsieur de Laval. Her sole desire was to marry him for status, prestige, and wealth." Aline smiled. "Of course, I don't need to tell you. You've met my daughter."

"You don't visit Lamont very often?"

"Non, she made it clear that she had no need for me and didn't want my influence to infect my grandchildren. But Marc-Claude calls me often and stops by when he's home. I take great comfort knowing I can count on him. Every so often Michelle sends cards." Aline shook her head. "That girl flits around like a bumblebee."

"Do you keep in touch with your brother, Louis de Fleury, and his family?"

"Non. I'm considered the black sheep of the family. When my father was drinking, he would imply that I was no daughter of his. My brother knew well the implications of those remarks and ignored me . . . unless he wanted a favor."

Claire sipped her coffee. She'd pried quite enough into Aline's life.

"In a way Marc-Claude is like me." Aline's face brightened. "Beneath the façade of a successful attorney lies an artist at heart, a soul that yearns to be free." She reached for Claire's hand, her golden eyes imploring her. "Help him find that freedom."

Claire placed her other hand over Aline's. "I will."

"Bless you. Now, let's have a bite of lunch."

"You don't need to do that."

"I want to. The kitchen is this way."

The pale yellow walls of the room made a perfect backdrop for the bright assortment of pottery around it, on the floor, on shelves and counters. A large window provided a view of a manicured lawn, bordered by flowers of red, orange, and gold. Water spilled over a fountain made of three copper basins of varying sizes. Four frolicking, yellow-breasted birds cavorted in the large one, splashing water on the ground.

After looking around the enchanting room and the garden beyond, Claire returned to stand beside Aline. "What can I do to help?" she asked.

"Chérie, you may set out the dishes." Aline waved her hand toward the glass doors of the cabinets. "We're having *blanquette de veau* over rice and salad."

The glazed earthenware plates were of a bold swirl design in the primary colors, red, yellow and blue. "What cheerful plates."

"Another hobby of mine."

"You designed these? They're wonderful."

"Oui." Aline nodded. "*Entrez*," she called in response to the tap at the door. "Lunch is ready."

Michelle came through the door and into the kitchen. "Do you need some help?"

"Non. Claire and I are just finishing up."

"It appears that you and Claire had a pleasant visit."

"We're fast friends already." Aline set the salad bowl on the table. "Shall we all be seated?"

During the meal, most of the conversation revolved around Aline's memories of her life in Montmartre.

After her last bite of crème brûlée, Michelle said, "Grand-mère, I wish we could stay longer, but we'd better go."

"It's been wonderful having you here," Aline said as she walked them to the car. "Claire, you're a real joy. Michelle, do come again and bring her with you. I meant what I said, you are always welcome here."

"Thank you." Claire patted Aline's hand and regretted she had to leave.

Aline hugged Michelle and then embraced Claire for a long moment.

After leaving Aline's house and reaching the city limits, Michelle set the cruise control at 85 mph. She glanced at Claire and said, "Felicity called while I was at *La Poste.* She sounded down and disheartened. So I said we'd stop by and cheer her up."

"Okay." Claire nodded. "I had hoped leaving Paris would help her."

"Eh, I don't know why she's panicked. If she doesn't get a grip, she'll need some Valium."

"It wouldn't hurt."

Michelle turned the black Cadillac into the Chateau Fleury

entrance. "Well, we'll know more when we talk to her."

"There she is . . . at the front door," Claire said, as Michelle parked in front of the house.

Felicity ran out and met them. "Come inside." Her heavy-handed application of blush didn't conceal the pallor of her skin. Her eyes, trimmed with brown eyeliner and mint eye shadow, looked like sunken glass. "I'm so glad you're here."

On the way to the house, Michelle put her arm around Felicity's waist. "How's your father?"

Felicity stifled a sniffle and looked away. "He's so frail that he's not expected to last the night."

"They're doing everything they can for him," Michelle consoled.

Felicity nodded and cleared her throat. "I know." After they were seated, she asked, "Would you like some tea?"

"Not for me. How about you, Claire?"

"No thanks."

"Let me know if you change your mind," Felicity said.

A tapping noise came from another room and Michelle looked toward the sound. "Have they started the green salon renovations already?"

"They began today . . . just an evaluation of how to proceed, I think."

Claire gestured toward the outside door leading to the rose garden. "The gardens here are quite extensive. Do you have plans for work on them?"

"Nothing definite yet. I'll show you around the chateau and the grounds now if you have time."

"I'd like that. I saw the rose garden the night of the fundraiser, but I'm sure it looks quite different in daylight."

"Oh, I'm sorry, Claire. We don't have time today," Michelle said. "I promised we'd pick up Jacques at the train station. Or I could pick him up and come back by for you. It's up to you."

"I guess it won't be today," Claire said to Felicity.

"I'll take you to Lamont on my way to see Père in the hospital," Felicity said. "I'll sit with him through the night."

"Are you sure you feel up to it today, or would another time be better?" Michelle asked.

"I'm sure," Felicity said with enthusiasm. "I need to keep busy."

Michelle rose. "If you're sure, I'll leave you to it."

As Claire stood by the door with Felicity and watched the big black car disappear from view, she began to have second thoughts. Perhaps she'd been too focused on exploring Chateau Fleury.

Chapter 22

Marc-Claude dropped his carry-on into the trunk of the Peugeot before he climbed into the driver's seat. Surrounded by vehicles in the Charles de Gaulle Airport parking lot, he sat for a moment before he picked up his mobile phone. "Inspector LaBeau, Marc-Claude Laval here."

"Monsieur de Laval, the chauffeur's body has been found."

Oh, my God, he's dead! "Where?"

"At the Quai d'Orléans about five miles from the warehouse."

"In the Seine?" Marc-Claude took a deep breath. "What was the cause of death?"

"Drowning. He had an ugly blow to the head but was still alive when he was thrown into the river," the inspector said. "Looks as though he was part of a drug smuggling ring."

"Using the wine cellar as a cover." Marc-Claude completed the sentence.

"Afraid so. Cocaine was found inside the cabinet with the collection of expensive wine."

"Zut, the de Fleurys are involved."

"The dead man in the tunnel has been identified as a member of a known drug ring. Lab tests confirmed cocaine residue in the box recovered in the tunnel by Mademoiselle Bennett."

Marc-Claude started the car, exited de Gaulle Airport, and headed toward Paris. He gripped the steering wheel until his knuckles turned white. The pieces of the puzzle began to fall into place. Felicity had arranged for her chauffeur to take Claire to the wine cellar. *Claire!* "Keep me informed," he said and abruptly ended the call. Frantic to warn Claire, he keyed in the number to Claire's phone. It rang and rang until his recorded message invited him to leave a message on his personal mobile. "Claire, you're in real danger. Give me a call as soon as you hear this message. I'm on my way! Under no circumstance leave Lamont before I get there."

Gritting his teeth, he mumbled out loud, "Great." He tried Michelle's phone and got her recorded greeting. *Where are they?* He pressed his sweaty palm against his shirt and phoned the Lamont residence. The butler answered, buzzed for Madame de Laval, and then for Monsieur de Laval. Neither one answered. Marc-Claude left another message with the man and hit the brakes just in time to avoid running into the back of a slow-moving tour bus. He passed the bus as soon as it was safe and tried Claire again. Still no answer!

By the time he got to Tours, he had exhausted every conceivable avenue he could think of to reach Claire. He exceeded the speed limit the rest of the way to Lamont. Upon arrival he jumped out of the car and dashed toward the house, past his black Cadillac parked in Michelle's spot. *They're back?* He almost collided with Michelle as he ran toward the stairs. "Where's Claire?"

Michelle flipped her hair back from her face. "Marc-Claude," she said in a patronizing voice. "For God's sake, calm down."

"Nom de Dieu, answer me!"

She frowned at him. "She'll be back soon."

"Where is she?"

"Chateau Fleury," Michelle said. "She wanted to see more of the chateau and gardens."

He turned without a word, ran to the Peugeot, and took off for Chateau Fleury. Adrenalin pumping, he forced himself to slow down and work out a plan. He'd have to be careful not to give Felicity a hint that he knew she was implicated in Claire's abduction.

By the time he reached the entrance to the chateau, he felt prepared for whatever challenge he found, although he hoped everything was tranquil. He parked near the gatehouse, opened and closed the car door, and made as little noise as possible. He moved along the gravel-covered driveway, hugging the edge of the road under the shadows of the trees. The element of surprise could be useful should Felicity be up to no good. Her behavior was sometimes erratic when things didn't go according to plan. He hoped for a chance to size up the situation inside. His first priority was to get Claire safely back to Lamont.

Lights shone through the arched stained-glass window above the weathered, green double doors in the library and from windows of two upper level rooms. Everything seemed normal until he approached the entry doors. One of them stood slightly ajar. He laid his hand on it and pressed until it opened a little farther. Light streamed from the library into the entry gallery. Again, he pushed just enough to squeeze through it.

The momentary serenity shattered at the sound of Felicity's agitated voice from the library, "Give it up, you conniving bitch. There's no escape!"

Marc-Claude moved quietly down the hall to the library just in time to see Felicity lunge at Claire with a dagger—the missing trousse! As if in slow motion, the lethal weapon seemed to advance toward Claire, who ducked behind a settee. Grayish puffs of stuffing spurted from an open gash in the sofa's cover as the knife slashed the expensive silk. Claire peeked around the settee, her face white, and stared at the wicked slash meant for her.

"Felicity!" Marc-Claude shouted as he wrestled the weapon from her. He glanced at Claire as Felicity dropped her arms in stunned silence.

Not one to give up easily, Felicity whipped a small pistol from her pocket and pointed it at him. "Damn you, Marc-Claude. Now I have to kill you too."

"Think this through . . . you don't want to be charged with murder."

"You don't think I'm that stupid . . . I hope," she hissed. "There won't be any proof that I did it. I'll make sure of that."

"The police already know about the drug ring and your warehouse. You're already implicated."

"Then I have nothing to lose by killing both of you." Her eyes darted to Marc-Claude and back to Claire.

In the split second Felicity took her eyes off him, Marc-Claude grabbed Claire's hand and dashed to the left side of the fireplace. A stray bullet zinged passed Claire's shoulder. Without hesitation, Marc-Claude pressed the letters F E U in the Fleury name on the decorative armorial crest. A second bullet whizzed by Claire's head just as a groan belched forth from a door-sized portion of the bookcase wall, which opened to reveal a means of escape.

Marc-Claude didn't pause, but pushed Claire ahead of him into the dark, narrow passage. It seemed an eternity before the door closed behind them. Bullets thudded against the library walls but didn't penetrate the passage.

"Fortunately, she's not a sharpshooter."

"Where are we?" Claire whispered. "It's so dark." She covered her mouth before she sneezed.

"I'm not sure," he said and turned on a small penlight attached to his key ring. Stone walls were on both sides. "We'll follow the passage." Reaching for her hand, he urged her to come with him. Sporadic gunfire and heavy thuds reverberated from the library. "She must have emptied the barrel by now."

"What *is* the matter with her?" Claire asked between breaths.

"I'll explain later." They ran for a good fifteen minutes until they almost collided with a door right in front of them. Marc-Claude grasped the knob and tried to push it open, but it didn't budge. He checked it but found no reason for it not to open. There was no lock requiring a key. He pressed his hand to his forehead and tried to recall what he had done in the library to get into the passage. *How'd I do that?* What were his moves? He couldn't remember. An image flashed through his head like a streak of lightning—enough of a glimpse to know that, with no conscious thought, he'd pressed the letters F E U on the armorial crest. *It must release levers or some such thing.* He shone the small light around the wall until he saw "Fleury" on a small crest beside the door. Once again, as in the library, he pressed the code and held his breath until the door scraped open long enough for them to escape.

He could make out the silhouette of the stables against the darkened evening sky. He paused long enough to get his bearings and then whispered, "This way. Don't make a sound." A sneeze now could be disastrous. No telling whether Felicity knew about the tunnel system—he certainly hadn't heard of it.

Marc-Claude grasped Claire's hand and started for the car. Good thing he'd parked away from the house. They froze in place when a large spotlight swept around the front of the chateau. It bounced up and down and back and forth, like a kid on a trampoline. He gauged the rhythm of the light from the chateau and timed his dashes among the trees to avoid the path of the light until he and Claire reached the road.

Then he heard a masculine voice carried through the evening air, "Circle back around this way."

"If they're still alive, they might be out here!" Felicity shrieked. "Keep looking."

The mix of voices receded into the distance as Marc-Claude

and Claire edged their way between trees until within sight of the car. The agitated sound of dogs barking and the roar of an engine near the chateau left little choice but to make a dash for the Peugeot. Once there Marc-Claude opened the driver-side door then waited for Claire to slip across onto the passenger's seat, almost sitting on her hand when he got in. "Désolé . . . sorry."

Claire let out an audible sigh. Things had turned ugly so suddenly for her.

High-beam headlights flashed on in the distance by the chateau. Marc-Claude backed out of the driveway, leaving his car lights off until reaching the highway. A few minutes later he glanced in the rearview mirror. "We're being followed." Confirming his statement, within minutes a bright beam of light shone into the car.

Claire twisted and strained against her seatbelt. "Oh, my God! That truck has a spotlight mounted on top."

"Hold onto my arm," Marc-Claude said as he rounded a curve and made a sharp turn onto what looked to be little more than a muddy wagon trail. The car sloshed around in the mud but pulled free. The truck headlights disappeared, only to reappear a few minutes later. Marc-Claude sped up. Sheep scattered in all directions as the spotlight disturbed their slumber.

Pop. Zing .Pop.

Gunshots shattered the silence of the tranquil meadow but missed their target.

"Get down." Marc-Claude pressed his hand on the back of Claire's neck to move her out of view. He shifted into reverse, turned around, and started up a hill in the opposite direction.

The car rumbled over potholes. At least the gunshots had stopped—for the moment. Claire raised her head enough to look out the passenger window. "Will your car handle this steep hill?"

"So far, so good," he said, keeping any doubts to himself. After another abrupt turn, the ride smoothed out. "We'll go to Blois. They'll expect us to head for Tours."

Claire straightened. "Any sign of them?"

"Non." Pulling his cell phone from his jacket, he thrust it into Claire's hand. "*Appelez de police . . . dix-sept*. Call seventeen."

Claire punched in the emergency number 17. "We're being chased and shot at by people in a black truck with a spotlight on top. I don't know the license number. . . We're on a dirt road, trying to make it to Blois . . . I don't know . . . Just a moment."

Claire handed the phone to Marc-Claude to answer more questions.

After concluding the call, he gave the phone back to her and slammed his fist onto his thigh. "I haven't seen the truck for a while. Felicity may be on her way to Lamont."

Marc-Claude knew his way around this backcountry—even if Felicity didn't. He relaxed a little and worked his way along a creek for several miles before he reached a crossroads. He kept on the road to Blois for a short distance before he made a sharp turn onto a less traveled road. "Call the police and let them know we're returning to Lamont."

Claire took the phone from his outstretched hand and did as he asked. Scraping and bumping sounds came from under the car when it bounced and hit an angry swirl of water. "Sorry. With the autumn rainy season begun, there's no telling how deep this creek is," he said. He accelerated and the vehicle jerked forward.

Claire sighed. "Do you think we've lost Felicity?"

Marc-Claude shifted his position and shrugged. "Hope so." When they reached the paved road, he took a left turn, and with a coordinated press of the accelerator, the car sped down the open road. "Almost there," he said before turning into the familiar private driveway to Lamont.

Claire tried without success to let go of the tension in her body. *Yeah, right into the arms of danger, if Felicity is here. What chance do we have with only an antique hunting knife?* She knitted her fingers together to release tension. She felt less safe here than on the back-woods trail. Glancing at Marc-Claude, she found him preoccupied. *Let's hope he has it figured out.*

Shortly, he pulled off the road into an opening under two low-hanging tree branches in the Lamont forest. The tips of branches brushed across the windshield and sides of the car. Driving deeper into the woods, he stopped the car behind a small shed. "Just to be safe, we'd better walk from here. We have to get to the house unseen." He went around the side of the car to meet her and put his arm around her waist. "Are you doing okay?"

Biting her bottom lip, she said, "So far." She was stretching the truth more than just a little. But there was nothing to do except press on and hope for the best. Menacing, grotesque shadows moved around them, threatening the calm she struggled to maintain. A group of startled night birds flapped their wings and flew off in fright. It took all her willpower not to make a sound in response.

The sudden iron grip of Marc-Claude's hand on her arm frightened her all over again. In a scarcely audible voice, he said, "There's someone ahead of us."

And then she heard it too. The sound of twigs cracking and snapping came from the other side of the road. A flashlight beam jiggled among the trees.

Felicity? Who else could it be?

"Back down the hill," Marc-Claude said as he grabbed her hand. "We'll have to go through the woods to La Notre's garden."

If there had been any doubt about who or what it was, the heavy footsteps that drew closer by the minute left no doubt. Short staccato bursts of bullets zoomed around them until they were sheltered in the bramble, brush, and trees.

After they were concealed under Mother Nature's protective cover, Marc-Claude stopped and faced Claire. The high-riding moon revealed perspiration beaded on his forehead. "Remember my childhood hiding place in the garden? Hide there while I go for help. And a gun."

Where are the police? Did I bungle our message? She couldn't be sure what she had told them.

The thicket of trees thinned into a park-like setting that she recognized. She could just make out the clipped yew hedge near the manicured area where Marc-Claude had told her about playing hide-and-seek. It would be a secure hiding place.

Marc-Claude stopped and pulled back the branches of the bushes. "Stay here . . . I'll be back for you." He watched until she wedged her way through the hedge niche behind the solid stone bench.

She pushed against the evergreens until she lay flat on the ground. It felt as if the pruned branches were puncturing her flesh. A car motor grew louder before falling silent again. She lay still and listened but heard no voices. Marc-Claude must be in the house by now. In her mind she retraced the steps he would take through the garden to get there. Had he gone around to the courtyard or up the stairs to the upper level and into the library? Her arms pinned by her sides kept her from seeing her watch. It felt as though she'd been there for an eternity, but it couldn't have been more than fifteen minutes. She had to move. Her arms felt numb.

Why hasn't he come back for me? Has a patrol car arrived?

Chapter 23

Claire flexed her arms and wiggled her fingers, seeking to restore circulation and feeling in her needles-and-pins digits. Panic edged her thoughts. *What delays Marc-Claude?* She had so little space to move that she wondered how difficult it would be to get out of her hiding place. *I have to get out of here.* She knew she'd have to back out of the hedge the way she'd gotten in—without the benefit of sight to keep on track. She inched her way out, feet first, while at the same time trying to gauge her progress.

"Ouch!" She shook her head to free her hair from the tenacious grip of a branch that caught it. Disrupting her snail's-pace movements, sharp, freshly trimmed limbs scratched her arms like an aggressive tomcat challenging his rival. She felt certain blood had been drawn.

After continuing to creep backward, she finally wiggled out of the hedge. While on her hands and knees, she turned and peeked around the bushes and bench in both directions. She saw no sign of life nearby and stood up on wobbly legs.

I must look a mess.

Shaking her prickly hands, she brushed off bits of leaf debris and evergreen needles that clung to her snagged pantsuit. She sighed— at least her brown clothes didn't show the dirt.

The scratches on her arms needed attention, but that would have to wait. She finger-combed her hair and tucked it behind her ears. Shrouded in the shadow of the wall of green, she worked her way along the edge of the path to the main part of the garden until the outline of the chateau came into view. She strained to identify what appeared to be huge mushrooms popped up in the grassy rectangles of the garden design. To her relief they turned out to be half-dome boxwood topiaries. Her heart nearly stopped when she detected movement beyond the ornamental boxwoods. Two grotesque silhouettes stood motionless.

They saw me!

Just as she started to turn to run into the woods, a stray puff of wind animated them. She hesitated and looked around. No one followed in pursuit. The wind must have blown the man-sized Italian cypresses.

How could she have been so jumpy as to mistake trees for people? She gulped and steeled herself to continue forward through the eerie night landscape toward the huge fountain, its mythical beasts perpetually spewing water from their mouths. After climbing the stairs to the upper-level terrace, she remained still for several minutes in order to calm down before venturing into the chateau. Lamps illuminated the library. She peeked through the windows but saw no one. Turning the handle on the French door, she opened it slowly and stuck her head inside.

Click!

The cold steel barrel of a gun against her temple caused her to stub her toe. Her pulse quickened.

"Give me a reason and you're dead."

Felicity!

Claire felt the gun rotate painfully, and Felicity increased the pressure. The library's lamps revealed Madame de Laval's ghostly-pale face in profile. She was seated in a straight-back chair in the center of the room, and a large multicolor scarf bound her hands behind her back.

Madame turned her heard towards Claire and wiggled in vain to free herself. "She's gone mad!" Madame de Laval's voice quavered. "She's tied my hands with my Loire Valley Hermès scarf. It's ruined!"

Claire made a sudden head movement when Felicity's hot breath blasted her face.

"You're trembling . . . afraid to die?"

Claire looked at Madame de Laval.

"Forget it. This pathetic hostage can't help you." Felicity slid the gun to Claire's back and shoved her. "Come on, you two. We'll check out Marc-Claude's apartment. You'll like that, won't you, Claire?"

"Felicity, what are you talking about?" Madame de Laval ventured in a small voice.

"Killing her and then, when it's safe to leave, taking you hostage, my dear."

"Taking me . . . where?"

"Stop your whining. You're going to see the world."

"You're a wicked woman."

Felicity gave her a push. "*Stupide*, how'd you like to take your vacation with a gunshot wound?" Felicity herded them out of the library and down the hallway until they reached the stairs to the third story. When Madame de Laval stumbled on the second step, Claire reached to steady her.

"Don't do that again." Felicity pressed the gun harder into Claire's back. "Keep on climbing. No sudden moves."

By the time Madame reached the landing, she was panting for air. Felicity prodded her to keep moving. "Is this the door to the off-limits apartment?"

Madame Laval nodded at her tormentor.

Felicity tried the knob but found the door locked. "*Merde*." She pushed the older woman and pointed to an exit at the end of the hall. "Where does that go?"

"An old storage room in the tower."

"The tower, eh? Madame, to the tower!" She gestured with the gun and shoved it into Claire's left shoulder. "Get going. You have very little time left to bask in your fond memories of Marc-Claude."

The final flight of stairs brought them into an unfinished storage turret set in the main tower—the donjon, the ancient stronghold of the castle. "Keep going," Felicity said, a hollow sound to her voice. "All the way inside." She pushed the door open.

The room contained centuries of accumulated Laval possessions, odd pieces of furniture, trunks, and boxes. Cobwebs and dust seemed to be the most recent additions. The three sets of fresh footprints in the powdery residue would leave a somber testimony to the night of terror that lay ahead.

A narrow catwalk could be seen through the open door across the room. Claire recognized the crenellation and parapet wall of the Tour de Laval, the oldest tower of the castle.

Agitated, Felicity pushed the gun harder against Claire's back. Without warning, she hustled Claire through the opening to the outside edge of the walkway around the pepper-pot roof. She paused as if relishing a game of cat and mouse. Ignoring Madame de Laval slumped against the inside wall, gasping to catch her breath, Felicity chided Claire, "No one can help you now."

Although droplets of perspiration beaded on Claire's upper lip, her hands felt cold. She didn't want to die. She just wanted a chance to tell Marc-Claude she'd be his wife. Jumbled images tumbled around in her head, threatening and teasing as if to chastise her for doubting him. She feared she might faint until a quiet clarity settled around her. *Marie!* She sensed her ancestor's presence, strength, and determination.

The entire Loire Valley lay in view beneath the pristine blue, star-studded sky.

I will fight for Marc-Claude. Get her talking!

Claire spoke with authority. "Felicity, you know you can't get away with this. Why even try?"

A guttural laugh rose from deep within Felicity's chest. "Poor naïve Claire."

"Why kill me?"

"If I can't have Marc-Claude, nobody will—especially you!" With a determined expression, Felicity said, "Marc-Claude and I were born to be together."

The hell they were! Marie's indignation sent a charged impulse through the space around them.

Felicity responded by glaring at Claire. "Ever since we were kids, we understood we would marry each other someday." A rapid swish of her hand dismissed Claire. "I don't need to explain anything to you."

Not to be silenced, Claire said, "Why on earth would you steal from the Lavals?"

"Shut up!" Felicity thrust the gun toward Claire. "My answers won't make any difference now."

Claire wished she could bat the gun from Felicity's hand, but she couldn't reach it. She whirled around and kicked her nemesis on the leg as hard as she could.

Okay, Marie, I hope this works.

Surprise, followed by pain and anger, registered on Felicity's face. She cocked the gun and squeezed the trigger as Claire ducked.

Poomb. Zing!

The bullet whizzed past Claire.

"Damn." Felicity cocked the gun and pulled the trigger again. The gun misfired. Claire grabbed Felicity's hand and bit it. The weapon fell to the floor with Claire on top of it. Felicity kicked her in the back and grabbed for the gun, but Claire yanked Felicity's hair with one hand and rose up with the firearm in the other.

Felicity slapped Claire across the face and pushed her against the guardrail chain. Angered by the sting from the slap, Claire dangled the gun over the edge of the parapet. She could always let go of it if necessary. She raised the weapon after she stopped shaking. "Step away and start talking. Why did you steal the de Laval's antiques?"

Felicity drew in a deep breath and slowly exhaled as she took a step back. "It wasn't supposed to end this way. Really, all I needed was the gun. But why leave behind the other treasures? They're priceless!"

"Needed the gun for what? Don't you own one?"

"You just don't get it, do you?" Felicity said, her voice raspy as she edged closer. "I'd shoot you with it and return it to Lamont. *Voila*, no connection to me. Leave it to Marc-Claude, the spoiler, to ruin another one of my plans."

Claire pushed against Felicity, but she couldn't get enough footing to move her. She waved the gun in the air. "If you want this, you'll just have to take it from me."

Felicity leaned forward and reached for the pistol in Claire's hand.

Pop! Pop! Pop!

Felicity took her eyes off her prey at the sound of the distant gunshots.

Claire's fear for Marc-Claude's safety outweighed that for her own. Who fired those shots? She leaned as far to the right as she could against the stone parapet to get a better view then watched in horror as Felicity overreached for the weapon and tumbled over the protective chain into the darkness of night.

The bitter taste of bile rose in Claire's throat. Her legs buckled. In shock she clung to the chain until she could scoot her body away from the edge of the crenellated roof walk. She had to find Marc-Claude. Voices drifted up to her, and she followed the sound until she saw five men huddled in the courtyard below. General de Laval issued orders, but she couldn't make out what he said. Nearby, she saw a body lying face down in the gravel.

In the excitement, Claire hadn't thought of Madame de Laval.

Is Madame okay?

Claire dashed back to the last place she'd seen her inside the turret room and found the woman dazed, still cowering in the corner where she'd left her. Putting the gun in her pocket, she untied Madame's hands and draped the large scarf around her shoulders. Then she slipped her arm around the older woman's waist. "Let's go downstairs."

Madame didn't resist. She clutched Claire's arm while they retraced their steps down to the second floor. From there they rode the elevator to the ground level.

"Do you want to come with me or wait here?" Claire asked. "I'll let them know where you are."

"I'll come with you." Color had begun to return to Madame's cheeks, forming scarlet splotches on her ashen face.

On their way to the courtyard, they met Marc-Claude coming their way. A blond, uniformed officer walked with him. Marc-Claude rushed to them, the tense lines on his face relaxing as he hugged Claire. "I've been frantic. I looked everywhere for you. Why did you leave the garden?" He turned to his mother, apparently unaware of her ordeal. "Have you seen Felicity?"

Madame de Laval collapsed into his arms and wept. Between sobs she said, "Dreadful, absolutely dreadful. She treated me with no respect."

Marc-Claude turned to Claire, "Let's take her inside. She's been traumatized by the shooting."

"Marc-Claude, Felicity tied me up and pistol whipped me," Madame said.

The policeman stepped forward. "Madame, do you know where she went?"

"No. I don't."

Claire said to Marc-Claude, "You go ahead. Your mother needs you now."

He'll find out about Felicity soon enough. It's better if the police inform him.

"Maman, is Felicity still in the house?" Marc-Claude asked as he took his mother's arm and led her to the chateau.

Claire responded to the policeman's question after Marc-Claude and his mother were out of earshot. "Felicity fell from the tower. We struggled . . . over this." She took the pistol from her pocket and thrust it into his hand. "She tried to kill me! And planned to take

Madame de Laval as a hostage."

The officer turned abruptly and approached Monsieur de Laval, who was with a heavy-set, middle-aged man. He huddled with them before looking back at Claire. He motioned to her to join them. "Show me where she is."

Claire followed him from the courtyard and heard Monsieur de Laval tell them that the gun was the one that had been stolen from them. She recoiled at the sight of the blood-soaked man on the ground. Three other uniformed officers moved around the area, while emergency personnel worked on the wounded man. Drops of blood from his body led toward the La Notre garden. She shuddered.

Was he watching me as I went to the house?

The blond policeman joined the other officers before motioning Claire ahead. The men followed in step with her as she led the way around the side of the house toward the tower. One of two ambulances trailed after them.

Stopping about twenty feet from the donjon, Claire pointed toward the parapet wall. "We, w . . ." She started to speak, but her voice cracked. She swallowed and tried again. "We were up there. We struggled for the gun." A wave of apprehension swept through her.

"Go on," the officer said.

"She lost her balance and fell."

"That will be all for now," the officer said.

The ambulance rounded the corner and the driver parked. The medical team jumped out and caught up with the officers. Walking in lockstep, the men moved ahead. Claire followed a few paces behind, dreading what they would find. The beam from their flashlights shone on Felicity's motionless body near the old Tour de Laval.

Chapter 24

Claire sat beside Marc-Claude on the sofa while the police continued their investigation of Felicity's death. She leaned her head against his chest, listening to the rhythm of his heartbeat, thankful they were alive and unharmed. Marc-Claude draped his arm around her shoulders and drew her close.

By the time the officers finished interviewing the family members, midnight had come and gone. Madame de Laval had taken a sedative and gone to bed after giving her statement. Monsieur de Laval looked tired, propped up in his recliner across from them, but he kept talking about the critical moments in the garden that had led up to the shooting. "Felicity's goon and I faced each other . . . weapons drawn. I fired—a misfire! I thought it was over when another shot rang out. The gendarmes had done the job for me."

"I met the officers when they arrived," Marc-Claude said. "We'd made a sweep of the gardens and were almost to the house. The gunman saw us and turned his weapon from you toward us. Luckily, he wasn't able to get off a shot."

Marc-Claude looked down at Claire. "Père talked to the police while I went to get you from your hiding place. How did Felicity find you?"

Claire pursed her lips. "She didn't. I got impatient and started for the house."

Marc-Claude shook his head at his father and said to Claire, "What can I say?"

Monsieur de Laval smiled as Marc-Claude leaned over and kissed Claire. "Enough talk for tonight. I can see you want to be alone. Bonne nuit." He rose and walked slowly from the room.

Stroking Claire's tousled hair, Marc-Claude said, "You know we're incredibly fortunate to be alive."

"I know." Claire snuggled closer to him. "Thank God we both survived and are physically okay."

Marc-Claude's lips tightened a fraction. "I keep asking myself why I missed the warning signs that Felicity posed a threat."

"You can't blame yourself." Claire ran her fingers along his hand and up his arm, taking in the reality of his presence before demanding another kiss. She straightened and held his gaze. "Remember that day at the boathouse when we talked about chivalry, and I said chivalry was dead?"

"Oui . . . so?"

"You proved me wrong. You've saved my life twice this week."

"Chivalry? I hardly think so," he said with quiet emphasis. "You saved your own life on the tower."

"I love you for being here for me," Claire said, understanding he had tried to protect her and would have if she'd stayed hidden as he asked.

"Is that the only reason?" Marc-Claude gave her an inquisitive look.

Claire ruffled his thick black hair and said, "Non, it's only one of many."

Marc-Claude's expression softened. "Wait here, I'll be right back." He brushed his lips across hers and stood. "I'm going to the kitchen to see what I can find for us to eat."

"What? You're thinking about food at a time like this?"

"Uh-huh."

After Marc-Claude left, Claire moved to the general's recliner, a sort of hybrid that looked like an easy chair. She sank into it, pressed the recline button until the chair reached a prone position, and closed her weary eyes. If Marc-Claude didn't get back soon, she'd sleep and he'd eat.

"Sleepy?" Marc-Claude patted her hand.

How had he gotten back so quickly? She had just closed her eyes, or so she thought. She raised the chair and stood, leaning deadweight against him. "Umm . . . not anymore."

"Shall we?" He gestured toward the door.

"Certainly."

He took her arm with one hand and picked up his small carry-on bag with the other.

"When did you bring that in?" Claire pointed to the overnight case.

"I got it from the car after I made your dinner." When he led her to her room and not toward his apartment, disappointment threatened to overcome her. She needed to be with him tonight, all night. Didn't he know that?

He's taking propriety too far!

He stopped by her bedroom door. "Pick up what you'll need for the night."

Her heart raced. He had understood. She hurriedly gathered a few essentials and eagerly joined him in the hall. "Ready." She wished she had Michelle's chemise and thong set rather than her floor length satin gown. But to her credit, she had presence of mind to bring her cosmetic bag and toothbrush.

This second time inside his apartment, Claire felt entirely different than she had during her clandestine visit with Michelle to search for her memoir. Now she could take the time to appreciate the apartment's comfort and harmony. She relaxed and began to feel as though she belonged. She hadn't fully realized the heavy weight she had carried, sneaking around behind his back.

Marc-Claude switched on the ceiling light and spun her around to face him. After giving her a hug, he asked, "Do you like it?"

She giggled. "Your hug . . . or your apartment?"

"Just answer the question."

"Yes . . . to both." She looked around the room with fresh eyes, taking in every detail. "It's wonderfully warm and inviting."

"I hoped you'd feel that way."

"It's so peaceful here."

His mouth curved into an unconscious smile.

"I imagine you're quite contented here," she said.

"Usually, I am." He reached for her hand and led her to the kitchen. The finish of the French provincial table and chairs complemented the rich brown-paneled wall at the end of the room. The delicately curved table legs rested on a blue and white rug. Plaid placemats and chair cushions coordinated with the rug, creating a light, informal ambience.

Marc-Claude removed a lunch bag from his carry-on. He opened the bag and pulled out two ham-and-cheese-stuffed baguettes. After he handed one to Claire, he poured two mugs of milk from a thermos.

"May I have my milk warmed?" she teased.

"*D'accord* . . . anything for you, chérie."

Claire smiled and shook her head. "Just kidding." She turned to gaze at the view across the wooded slope toward the highway. The silhouette of the forest formed an obsidian overlay across the horizon of the star-lit sky. She returned her gaze to find Marc-Claude watching her, a serious expression on his handsome face. "You're not eating. Is something wrong?"

He stood and moved behind her chair to hide his emotions. He leaned forward to kiss her ear and said with quiet emphasis, "Much has changed today. Life is full of uncertainty." He straightened, moved around to face her, and looked into her eyes. He held her hands in his. "We should get married as soon as possible . . . that is, if it's agreeable with you. There's no reason to wait until summer."

She saw his mellow, golden eyes were no longer the unreadable eyes of their first meeting.

There's no reason to wait any longer—I've waited centuries for you.

"I know . . . I've been thinking the same thing," she said, her voice choked with emotion.

He pulled his chair by hers and sat beside her. "And what are your thoughts?"

"What do you say to a mid-November wedding?"

With a playful look, he said, "Why wait so long? Maybe we should elope."

She gently slapped his hand. "I don't think so. I have the Cathedral of Tours in mind for our wedding."

Marc-Claude raised an eyebrow. "Not in Boise?"

"No, I have a deep love for the cathedral—and you."

"A happy bride is my top priority."

Claire nodded. "I have to let Mom know that we're getting married as soon as possible."

Marc-Claude handed her his cell phone.

Claire pressed in the numbers and waited for her mother's familiar voice. "Mom, it's a wake-up call from France," she said.

"Is everything okay?"

"It couldn't be better," Claire said, a lilt in her voice. "Why do you ask?"

"I expected a call, but not at this hour."

"Marc-Claude and I are going to be married as soon as we can schedule the cathedral here in Tours."

"The cathedral . . . you're going to be married there? Oh, Claire, it's not like you to be hasty."

"Mom, I have waited my entire life for him. I don't intend to waste one more precious moment."

"Why are you talking this way? What has happened?"

"It's a long story. Just be happy for us and get here within the next couple of weeks. Here's Marc-Claude." She handed the phone to him.

"Mrs. Bennett, it is my pleasure to speak with you," Marc-Claude said. "Rest assured that my life will be devoted to the happiness of your daughter."

"I . . . hope so," Claire's mother said, a note of uncertainty evident in her voice. "I look forward to meeting you and your family."

Claire reached for the phone. "Mom, I'm so very happy. Trust me and be happy for us. Talk to you later." She flipped the phone closed and set it down. She studied Marc-Claude's expression and laid her hand on his arm. The respect he had shown to her mother warmed her heart. "I love you more than you can imagine. Just wait until Mom meets you. She'll be as charmed as I am."

But how will Madame de Laval react?

"I'll do my best." Marc-Claude rose. "It's time to get a few hours of sleep while we can. But after a day like this, we'll need a shower. The bathroom is the first door on the left."

Claire stood and reached for Marc-Claude's hand, an impish smile on her face. "Want to join me? It'll save time."

"*Bien sûr,* my lovely," he said.

His bathroom was light and airy with design elements that gave a nod to the chateau's history. The clear shower door led the eye to mosaic walls of French blue vines and flowers on a white background. For some reason Claire hadn't expected such elegance. *I should have, though, after seeing his beautiful Paris apartment.*

After they had showered and playfully dried off, they held hands and pattered to the bedroom. Marc-Claude lifted her and placed her on the bed.

She shivered with anticipation as he lay down beside her.

Five hours later, sunlight spilled across the hardwood floor. Claire stirred from sleep and extended an arm, wanting to snuggle against Marc-Claude.

Uhhh . . . where is he?

The last thing she recalled was spooning against his warm body. She sat up and looked around. "Where are you?" Again she called out, "Marc-Claude?"

He poked his head in the door. "Bonjour, chérie." He came in, sat on the side of the bed, and kissed her on the cheek. "Café?"

"Sounds good. Where were you?"

"In the study. I didn't want to disturb you."

"I missed you."

"Well, that's good news." He leaned forward, kissed her lips, and stood quickly. "I'll get the coffee and fill you in on my conversations with Inspector LaBeau and Dr. Sartre from the Genetics Research Center."

"Hurry back," Claire called after him. "I can't wait."

"Okay." A few minutes later he returned with a tray prepared for their morning coffee. In his left hand he carried a silver bud vase with one perfect red rose bud. *"Pour ma bien-aimée."* After he placed the rose on the nightstand, he poured the fresh brew and sat in the chair beside the bed.

She folded her pillow in half, propped herself up, and sipped her java. "This is delicious. What did LaBeau have to say?" The longer she could delay a discussion about Dr. Sartre's genetic research results, the better—not that it mattered as much now.

But she needed validation of Marie and Janine's writings! She didn't know how she'd cope if for some reason the results didn't support their authenticity.

"More coffee?" Marc-Claude asked.

She nodded. "Half a cup."

"LaBeau explained that the drug squad has worked aspects of this case for a couple of years. Now, with the de Fleury warehouse connection, they have the missing link." Marc-Claude paused to take a sip of his steaming beverage. "Street dealers are usually only able to inform on the next level up, leaving the top people in the organization out of reach. The drug squad cleans up one hotbed of activity, only to find the ring resurfaced in another location. At times they hold off on arrests, hoping to flush out the organizational masterminds before their next move."

"Was Felicity one of the masterminds?" Claire asked.

"Yes. The rare wine collection contained more cocaine than it did vintage wine."

Claire set her cup on the nightstand and reached for Marc-Claude's hand. "Why in the world would she be involved in that?"

"Money . . . I would guess. About ten years ago, the Chateau Fleury vineyards were severely damaged by a virus."

Claire shook her head, refusing to believe Felicity had no other options.

"Apparently, Felicity and Yasin were partners. She lived a double life. I had no clue what they were doing, although I never liked the man. I didn't see much of her, either. The drug squad located a house of Yasin's in Paris. In the basement they found a fully equipped drug-cooking laboratory and cocaine packets loaded into Fleury wine cartons. Ready to be moved to the warehouse, *probablement*."

"Who killed Yasin?"

"Felicity could have arranged it, or another of his many enemies could be responsible. As part of his empire, Yasin was mixed up with a money-laundering ring in Corsica."

"Any connection with the unidentified body in the catacombs?"

"Yes. A small-time drug dealer that had been picked up and questioned by the *flics* . . . eh, cops."

"I still can't believe what happened. Where will it end?" Claire shook her head. "I better get up." She swung her legs out of the bed and sat on the side of it. "I'll imagine the drug squad will be disappointed that two of the ringleaders are dead and won't stand trial."

"There'll be other arrests made with an organization like this one. It most certainly is international in scope. The authorities are working on how the drug operation has infiltrated our nation."

Claire stood and encircled her arms around Marc-Claude, kissing his neck, his ear, and forehead on a sensual path to his mouth.

"What do you have in mind now?" he managed to murmur.

The phone's ring tone startled her.

Marc-Claude seemed to be torn between answering it and ignoring it. With a sigh, he picked it up. "Allo?"

"Marc-Claude, this is Grand-mère Maille."

"Grand-mère! Ça va?"

"Pas mal. Not bad. Just shocked by the news. The de Fleury family's attorney called about Felicity's and the Count's deaths. I'm the closest living relative and will need to make funeral arrangements for her. Then there are the estate's financial affairs that need my attention."

Marc-Claude frowned. "You're the closest living relative? Doesn't the count have a brother?"

"The count and I had a brother who died when he was young. There were only the three of us. Will you help me through this legal maze?"

"Bien sûr. Of course, I will."

"Could you come to see me today?"

Marc-Claude glanced at Claire. "This afternoon . . . about one-thirty."

"Merci."

Marc-Claude ended the call and flipped the phone closed. "As soon as you are ready, we can go down to breakfast and share our good news with the family."

"As you wish." Claire slipped on the robe Marc-Claude took from the closet and handed to her. "What did Dr. Sartre say?"

"They've completed their report. We have an appointment with them Thursday afternoon at two. That'll give me time enough to check in with the office and take care of pressing matters after we return to Paris."

Chapter 25

Claire clasped Marc-Claude's hand while they walked down the stairs to breakfast. She marveled at the calming effect he had on her. Ideally, she should be filled with happy wedding plans, but the horrors of the last few days weighed heavily on her heart. Now she felt she understood the pain that had strengthened Marie and Andre's love. She and Marc-Claude couldn't afford to squander their second chance at happiness. No matter what the results were from the DNA testing, she gloried in the promise of their future together.

Madame de Laval's footsteps echoed on the stone floor before she came into view. She approached the staircase, wearing a pink shell under a gray suit. Madame's appearance gave no indication of her dreadful experience the previous day. She started up the stairs and paused as she drew closer. "Bonjour. Claire, ça va?"

"Ça va bien, merci," Claire said, pleased with Madame's cordial greeting.

"Maman, you're looking well this morning. Won't you join us for breakfast?"

"Merci, non. I've just finished *le petit déjeuner*." She stopped on the step below them. Taking Claire's hand, she studied her face. "I'm so thankful you weren't harmed."

Claire nodded and smiled at the change of attitude. "Thank you. I'm glad you've recovered from the ordeal."

"Indeed," Madame said as she started back up the stairs.

Upon their arrival in the gold, sunlit morning room, Claire noticed Michelle alone at a table against the far wall. Ribbons of steam spiraled from the cup in her hand. A pen and tablet lay on the table to the side of her plate.

Michelle looked in their direction and rose. She rushed to their side and clasped Claire's hands. "Mon Dieu! Père told me what happened last night. It's horrible. You could have been killed."

"It has been a shock, all right," Marc-Claude said after a quick intake of breath. "But we're alive. That's what counts."

"Let's sit and have a little breakfast," Claire said, hooking arms with Michelle.

Marc-Claude continued to the buffet and soon returned with a selection of croissants, fruits, and coffee. Taking Claire's hand and kissing it, he said to Michelle, "May I introduce my future wife."

"I knew it!" Michelle jumped up so fast she knocked over her cup and kissed each of them on the cheek. "Well, I guess congratulations are in order." She moved the dishes quickly to the next table, rolled up the coffee-stained, checkered tablecloth, and set it aside. "When's the wedding?" she said as she sat back down.

"Probably early November." Marc-Claude set the breakfast platter on the table and took the chair across from Michelle.

"After last night, we decided not to wait," Claire volunteered.

Michelle shook her head, momentarily pensive. As if aware of the conflicting emotions she reflected, she smiled at them. "I'm so excited and happy for you. Do Maman and Père know?"

"Not yet." Marc-Claude lifted his coffee mug. "I don't think it'll come as any surprise."

Michelle rose, picked up the empty tray from the next table, and put her dishes on it. "Let's go find them."

"Before we finish eating?" Marc-Claude chided his sister.

"I didn't mean that," she scoffed. "When are we going to tell them?" she asked, her eyes sharp and assessing.

"Right after breakfast," he said.

Apparently satisfied, Michelle carried her tray to the servant's station behind the buffet.

Claire wondered whether Michelle sought to take her mind off Felicity's death and the shocking revelation about her illegal activities. The de Laval family wouldn't go unscathed when the news accounts of the story broke.

Marc-Claude shook his head. "Michelle continued to think she is in charge of our lives, but she is correct about one thing. We need to share our good news with Maman and Père."

"Will you please hurry up?" Michelle chided as she approached and sat down across from them, watching their every bite.

Privately, Claire questioned why her friend was so eager to

have her parents know of Marc-Claude's marriage plans. Did she just want to provide a diversion from the tragedy of the previous day? She decided to leave it in Marc-Claude's hands to make the announcement to the de Lavals. The uncertainty of his parents' reactions affected her appetite. She pushed her plate away, to the delight of Michelle. Apparently unruffled by the prospect, Marc-Claude continued to eat until he'd finished his meal. He gave no indication whether he felt nervous about their announcement.

When Marc-Claude finally finished eating, Michelle placed the last plate on the tray with the mugs, carried them across the room, then caught up with her brother and Claire on their way to the ground-level gathering room where Monsieur and Madame de Laval usually read the morning newspapers and went over the day's activities.

Marc-Claude offered his arm to Claire as they entered the casual room where they'd spent torturous hours with the gendarmes the night before.

Rather than reading, General de Laval was speaking tenderly to his wife. "We'll take each day as it comes. What is done is done, non?"

Madame daubed her eyes with a lace-trimmed handkerchief. "I can't bear the thought of facing my friends. Our reputation is sullied."

Marc-Claude cleared his throat. "May we join you?"

His father looked relieved at the distraction. "Come in. Your mother can use cheering up."

Marc-Claude and Claire sat on the sofa where they'd been a few hours earlier. Michelle settled down beside her mother on the loveseat. "You look lovely this morning," she said, giving her mother an affectionate kiss on the cheek.

"Merci," Madame smiled at her daughter. "I am fortunate to have my wonderful family by my side." She wiped a tear from her cheek. "Claire, thank you for your kindness to me yesterday."

"*De rein*, don't mention it."

"Claire and I have good news," Marc-Claude told his parents. "We're getting married within the next month or so."

"Congratulations to you both. You have my blessing," Monsieur de Laval said.

"Oh . . . it's so sudden." Madame looked first at Claire with a frown and then at her son. She shook her head. "Too much is happening all at once."

"It's fine. I'll help you." Michelle patted her mother's hand. "It's so exciting. A de Laval wedding! Can you imagine? Marc-Claude is going to take the plunge?"

"Claire and I will be married in Tours Cathedral," Marc-Claude stated with finality. "After Claire's mother arrives, we'll work out the details."

Madame twisted her handkerchief around her index finger. "Michelle tells me you found Claire's memoir."

Marc-Claude's expression stilled and grew serious. "What?"

Claire looked reproachfully at Michelle then she shifted to damage control. Had Madame de Laval set about to make trouble between them? "Michelle and I found it in a drawer in your room," she confessed to Marc-Claude.

For a moment he studied her intently. "You searched my apartment and didn't tell me? Why not?"

Before Claire could respond, Madame rose and stood in front of Marc-Claude, looking him in the eye. "Don't take this out on Claire. The entire mess is my fault. I'm the one who took the diary . . . just to read."

Marc-Claude stared at his mother in disbelief and turned to Claire. "I'm sorry for all the trouble Maman caused," he said and reached for her hand.

Madame went on, "I returned it to your room and slipped it into a drawer. I thought you'd find it and believe you'd put it there. Can you forgive me?"

Marc-Claude sighed. "I can. I hope that Claire can too." He went to his mother and hugged her. "Thank you for telling us. I know it wasn't easy."

As Claire watched them, she wondered whether Madame de Laval would ever accept her into the family. At least she had the decency to admit what she'd done. She could have allowed the doubt to exist between her son and his future wife.

Marc-Claude glanced at his watch. "We better get going. I have a couple of stops to make before we go to Grand-mère Maille's.

Madame de Laval said, "I suppose you do need to tell her about the wedding."

"That goes without saying." Marc-Claude stepped away from

her. "She *is* family, whether you act like it or not."

By the time Marc-Claude and Claire departed from the Cathedral and had a bite of lunch, they arrived at Aline's with no extra time to spare before the one-thirty appointed time. A gray mist hung in the air and dulled the vibrant colors of Aline's flower garden but did nothing to dampen Claire's pleasure of visiting again. She and Marc-Claude wended their way along the flower-edged path to the vine-covered house.

"I'm pleased you like Grand-mère," Marc-Claude said, "She's a free spirit."

"Yes. She finds joy in life."

After opening the door, Aline's eyes went to their entwined hands. She nodded and said, "C'est bon. Perfect." She wrapped her arms around Marc-Claude. "It's been too long since we've seen each other. I'm happy you brought Claire with you. Come in and sit wherever you like."

Claire felt no inhibition about showing her affection for Marc-Claude in front of Aline. It seemed so natural. She circled her index finger around his, an intimate hint at their emotional bond, as they followed his grandmother into the salon and were seated.

The gesture wasn't lost on Aline. Her face glowed.

Marc-Claude smiled. "Grand-mère, I knew you would approve," he said, his expression contented. "Claire and I plan to get married early next month."

"It's so right. Tell me more. Where will you marry? Where will you live?"

Claire snuggled against his chest. "We want to be married here in the cathedral."

Aline rose and went to her desk. She returned with her red leather appointment book in hand and sat beside her grandson. She opened it and said, as if to herself while printing in large block letters across the page of November 7, "Cathedral wedding of Marc-Claude and Claire." With a flourish of her pen she underscored it with an elaborate scroll of an entwined MC and C.

Marc-Claude gave her a questioning look. "Grand-mère, we don't have a definite date yet."

She set the calendar down and held his gaze. "Trust me, it is November seventh. All of these years I allowed your mother to keep me away from you . . . but I knew someday I'd have you back again."

Marc-Claude slipped his arm around Aline. "It'll be up to Maman whether she wants to be part of our life. But after last night, I think she just might."

Seeing the two of them together, Claire marveled at how alike they were—cut from the same fabric.

"Excuse-moi, I've forgotten my manners," Aline said, "Come into the kitchen. We'll talk over a cup of coffee."

After filling the cups, she placed the carafe on the table and sat across from Marc-Claude. Aline twisted the wide silver bracelet on her arm and with a thoughtful expression said, "Over the years I haven't been close with Louis and his family. I was caught by surprise when the de Fleury family attorney phoned this morning." With a faraway look, she gazed out of the window. "When Louis and I were kids, we used to play in the rose garden while Père worked on legal matters, or so he told us. He'd call Louis inside to talk about the estate and leave me outside." A cloud of sadness passed across her usually serene face. "I've been outside most of my life."

"Sometimes, fathers don't realize the impact they have on their children," Marc Claude said. "I'd like to think if they did, they'd change their behavior."

Aline nodded. "I'd hope so."

Marc-Claude patted Aline's arm. "What did the attorney say?"

"That I'm the heir to Chateau Fleury. He asked whether I would be able to handle the day-to-day affairs of the estate." Aline cleared her throat. "Of course, under the circumstances of Felicity's death, the funeral arrangements must be planned with little fanfare."

"You won't be faced with that alone. I'm here to help you," Marc-Claude assured her.

"Merci. I really worried that I might not get it right."

"Together, we'll take care of it." Marc-Claude frowned. "Did the attorney caution you not to accept the *patrimoine* before knowing whether there are excessive debts attached to the inheritance?"

"Non, he just arranged a meeting later in the week. Now, with the death of the count, there's a lot to discuss."

"Under no circumstance should you accept the inheritance until you and I have gone over it."

"What are my choices?"

"As heir you have three options. First, you may accept the inheritance without reservation. But if you do so, you'll be liable for the debts as well. Second, you may accept *sous bénéfice d'inventaire*. With this option you have three months to compile an inventory and an additional forty days to accept or reject. The last option is that you may reject the inheritance."

"Marc-Claude, I'll need your guidance throughout this process."

"You can count on me. After your initial meeting with the attorney, I'll work with you to do what is needed."

Autumn leaves scampered down the Parisian street toward Marc-Claude and Claire as if rushing to greet them. *Could that be a good omen about the news Dr. Sartre has for me?* Claire wondered. She paused and looked up at the pristine, modern, glass-and-steel building that housed the research team's offices. She knew in her heart that the blood in her veins carried genetic material inherited from the Marquise de Fleury. But what if one of the samples was contaminated? In that case the results would condemn her claim, and Marc-Claude might resent her persistence in making it.

Oh, why did I go ahead with this crazy scheme?

"What are you waiting for?" A smile ruffled Marc-Claude's mouth. "For what it's worth, I believe I have more to lose than you do."

"I don't know whether this DNA testing is reliable."

"Come on. It's important. Dr. Sartre is one of the best in the field. His research protocol is impeccable." Marc-Claude reached for her hand. "What really matters is that we have each other."

Marc-Claude didn't seem to dread the results of the test. Why should she? Claire squeezed his hand. "With you by my side, I can face anything."

They went inside and walked along the corridors, past technicians in masks and lab coats, before reaching the Center for Human Genetics and the offices of Dr. Sartre and his molecular diagnostics research team.

Dr. Sartre stood at his office door as they approached. "Bonjour. Come in and have a seat," he said, warmth evident in his voice. "I have your report right here." He closed the open folder on his desk and pushed it aside. "We have promising results from our cancer research." He smiled. "But I won't take any more of your time by talking about my hopes for the future based on our current projects."

He reached for a second folder and reviewed its contents. "Perhaps you'll read about our new research results in the newspapers in the not-so-distant future," he said, apparently still in awe of the breakthrough in his cancer research.

"If the past is any indication of the future," Marc-Claude said, "I'm confident that we will."

"You're very kind." The doctor cleared his throat and spoke slowly as he looked at the report. "The mitochondrial DNA-repeated sequences of bases from Mademoiselle Claire Bennett's blood sample and those from the strands of hair sample from Marquise Marie de Fleury, successfully removed from the sealed locket, are matched perfectly. The mtDNA signatures are identical, leaving no ambiguity about the results."

Claire rested her head in her hands. "Ooh, my God." She looked up and turned to Marc-Claude.

What is he feeling right now?

Their eyes met. She saw only tenderness in his golden eyes, as they melted into hers.

"*Il ne fait aucun doute,*" Dr. Sartre said, "Mademoiselle Bennett, there is no doubt your mtDNA is from the maternal line of Marquise Marie de Fleury."

Marc-Claude leaned forward and kissed Claire on the cheek. "I'm relieved that after all these years technology has provided closure for Marquise de Fleury and your family."

Chapter 26

On the way to de Gaulle Airport, Claire pondered the irony of the outcome of her situation. Her DNA tests validated the diary account of the false claim to Chateau Fleury. Janine de Fleury, her ancestor, was the daughter of the legitimate owners of the chateau. Now Claire would soon marry the grandson of the imposter's heir. What a convoluted twist of events. In a way their marriage provided poetic justice for the Marquis and Marquise de Fleury.

"I was thinking," Claire said to Marc-Claude, "I'm going to invite Aline to go shopping with Mother and me for my wedding dress. Do you think I should invite your mother, too?"

"Oui. You don't want your mother-in-law to feel excluded."

"You think she'll come?"

"I don't know. She's faced with some tough decisions about her role in the family."

"I hope she will join us, but I'm nervous about how she'll respond," Claire admitted as the Peugeot slid into an open parking space outside of the international terminal.

"Their flight should be here by now," Marc-Claude said, as he opened the car door for Claire. They walked briskly into the building and checked the arrivals column on the board. "Your family might be inside now."

Claire sat while Marc-Claude went for coffee at a café near the customs exit of the terminal. She stayed to watch for her mother and brother when they cleared customs, but there was still no sign of her family when Marc-Claude returned with their drinks. "I wonder what's keeping them so long," Claire said as she reached for the cup. She looked forward to the support of her family. Somehow, their presence seemed to tip the balance in her favor. Surprised at the strength of her feelings, she determined that she'd stand up to Madame de Laval. She had to admit that Madame had succeeded in undermining her self-confidence in the past.

A new day has dawned!

"We haven't been here more than thirty minutes. Sometimes the lines move slowly." Marc-Claude pulled out a chair and sat. "We may have another thirty to wait."

After ten minutes had gone by, Claire finished her coffee and got up. "I'm sorry, I have to pace for a while. There's no need for you to come with me. I'll bring them here to meet you."

Marc-Claude rose. "Non, I'm coming with you."

"Okay," she said, happy that he wanted to be there for her family.

After a short fifteen-minute wait, Claire's heart lurched at the familiar sight of her mother's loving face. Her brother, John, followed his mother with their luggage cart.

"Claire!" Mrs. Bennett rushed into the open arms of her daughter then turned to gaze at Marc-Claude.

Claire reached for his hand and drew him closer. "Mother, this is Marc-Claude."

"I'm happy to meet you," Mrs. Bennett said, holding his hand a little longer than necessary. Apparently, she was charmed by the French customary *faire la bise*, the kiss he placed on each of her cheeks.

Claire stepped forward and gave her brother a quick hug when he approached. "Marc-Claude, please say hello to my *little* brother, John Bennett," Claire said as she looked up at her brother with pride.

"John, it's good to meet you." Marc-Claude extended his hand. "Claire speaks of you with great affection."

"The pleasure is mine." John picked up the two large pieces of luggage.

"Let me give you a hand with that." Marc-Claude took one of the bags from him.

Claire reached for her mother's small, forest-print case. With a grin, she said, "Your purse is as big as this."

The drive to the Loire Valley went smoothly. After a short detour around Tours to see the cathedral, they arrived at Lamont before noon. General and Madame de Laval met them in the courtyard, patiently waiting while the passengers got out of the car. Marc-Claude made the introductions before they went inside to the ground-level gathering room.

"Bienvenue." Madame gestured toward the chairs and sofas. "Please make yourselves comfortable while we wait for the butler to deliver your baggage. I'm sure you'll want to freshen up before lunch.

Marc-Claude, I'd like you and Claire to see Madame Bennett and John to their rooms in the east wing."

"Bien sûr."

After the guests were seated, Monsieur de Laval settled into his recliner and said to John, "How was your flight?"

"Uneventful."

The general nodded. "Bon."

They chatted amiably for ten or so minutes before Marc-Claude stood. "Mrs. Bennett, we'll show you to your rooms now."

Madame de Laval said, "Lunch will be served at one-thirty. Michelle and Jacques expect to be here in time to join us."

Pausing at the door, Claire said to Madame. "I'd like a word with you when we come back down."

"I'll be right here."

On their way downstairs, Claire said to Marc-Claude, "I want to have a woman-to-woman talk with your mother to invite her on my wedding-gown excursion. She needs to know that Aline will be with us."

Marc-Claude sighed. "Good luck."

Claire continued to the gathering room while Marc-Claude stopped in the hall to talk with his father. When Claire entered the room, she found Madame de Laval waiting for her. She sat closer to Madame than her comfort zone dictated only because the moment required it. The woman would soon be her mother-in-law. The tone of their new relationship should be set today. But Claire hesitated a moment too long to start her rehearsed remarks.

"Claire, I've planned a small gathering next week for our de Laval friends. It provides an occasion for the announcement of Marc-Claude's and your wedding plans. And it will be a good opportunity for your mother and brother to meet some of the prominent families of the Loire Valley."

"I appreciate your thoughtfulness, but you failed to talk with Marc-Claude and me about our wishes. I'll speak to Marc-Claude and let you know whether next week is convenient for us."

"I'm sorry you feel that way. I've spent much time making the plans to help you. Rather than a thank you, I am rebuffed."

"You will recall that I asked to meet with you. I did so because I wanted to extend an invitation for you to shop with me for my wedding dress. Michelle, my mother, and Aline will join us."

Marc-Claude's mother remained silent and stoic for a long moment before she said, "I'm unable to accept. My mother and I have been estranged for years. Such a venture would jeopardize a happy time for you. Believe it or not, I don't want it to be unpleasant because of our inability to get along.

"But I do need to get some things off my chest. I cannot deny that the ideal wife for my son, the future Duc de Laval, would be an aristocratic French woman. But since that is not to be, I am satisfied that you will make him happy. I can see the love that flows between you, and I want the very best for you both. Who knows? Maybe mother and I can mend our broken relationship."

The bright sunny morning found Claire in her wedding gown in the bridal dressing room at the Cathedral of Tours. How swiftly November seventh had come. Somehow, all of the wedding arrangements were in place, thanks to Aline, Madame de Laval, Mrs. Bennett, and wedding planner par excellence, Michelle, her maid of honor. Under Michelle's direction, the men of the two families had also taken care of the things that were traditionally male responsibilities.

Claire removed her engagement ring from her left ring finger and transferred it to the right hand. The ring—a three-carat, yellow diamond surrounded by teardrop emeralds—reminded her of the beautiful Loire Valley. She eagerly anticipated her new husband slipping her wedding ring onto the third finger of her left hand.

Michelle studied her own reflection in the mirror before she again rearranged Claire's wedding gown. She adjusted and readjusted the semi-cathedral train on the layers of white satin. "This crystal beadwork and embroidered lace is *magnifique*."

"Without your help, I wouldn't have found it. It's perfect."

Little more than one month had passed since she first visited the cathedral and relived the wedding of Marie de Conde to Marquis André de Fleury. Today Claire Bennett, the bride of Marc-Claude de Laval, not Marie, looked back at her from the mirror.

Marc-Claude's and my wedding day—our life to live!

"I'm so excited." Michelle purred. "Maybe Jacques and I should get married. Don't worry, I won't mention it to him unless I'm sure." Michelle ran her hand lightly along Claire's shoulders as if giving her final stamp of approval. "You look ravishing. Marc-Claude will be captivated." She laughed. "If he's not sufficiently so already."

Claire and Michelle left the dressing room and joined the bridal party. After her maid of honor went down the aisle, Claire linked arms with her brother while he escorted her to her groom. His presence helped steady her as she thought how her father would have been so proud of his children. She looked around the church and caught her mother's eye—her loving mother and best friend, who had fallen under Marc-Claude's spell the day she met him.

She thought of how Madame de Laval finally accepted her own mother and her new American daughter-in-law. She had told Claire repeatedly how wrong she had been about Felicity, and that she approved of Marc-Claude's choice for his bride. And, as if a divine frosting on the cake, Aline, dear Aline, had given them title to Chateau Fleury as a wedding gift.

But enough of that—her groom awaited. Marc-Claude beckoned her. The sweet perfume of the white lilies on the altar grew more aromatic as she came closer. She felt as though she might float off the floor. In response, she had the strangest desire to fly down the aisle to him.

The next thing she registered was her voice saying, "I do."

Marc-Claude retrieved the two-toned gold filigree wedding band from Jacques' hand. He slipped it on Claire's finger while he spoke, "Claire, take this ring as a sign of my love and fidelity."

At 10:20 that morning, the priest declared, "I pronounce you man and wife."

An unexplained, ethereal voice chanted, "Ah. . .ah. . .ah. . .ah. . .lay. . .a. . .lu. . .ou. . .ou. . .ou. . .yah"

And then the church bell struck once.

Moments slipped past before the priest recovered enough to say, "I present to you Monsieur and Madame Marc-Claude Georges de Laval."

Marc-Claude whispered in Claire's ear, "*Mon ange* . . . my angel."

Claire smiled and nodded to their guests as she walked down

243

the aisle with her new husband. Gratitude filled her heart to be united with the one her soul loved.

Together again . . . my beloved soul mate and I!

Epilogue

I watch the light play on strands of Aline's upswept silver hair. She raises her champagne glass and proposes a toast to Marc-Claude and me in celebration of our fifth wedding anniversary. I wonder what she'll say. She's such a blessing in our life.

I wait no more. She speaks now. "As Homer wrote in the *Odyssey*, 'There is nothing nobler or more admirable than when two people who see eye to eye keep house as man and wife, confounding their enemies and delighting their friends.' Today, Marc-Claude and Claire's family and friends delight in observing the enrichment they bring to each other's lives while unselfishly sharing their talents to make the world a better place for all."

Aline smiles and lifts her glass. After the clinking of glass and the sipping of champagne, the room echoes with calls of *"Santé."*

Strains of "Plaisir d'Amour"—our song—performed by the three-piece ensemble—violin, cello and piano—cascade through the Chateau Fleury blue salon. "Happy anniversary, *mon amour*," Marc-Claude whispers. We embrace and kiss with deep emotion, lost in the moment. He reaches for my hand and leads me to the center of the room.

We dance and others join us. I lay the side of my face against his. "The day we wed, I thought it was impossible to love you more," I tell him. "Now, five years and two children later, I find I love you more than ever."

"I've worshiped you through the ages." Marc-Claude's arm tightens around my waist as he draws me against his body. "And will go on loving you always."

I breathe in the familiar woodland scent of him and feel as if my heart will burst with wonder.

I have it all . . . a wonderful family, fulfilling career, and my wonderful soul mate by my side.

I know that Marc-Claude has adjusted his professional life and goals to coordinate with the demands of my position as Executive

Director for the International Conference for the Education of Women. He supports me in the work I love. We spend most of our time in Paris, but savor time at Chateau Fleury during the summer and holidays. Aline is a key member of the household. She lives with us and basks in caring for the children while we work.

We share our love of Chateau Fleury by opening it to public tours while we are in Paris. Each summer here at Chateau Fleury, Nadia and I sponsor a six-week life skills training conference for abused women. Many of our graduates return to train others.

The music stops, and now it is time we greet our well-wishers.

I look around the room for Michelle and my mother-in-law, Madame de Laval. I don't see them and wonder where they are. Someone is running.

Tap. Tap. Tap.

I turn and see our adorable, four-year-old Marc-Andre approach, his shoes smacking the wooden floor each step of the way. Michelle is close on his heels.

"Look what Mimi gave me." He holds out a bright red army tank and thrusts it into his daddy's waiting hand.

Marc-Claude lifts him onto his lap, one arm around his son, leaving the other one free to examine the toy. He looks at Michelle. "Now he'll want to play all night." My husband feigns disapproval.

"Oh, give him some space, Dad." Michelle says as she pats our son's head.

My mother-in-law and I have developed an understanding—of sorts. Although I know I'll never be *French* in her eyes, I can tell she's given her heart to her *French* grandchildren. Here she comes now with our tiny, one-month old Janine-Marie. She's taking her time giving the baby to me, showing off her granddaughter to everyone in the room. I wouldn't have it any other way.

She's finally here.

Her eyebrows rise inquiringly. "What's the family conference about?" she asks. She ignores my outstretched arms, which forces me to take my daughter from her.

Janine-Marie's tiny body is now cradled in my arms while Marc-Claude restrains Marc-Andre long enough to sit with us. Jacques snaps two family portraits before our little boy jumps down and runs to his grandfather and then quickly dashes off. The child screams with delight as General de Laval chases him.

Aline reaches behind her chair and hands Marc-Claude a large package wrapped in shimmering white paper with an iridescent confetti pattern.

"Open it," she says with enthusiasm. "I painted it especially for you and Claire."

I unfasten the wrappings and ribbon while Marc-Claude holds the large box. He opens it and pulls an Impressionist-style painting from inside. My eyes follow architectural images of the eighteenth-century Chateau Fleury and an American southern plantation house before resting on the focal point, present-day Chateau Fleury.

I'm speechless. How did Aline know such detail? I brush away a tear of gratitude clouding my vision. Suddenly, I have no doubt about the truth of what I have felt since I first met her. I wrap my arms around her and look into her precious face. "You do remember, don't you?" I reach for Marc-Claude's hand and draw him to Aline and me.

Aline nods. "Oui."

"When did you first know?" I ask.

"Always." Aline smiled with candor.

We three have come full circle.

After more than two centuries, Marie, André, and Janine have returned to Chateau Fleury—whether Marc-Claude really believes it doesn't change a thing.

Historical Notes

The notes that follow trace the Houses of Bourbon and d'Orléans to the time of the French Revolution and the end of the French absolute monarchy.

House of Valois

A monarch of the House of Valois, King Louis XI of France ruled from 1498 to 1515. He was the son of Charles, Duke of Orleans. Before he ascended to the throne, he was known as Louis of Orleans and was forced to marry his disabled and supposedly sterile cousin, Joan. As King Louis XI, he hoped to extinguish the Orleans cadet branch of the House of Valois. He died in 1515 without a male heir and was succeeded by his cousin Francis from the Angoulême cadet branch of the House of Valois.

House of Bourbon

A branch of the Capetian dynasty, the Bourbon kings first ruled France and Navarre in the sixteenth century. The dynasty originated in 1272 when the heiress of the lordship of Bourbon married a younger son of King Louis IX. The House continued as a cadet branch until Henry IV became the first Bourbon king of France in 1589.

Louis XIII – King of France –1610-1643

Louis XIII was a monarch of the House of Bourbon and became King of France at the age of nine after the assassination of his father, Henry IV. His mother, Marie de Medici, acted as regent during his minority. Because she wouldn't relinquish power when Louis came of age, he staged a coup d'état, exiled his mother, and assumed his rightful place as king. His brother Gaston, Duc d'Orléans, stood next in line to the throne until Louis's two sons were born—the future Louis XIV and Philippe I, Duc d'Orléans.

Reign of Louis XIV—the Sun King -1643-1715

During the early years of the seventeenth century, France had seen the rise of royal absolutism and diminishing importance of the Estates General, the national parliament.

In 1643, at the age of five, Louis inherited the central issue that had dogged France for over one hundred years—the aristocracy that resented the increasing power of the monarchy. The new king embraced the political philosophy of the divine right of kings—that is, the belief that the monarch held God-given rights. He believed he answered to a higher power rather than earthly political or religious authority. "L'etat, c'est moi" (I am the state) is attributed to the king.

Louis built his lavish Palace of Versailles thirteen miles from Paris to create awe and to centralize power. As a means to eliminate feudalism, he compelled many members of the nobility to serve him and inhabit his palace. Not to be denied, he lured or ruined provincial aristocrats to accomplish his objectives. He sought personal glory through warfare. France was either at war or planning one as Louis concentrated on building a strong military. By these means he became one of the most powerful French monarchs and consolidated a system of absolute monarchical rule in France.

As the old king lay near death, he summoned his five-year old great grandson to his bedside and said, "My child, you are about to become the greatest king in the world. Never forget your duty to God. Do not copy me in my taste for war." He kissed the Dauphin, blessed him, and burst into tears.

During the seventy-two-year reign of Louis XIV, the Bourbon monarchy—a branch of the Capetian dynasty—France became the leading power of Europe.

Reign of Louis XV—The Well Loved – King 1710 -1774

Louis XV succeeded his great grandfather Louis XIV at the age of five, and the Duc d' Orleans became regent. After his regent's death, the young king relied on his former tutor, Cardinal Fleury, who became his chief minister. Fleury provided governmental stability over the next seventeen years. After Fleury's death, Louis took little interest in government and was greatly influenced in all matters by his mistress, Madame de Pompadour, and later by the Comtesse du Berry.

In 1733 France joined in the War of the Polish Succession to restore Stanislaus Leszczynska—the father of the king's wife—to the Polish throne. Their effort failed.

In 1740 France allied with Prussia against Britain and Austria in the War of the Austrian Succession. After winning battles and occupying the Austrian Netherlands, Louis returned the territory to Austria, much to the chagrin of his subjects.

During the Seven Years War, France allied with Austria against Britain and Prussia. The French defeat exacted the loss of most of her colonies to Britain. By the end of Louis's reign, the huge expense of decades of warfare, mistresses, and lavish living left the monarchy and government weakened. It was said that after the disastrous Battle of Rossbach in 1757, the king remarked, "Après moi, le deluge."(After me, comes the flood). How prophetic! The charismatic Louis le Bien-Aimé no longer retained the respect and affection of his subjects. Had he recognized the damage done?

Louis XVI – King 1774-1793

On May 10, 1774, Louis Auguste became Louis XVI upon the death of his grandfather.

The twenty-year-old king lacked the self-confidence and charisma of his predecessor. Louis wanted to be a good king and help his subjects but was ill equipped to face the many problems created by the previous monarch. He lacked sufficient strength and decisiveness to combat the influence of court factions and was unable to support reformers in their efforts to improve the French government.

His early foreign policy success came from supporting the American colonies' fight for independence from France's nemesis—Great Britain. However, that success almost bankrupted the country. By the mid-1780s the king found it necessary to support radical fiscal reforms opposed by his subjects. As the pressures built, he withdrew to pleasurable activities, such as hunting and tinkering with clocks and locks.

By 1789 he could no longer ignore the fiscal crisis. In May he convened the Estates General, an advisory assembly of different estates or socio-economic classes—the clergy, the nobility, and the commoners. By June the commoners' estate declared itself the National Assembly and began work on a constitution. Initially, the king attempted to put the rebellion down, but by July he was forced to acknowledge the Assembly. On July 14, riots broke out in Paris. Mobs stormed the Bastille prison, an act in defiance of the king. Although Louis announced he would acquiesce to their demands, he resisted doing so. On October 6, 1789, the royal family was forced to leave Versailles and return to the city. They moved to Tuileries Palace in the heart of Paris, not far from the Palais Royal, the stronghold of intrigue and resistance supported by his cousin Phillipe II d'Orléans.

On September 21, 1792, the Legislative Assembly proclaimed the First French Republic. In November the king and his family were charged with treason, found guilty by the National Assembly, and condemned to death. Louis XVI faced the guillotine in the Place de la Révolution on January 21, 1793. Nine months later his wife, Marie Antoinette, was executed.

Louis Philippe II, fifth Duke d'Orléans, Philippe-Egalité

During the *ancien régime*, it became a tradition that the duchy of Orleans be granted to a younger son of the king. While each of the Orleans branches thus descended from a junior prince, they were always among the king's nearest relatives in the male line.

The title Duc d'Orléans, reserved for French royalty, was first created in 1344 by Philippe VI in favor of his son Philippe of Valois. Known as princes of the blood (*princes du sang*), the title passed to the oldest brother of the king, if there was one. Those princes became a collateral line of the French royal family with an eventual right to succeed to the throne should more senior princes of the blood die out.

The Orléans branch of the House of Valois came to the throne with Louis XII in the fifteenth century. The last cadet branch to hold the ducal title descended from the younger son of Louis XIII. It was known as the House of Bourbon-Orléans. From 1709 until the French Revolution, the Orleans dukes were next in the order of succession to the French throne after those descended from Louis XIV.

In November 1785 Louis Philippe d'Orléans became the head of the House of Orléans, one of the wealthiest families in France. He stood next in line to the throne should the senior Bourbon line die out.

His marriage to his cousin Louise Marie de Bourbon, the sole heiress of the House of Bourbon-Penthièvre, combined her vast fortune with his own. Three years after their marriage, he began a secret relationship with the Countess of Genlis, his wife's lady-in-waiting.

In 1778 Philippe served in the squadron of the Count of Orvilliers. He was present in the Battle of Ushant on July 27, 1778, a naval battle against the British during the American War of Independence. As a result of his actions during the battle, he was dismissed from the navy because of incompetence and alleged cowardice.

He used his centrally located palace to stage revolutionary plots and rebellion against the crown. His final action of betrayal of his cousin was to vote for King Louis' death. In 1793, as the revolutionary frenzy grew more bloodthirsty, Phillip II d'Orléans felt the guillotine blade.

Further Reading on this Time Period

Listed below are source books I found useful as reference material for *Return to Chateau Fleury:*

Memoirs of the Duc de Lauzun (first published 1928)

Nesta H. Webster, *The Chevalier de Boufflers: a romance of the French Revolution* (1916)

Memoires de Madame La Comtesse de Genlis, (1825)

Memoirs of Madame de La Tour du Pin, (1971)

Zoe or The Martel Papers: a manuscript of the Conciergerie (1865)

Francis Scarfe, *André Chénier: His Life and Work,* (1965)

Simon Schama, *Citizens: A Chronical of the French Revolution* (1989

Desmond Seward, *The Bourbon Kings of France* (1976)

Christopher Hibbert, *The Days of the French Revolution* (1980)

Antonia Fraser, *Marie Antoinette* (2001)

James Tipton, *Annette Fallon* (2007)

Diana Reid Haig, *Walks Through Marie Antoinette's Paris* (2006)

Catherine Delors, *Mistress of the Revolution* (2008)

Tom Ambrose, *Godfather of the Revolution: The Life of Philippe Egalite Duc D'Orléans* (2008)

Imbert de Saint Amand, *Marie Antoinette,* Volumes I-III
    The End of the Old Regime (1890)
    The Downfall of Royalty (1891)
    Marie Antoinette at the Tuileries (1891)

Claude Manceron, *Age of the French Revolution*, Volumes I-V
    Twilight of the Old Order (translated 1977)
    The Wind from America (translated 1978)
    Their Gracious Pleasure (translated 1980)
    Toward the Brink (translated 1982)
    Blood of the Bastille (translated 1989)

www.ingramcontent.com/pod-product-compliance
Lightning Source LLC
Chambersburg PA
CBHW070902180626
46817CB00003B/887